P9-DNT-330

PRAISE FOR
THE *NEW YORK TIMES* BESTSELLING
FLOWER SHOP MYSTERIES

"Kate Collins continues to create flat-out fun mysteries with characters you love and some you love to hate. Bravo on this latest installment."
— Leann Sweeney, *New York Times* bestselling author of the Cats in Trouble Mysteries

"Colorful characters, a sharp and funny heroine, and a sexy hunk boyfriend."
— Maggie Sefton, national bestselling author of the Knitting Mysteries

"The Flower Shop Mystery series stays fresh and keeps getting better. Collins has created a small-town community that readers feel part of." — *RT Book Reviews*

"Kate Collins delivers an entertaining, amusing, and deliciously suspenseful mystery."
— Cleo Coyle, *New York Times* bestselling author of the Coffeehouse Mysteries

"A delightful, lighthearted cozy." — The Best Reviews

"A nimble, well-crafted plot with forget-me-not characters."
— Laura Childs, *New York Times* bestselling author of the Tea Shop Mysteries

continued . . .

"Kate Collins has played a major role in shaping the off-shoot of the 'cozy' mystery into a growing entity of its own, the romantic mystery. I, for one, am grateful."
—Once Upon a Romance

"One of my favorite mystery series."
—Kate Carlisle, *New York Times* bestselling author of the Bibliophile Mysteries

"Kate Collins never fails to deliver a spectacular story . . . another triumph."
—Lorna Barrett, *New York Times* bestselling author of the Booktown Mysteries

"A clever, fast-moving plot and distinctive characters."
—JoAnna Carl, national bestselling author of the Chocoholic Mysteries

"An excellent heroine."   —The Mystery Reader

"As fresh as a daisy, with a bouquet of irresistible characters."
—Elaine Viets, national bestselling author of the Dead-End Job Mysteries

"Ms. Collins's writing style is crisp, her characters fun . . . and her stories are well thought-out and engaging."
—Fresh Fiction

Other Flower Shop Mysteries

Mum's the Word

Slay It with Flowers

Dearly Depotted

Snipped in the Bud

Acts of Violets

A Rose from the Dead

Shoots to Kill

Evil in Carnations

Sleeping with Anemone

Dirty Rotten Tendrils

Night of the Living Dandelion

To Catch a Leaf

Nightshade on Elm Street

Seed No Evil

Throw in the Trowel

A Root Awakening

Florist Grump

A Flower Shop Mystery

Kate Collins

AN OBSIDIAN MYSTERY

OBSIDIAN
Published by the Penguin Group
Penguin Group (USA) LLC, 375 Hudson Street,
New York, New York 10014

USA | Canada | UK | Ireland | Australia | New Zealand | India | South Africa | China
penguin.com
A Penguin Random House Company

First published by Obsidian, an imprint of New American Library,
a division of Penguin Group (USA) LLC

First Printing, November 2015

Copyright © Linda Tsoutsouris, 2015

Penguin supports copyright. Copyright fuels creativity, encourages diverse voices,
promotes free speech, and creates a vibrant culture. Thank you for buying an
authorized edition of this book and for complying with copyright laws by not
reproducing, scanning, or distributing any part of it in any form without permis-
sion. You are supporting writers and allowing Penguin to continue to publish
books for every reader.

OBSIDIAN and logo are trademarks of Penguin Group (USA) LLC.

ISBN 978-0-451-47343-1

Printed in the United States of America
10   9   8   7   6   5   4   3   2   1

PUBLISHER'S NOTE
This is a work of fiction. Names, characters, places, and incidents either are the
product of the author's imagination or are used fictitiously, and any resemblance
to actual persons, living or dead, business establishments, events, or locales is
entirely coincidental.

If you purchased this book without a cover you should be aware that this book
is stolen property. It was reported as "unsold and destroyed" to the publisher and
neither the author nor the publisher has received any payment for this "stripped
book."

Acknowledgments

Any one thing in the creation is sufficient to demonstrate a Providence to a humble and grateful mind.
—Epictetus (AD c. 50–c. 138)

As an author, I am always humbled by and grateful for the people who play important roles in a book's production, whether through their expertise, encouragement, or contributions. For *Florist Grump*, these are:

My editor, Ellen Edwards; my agent, Karen Solem; my son/author assistant, Jason Eberhardt; my daughter, Julia Eberhardt; my best friend to the end, Barbara Ferrari; my family; my friends in the 'hood; and my fellow Cozy Chicks Author buddies: Ellery Adams, Lorraine Bartlett, Duffy Brown, Mary Kennedy, M. J. Maffini, Maggie Sefton, and Leann Sweeney.

Thanks are due to dedicated reader Lynn Cotner for coming up with the winning name for Jillian's baby. I would also like to acknowledge the following readers for their winning entries in my WORST TITLE EVER contest, which are sprinkled throughout the story and add greatly to its humor: Peggy Glennie, Sheila Korman, Karen Gorny, Nancy Roessner, and Mary Davern. Florist Pam Kutchey (Kutchey's Flowers, Key West, Florida) provided helpful tips and tidbits.

Florist Grump is dedicated to my husband and eternal soul mate, Jim, who still guides and inspires me from above.

CHAPTER ONE

Monday

I used to like Monday mornings. They were the opening ceremonies of the Olympic Games, revving up my enthusiasm for the challenges of the week ahead, or the starting pistol at the horse races, sending me out of the gate with a burst of energy, ready to run the course no matter how much mud was on the track.

Sadly, those days were over, a fading vision in my rearview mirror, a reminder that life is ever changing—and not always for the better. And it wasn't only the beginning of the week that fate had fumbled. It was every morning of every day. Every. Day.

This morning was a prime example. I'd risen at seven o'clock, showered, put on mascara, a little blush, skipped the concealer—nothing covered my freckles—and tamed the red beast that many called my hair. Marco had already walked our rescue dog, Seedy, and brought me a cup of coffee laced with half-and-half, just the way I liked it. After seven months of marriage, this small token of love still amazed me.

Then we'd proceeded to the kitchen for breakfast.

The Olympic torch had barely been lit when its bright flame began to flicker.

The previous September I had become Abigail Knight Salvare, wife of Marco Salvare, the former Army Ranger/current owner of Down the Hatch Bar and Grill and the sexiest man in town. He had dark hair, soulful brown eyes, a strong jaw, an olive complexion with a faint five-o'clock shadow, muscular arms, and trim hips—honestly, he could have been a cover model for *GQ*. What he saw in a busty, five-foot-two, Irish-tempered redhead was a mystery to me.

In addition to being Marco's wife, I was the owner of Bloomers Flower Shop, located on the square in New Chapel, Indiana. I had also recently become Marco's partner in the Salvare Detective Agency, and together we had helped solve sixteen murder cases. There was a lot on my plate, but I loved it all.

Then, after several long months of being crammed into Marco's bachelor pad, and with his lease up for renewal, we'd embarked on a laborious and tangled house hunt. By "laborious" I mean that my cousin Jillian went into false labor three times while assisting us with the hunt, and by "tangled" I mean that we got ourselves into quite a knot of a murder investigation.

Thanks to my budding sleuthing skills, the murder case had been resolved, but not the house hunt. So we'd decided to build. Because of *that* decision, we needed to save money and find a temporary place to live, so—*deep breath, Abby*—we'd moved in with my parents.

To be honest, I wasn't in favor of it, but they'd insisted, and Marco had accepted for both of us, something I believed he had come to regret. In any case, we were now

ensconced in my childhood bedroom, still painted screaming yellow with purple accents and decorated with plaster
of paris handprints I made in kindergarten, a silhouette of
my ten-year-old head, framed awards for perfect attendance (the only awards I'd ever received), and posters of
my favorite childhood movies. Basically, I was living in a
flashback.

Now the room that had once been my punishment—as
in, "Go to your room, young lady—you are grounded!"—
had become my sanctuary. It was the only place in the
house where Marco and I had any privacy, and even then,
we had our little Seedy packed in with us.

In my parents' kitchen, which was spacious enough for
a long, farm-style table and eight chairs, Marco made oatmeal for himself and I had a second cup of coffee. I never
ate at home on Mondays because my assistant, Lottie, always served up her famous skillet breakfast at Bloomers
that day. We were joined in short order by my mom, Maureen "Mad Mo" Knight, a kindergarten teacher and weekend artist who managed her household with the same firm
hand with which she ran her classroom.

This morning, Mom had made a new dish involving
eggs, tomatoes, something, and something for herself and
Dad, and now she insisted I eat it. I told her up front I
didn't want any, and she knew very well why. Even so, a
battle of wills ensued, with my mother maintaining that I
was not getting out of the house without trying her omelet. The stalemate was broken by my dad, who had rolled
his wheelchair into the kitchen to eat breakfast and instead found himself initiating what amounted to hostage
negotiations, one of Dad's areas of expertise.

"Take a seat, Maureen," he began, scooting out a chair
for her. "Right here, across from your daughter."

My father, Sergeant Jeffrey Knight, had been a cop for twenty years before a drug dealer's bullet blew a hole through his leg and landed him in the hospital. Then surgery to remove the bullet caused a partial paralysis of his legs that confined him mostly to the wheelchair. He'd retired from the force soon after, but he would always and forever be a cop. Thus the negotiations.

"Now, Mo," Dad said, one hand on her shoulder, "you know Abracadabra has breakfast at Bloomers on Mondays, right?"

This got a reluctant yes from my mother. I suspected he had used my childhood nickname to remind Mom of the adorable cherub I had once been. I think she and I would have agreed that was a debatable point.

"And, Ab, you know that all you have to do is eat a few forkfuls to make Mom happy, right?"

I shrugged, indicating ambivalence. Bad move on my part. Dad was looking for total capitulation.

"Come on, Abby," he said. "You know your mother is only acting in your best interests."

"Yes, Dad, I know that." I glanced at Marco, seated across the table from me, and rolled my eyes. He shook his head as though to say, *Nope. I'm out of it.*

"Now, who is willing to compromise here so we can move on to a pleasant topic of conversation?" Dad asked.

Not me. I wasn't about to give in. That was just what Mom wanted.

Wait, what had I just said? A shiver raced up my spine. *Dear God, it's like I never moved away from home.* It was as though the years after high school graduation, through college, through my failed attempt at law school, through two years of owning Bloomers, had vanished once I'd stepped back into my old bedroom.

I had to get that new house built fast.

"This is my last word on the subject, Abigail," Mom said. "A little protein will make you feel better until you can have breakfast at Bloomers. You know how you crash and burn when you're overly hungry."

"I'll be fine," I said, then sipped my coffee. Marco finished his oatmeal silently, his gaze seeking out the clock on the wall.

At that point Dad began his new ritual wherein he read aloud articles from the morning newspaper.

"Here's something for you, Abracadabra," he said, and began reading. I rolled my eyes at Marco again and pulled out my cell phone, ostensibly to check messages but actually to play a game so I could tune Dad out.

My phone rang in the middle of my losing the game, so I paused to check the screen and noticed that Mom and Dad were both waiting to hear who my caller was.

"Just Jillian," I said, then left the room to take the call. My cousin Jillian was the unbearably proud mother of a one-month-old baby girl named Harper Abigail Lynne Osborne, whose initials by no coincidence spelled *HALO*. The child was Jillian's little angel and even had a "halo" of white seed pearls that Jillian put on her tiny head like a sweatband every time a photo op presented itself.

I couldn't very well complain, however, since Jillian had chosen Harper's middle name as a tribute to me, the loyal cousin who'd stuck by crazy Jillian through thick and thin. And while I appreciated her having a healthy, adorable baby, it seemed a little too early in the game to declare presidential aspirations for Harper.

"Abs, you won't believe what Harper did," Jillian said. This was her daily mantra, and I was tired of it. "Let me guess. She woke up, nursed, pooped, and went back to sleep."

Seriously, what else did month-old babies do? I tuned Jillian out, too.

Fifteen minutes later, Marco and I broke free and headed for the town square in my refurbished banana yellow 1960 Corvette. I'd gotten the car for a steal after it had been found languishing in a barn under a huge collection of junk. When the farmer who owned the property died, the family had wanted to get rid of everything, making the sporty little car totally affordable for an impoverished law school flunk-out. The poor 'Vette had been horribly mistreated, but a good paint job had fixed most of that.

Had it been my choice, I would have been the one driving, something I loved passionately. But Marco always got behind the wheel first, so I had to let it go because I loved him *more* passionately. I also would have cranked up the volume on the radio and sung along, ragtop down, wind blowing my hair, feeling as free as a cloud in the sky, but I felt self-conscious with Marco there.

I decided to stay mum about it, however, since his green Prius had been totaled just a month earlier while he was trying to save me from a killer. He hadn't bought another vehicle yet because he was certain we could save money by carpooling.

He parked in a public lot a block off the square and we walked to Franklin Street, where both of us had businesses. Seedy hobbled happily along with us, pausing as we stopped midway between our shops for a kiss.

"Dinner at the bar after work?" Marco asked, brushing a strand of hair off my face.

"You bet. And maybe we should start having breakfast out, too."

"Your parents aren't that bad, Sunshine."

"Marco, do you really like having someone read the paper to you? Or insist you eat their food when you're not even hungry?"

"You're always hungry when you wake up. And we're not going to live with them forever."

"It just feels that way," I said with an exasperated sigh.

Marco looked deep into my eyes. "Be grateful you have them."

I couldn't argue. Marco's father had died when he was a teenager, and he still felt the loss. Besides, I was starving and just wanted to get to Bloomers so I could eat. I kissed him again, then headed down the block while he headed up.

Franklin was one of four streets that made up New Chapel's courthouse square. The five-story white limestone county seat was situated in the middle of a large expanse of green lawn, with cement planters at all four corners and cedar benches placed along the sidewalks. The courthouse was the heart of the town, making it a bustling place.

Normally at that time of the morning not much was happening, however, as most shops wouldn't open for another hour and the courthouse staff wouldn't roll in until eight thirty. But something was about to happen this morning, and by the looks of it, I was guessing a press conference. Workers were setting up microphones at the top of the wide courthouse steps, hanging banners from the portico, and cordoning off an area with thick burgundy ropes for whatever VIPs were going to be there.

Other than the workers and a few men in dark suits huddled near the mics, the only other person out that early was Jingles, the old window washer, who was squeegeeing off the windows of the business next to mine.

Jingles, so named for the coins in his pocket that he rattled when he talked, had been washing windows for as long as I'd been coming down to the square. With his old tin pail and trusty squeegee, his worn jeans, gray sweatshirt jacket, and scuffed black work boots, the seventy-five-year-old senior was as much a fixture as the courthouse.

But as we approached Bloomers, Seedy saw Jingles and scurried behind me, causing the leash to wind around my ankles, nearly bringing me down. Her reaction wasn't unusual. The abuse she'd suffered from her previous owner had left her with a fear of most people, especially men.

"Seedy, stop. Hold still." As I untangled my legs, my phone beeped, so before I scooped her up I pulled out my cell and saw a text from Jillian: *Call me.*

"Not going to happen," I muttered, then nearly stepped into a bucket of sudsy water that Jingles had set on the sidewalk.

"Sorry, Jingles," I called as my thumbs flew over the buttons on my phone: *Busy now. Maybe later.* With a huff of annoyance, I dropped the phone into my purse and picked up my dog. I had no time for Jillian's nonsense.

I opened the yellow frame door and stepped inside the loveliest shop on the square. Did it matter that I had mortgaged Bloomers to the hilt? *My* name, not the bank's, was on the sign above the door. But just to be certain bank gremlins hadn't repossessed it overnight, I put Seedy down, then peeked through the glass pane for a quick look up.

BLOOMERS FLOWER SHOP
Abby Knight, Proprietor

Oops. I had to remember to order a sign with my new name on it.

"Morning, love," Grace called, coming out of the coffee-and-tea parlor, a charming Victorian-themed café I'd added to lure more people into Bloomers. Grace Bingham, an elegant sixtysomething expat from Great Britain, not only ran the parlor, but also baked fresh scones daily and made the best gourmet coffee in town. "Shall I pour your coffee now or wait until Lottie calls us to the kitchen for breakfast?"

I crouched down to detach the leash from Seedy's collar. "Now, please."

"You did remember to buy the eggs, didn't you?"

"Was I supposed to buy eggs?"

"Lottie mentioned we were out last Friday, and you said you'd take care of it."

I really needed to start paying more attention when people were talking to me. Make that *certain* people.

"I'll run to the grocery store right now." I let Seedy off her leash, and she hobbled to the big bay window and jumped up—an amazing feat for a three-legged dog. She loved to watch the comings and goings on the court-house square across the street.

"There won't be enough time for a grocery run, dear," Grace said. "You've got an appointment at eight forty-five—another wedding consultation. And we have flower orders for two funerals today, so it's all hands on deck. We'll have to skip breakfast today."

A wave of nausea rolled through my empty stomach. Skipping breakfast was not an option. My body required two things to operate efficiently: regular meals and seven hours of sleep. Deprived of either or both, Abigail Christine Knight Salvare turned into an actual redheaded beast.

At once, my mom's words resounded in my head: *You know how you crash and burn when you're hungry.*

Well, I would just prove her wrong. There would be no crashing or burning.

"The Old World Deli has breakfast sandwiches," I said, pulling out my cell phone. "I'll order egg and sausages for all of us, then dash over and pick them up."

That was one of the benefits of working on the town square. Everything one needed was only five minutes away.

While I was on the phone, Seedy began to whine and paw the window. Then she jumped down and hobbled to the front door, putting her paw on it and looking over at me.

"It appears you'll have company on your walk to the deli," Grace said.

I snapped Seedy's leash on, picked her up, and headed back outside. As soon as we'd crossed Franklin Street, I set her down again so we could head right, circling around the front of the courthouse to reach the deli on the opposite side. Seedy had other ideas, however, and pulled me toward the left, aiming for the budding lilac bushes that nearly obliterated the courthouse's rarely used side entrance.

In the days before videoconferencing, inmates were bused over from the jail five blocks away and hustled in through the side door, where they could be taken straight to the courtroom. Nowadays, the side entrance was used only when a VIP came to town and wanted to slip into the courthouse unnoticed. Since New Chapel was a small college town in northwest Indiana, this was a rare event, which was why the shrubs were overgrown.

I pulled her back. "Not now, Seedy. We need to keep moving."

My phone beeped again, so I checked the screen and saw that my fourteen-year-old niece had sent me a text: *Need your advice. After school OK?*

Seedy had stopped to sniff a piece of material lying in the grass, so I took a second to text back: *Sure.* Afternoons were busy at Bloomers, especially because Rosa Marin, my part-time help, wasn't around then. But how could I say no? What was an aunt for if not to give advice? I'd just have to squeeze in five minutes to talk to her.

"Come on, Seedy," I said, giving her leash a gentle tug. "We don't have time to play this morning." Especially not with someone's cast-off necktie. Rather, a piece of a necktie, as it appeared to be just the knot. Someone was obviously in a hurry to disrobe.

The flurry of activity was increasing as workers set up folding chairs and more men in suits gathered at the top of the stairs. I spotted the mayor and paused. What was going on?

A worker passed by with a push broom, so I called, "Hey, what's up?"

"Press conference at nine."

"What for?"

"Big announcement about the New Chapel Savings Bank partnering with the city to build an entertainment venue downtown. It was the lead story in the newspaper this morning."

Well, that explained a lot. I watched the activity for a few minutes, then looked around, trying to guess where the venue might go. But at a menacing growl from my stomach, I remembered my mission and set off, the two of us dodging the people now drifting in. We finally made it to the other side and, after letting several cars pass, crossed the side street. We were nearly at the deli when pounding footsteps sounded behind me.

I turned to see a woman in a black trench coat and tall black boots, her thick auburn hair sprayed so stiffly that it stood four inches above her head, running across the street heading straight for me. She was stuffing something into her purse, not looking where she was going, and it was only my shout of "Hey!" that kept us from colliding.

Startled, she jerked to a stop, muttered an apology, and hurried around us. I stooped down to calm my trembling pet, heard a bang, and looked up to see that the lady had smacked into the deli's glass door and stumbled backward. Rubbing her forehead, she glanced around to see whether anyone had witnessed her accident, gave me a weak smile, then entered the shop.

"That's what happens when you don't pay attention, Seedy," I said, rising. "Let's go get our sandwiches. I'm starv—a little hungry."

"Morning, Abby," called Jennifer, the friendly woman behind the counter, when I walked into the deli. "Sandwiches will be ready in a few minutes."

I caught sight of the lady with the big hair standing in front of the meat case near the back of the shop. She kept glancing around, trying to see out the front window as though looking for someone, her fingers in tight fists at her sides.

When a clerk handed her a white bag, the woman glanced inside, then snapped, "Where's the receipt? I need a receipt."

"I'm getting it for you now."

The impatient woman jerked it from the clerk's hand, stuffed it in her bag, then hurried past me and out the door just as Jennifer came out from behind the counter with my order. "Wow. *She* was certainly in a hurry. Sorry for the delay, Abby. We've had quite a crowd this morning. Of course it helps that we're the only ones open this early. And look what I have for you, Seedy." She held out her hand to reveal a piece of ham in her palm. Seedy wagged her tail and yipped, happy to take the gift.

Most of the shop owners around the square had come to know and love Seedy in the short time I'd had her, even though all agreed she was the ugliest mutt anyone had ever seen. She had a small body covered with long, patchy white, brown, and tan fur, big butterfly wing ears with tufts of hair sticking out of the tops, a pointed, bristly muzzle, an underbite, and only three legs.

I'd first noticed Seedy at the animal shelter, where she was next in line to be euthanized because no one would adopt her. I'd tried to find her a home, never intending to take her myself. But when she'd looked at me with big brown eyes brimming with love—and more than that, trust—my heart had melted.

I settled up at the cash register, then, with the white bag in hand, led Seedy out the door. As we crossed the street and started across the wide expanse of lawn, I could see people heading toward something on the other side of the courthouse. As we drew nearer, two squad cars raced up Franklin Street and stopped in front of Bloomers, their lights flashing and sirens blaring. Right behind them was an emergency medical vehicle.

My heart began to pound. Had something happened to Grace or Lottie? But all the uniformed men were racing toward the far side of the courthouse. Seeing the men, Seedy stopped and tried to get behind me, so I crouched down to stroke her fur. "It's okay, baby. Look — there's our friend Reilly."

I tried to point out Marco's buddy on the force, but Seedy was too frightened, so I picked her up and hurried on. Marco came out of the bar then and headed toward the crowd. I finally got close enough to see that the EMTs and cops were on either side of a man in a dark suit sitting on the cement steps holding his hands over his ears.

"Hey," Marco said, giving Seedy's head a rub. She peered out from under my arm long enough to lick his hand, then tucked her head again.

"Abby," Reilly said with a nod of greeting.

Sergeant Sean Reilly was a good-looking, six-foot, forty-two-year-old with brown hair, light brown eyes that crinkled at the corners, and a good heart. He was a cop to be trusted and had helped Marco and me on many investigations, bending rules only when our safety was at stake. The sole issue I had with him was that he referred to me as the town's trouble magnet. I didn't attract trouble. It was more like I bumped into it.

"What happened to the man?" I asked. "Stroke? Seizure?"

"I wish," Reilly said.

"That's not nice," I said with a scowl. I couldn't help it. My stomach was angry.

"The man's been strangled, Abby," Marco said.

"Oh, my God! And he survived?" I asked.

Reilly shook his head, surveying the people gathering around with a critical eye. "This guy's been dead a while."

"What?" I tried to get another look, but there were

too many people crowding around the steps. "But he's sitting up."

"Rigor mortis," Marco said. "That's the position he was left in after he died."

The thought of what that poor man must have suffered made me shudder. "That body has been sitting on the courthouse steps for an entire day, and no one noticed?"

"No one noticed because he wasn't there," Reilly said. "Someone placed him there this morning sometime after five a.m. That was the last time one of my men patrolled the area. We received an emergency call about it ten minutes ago."

"What possible motive would a person have to kill someone and then carry the body to a public location?" I asked.

"That's a problem for the detectives to work out," Reilly said, glancing around again. "My problem is that we've got a murderer in town."

CHAPTER TWO

"I wonder if that's what Seedy wanted to investigate," I said. "She tried to lead me toward the side steps, but I was in a hurry to get to the deli and didn't stop."

"Why were you on your way to the deli?" Marco asked.

I held up the bag. "I had to buy breakfast sandwiches. I forgot to bring eggs this morning."

"Bet you wish you'd eaten that forkful of omelet now," Marco said.

"I'm not hungry. Grace and Lottie are. Here, take her." I handed Seedy over so I could move in for a closer view. But the gruesome sight told me that was not the smartest thing I'd ever done, especially considering my empty stomach.

The victim appeared to be middle aged, with dark hair that had gone silver at the temples. He wore a black suit, white button-down shirt, and polished black dress shoes. He was hunched over with his head tipped back as though he were gazing at the sky, revealing a ring of dark bruises on his throat. His elbows were pressed into his ribs and his hands were flat against his ears, almost as if he'd been squeezed into a box. His skin was bloated, with a waxy blue tint to it.

Officers were moving the crowd back so they could

cordon off the area, and a police photographer was taking photos of the body, so I returned to Marco and Reilly just as a young policeman wearing disposable gloves brought over a wallet he'd removed from the man's suit coat pocket.

"The victim's name is Dallas Stone," the cop said, reading off the driver's license. "Age fifty-one. Not an organ donor. He has a local address."

"Are the detectives here yet?" Reilly asked him, glancing around.

"Not yet," the cop answered.

"Oh, my God," I heard a woman cry. "I know him."

"Bring that woman over here, Kane," Reilly said to the young cop. "And did you locate the person who made the nine-one-one call yet?"

"No, sir."

The young officer returned with a stumpy little woman in her late forties. She had a round face and short brown hair, and wore a brown tweed coat. Reilly introduced himself, then asked for her name.

"June Griffin," the woman said. She kept looking back at the scene in horror.

"Mrs. Griffin, do you know the man on the steps?" Reilly asked her.

"Yes, I work with Mr. Stone at the savings and loan. What happened to him?"

"We haven't determined the exact cause of his death," Reilly said. "Are you on your way to work?"

June tapped the face of her watch. "Yes, and I have to be there at eight thirty."

"I'll need to ask you a few questions first," Reilly said. "It shouldn't take long."

"I hope not," she said. "My supervisor gets upset when

someone is late. I'm always on time, though, so she'd better not complain. Thirty years of being on time, to be exact. Of course, when *she's* late—"

Reilly cut into her monologue. "Is that what time Mr. Stone usually gets to work?"

"Yes, but all the upper management was supposed to be here at eight for the press conference." June gave a hard shudder and rubbed her arms. "I can't believe he's dead."

Reilly had his notepad out and was writing. "Any family that you know of?"

"He's not married. I know that much. But Mr. Stone didn't talk about his personal life—well, except to brag when he had a new suit. He loved his fancy suits." As though something clicked in her head, she glanced at the body again. "He doesn't have his tie on. Mr. Stone always wears a tie. He buys those hand-painted ones from David's Men's Store and pays a lot of money for them. He's such a sharp dresser—I mean, he was."

Remembering the material Seedy had sniffed, I said quietly, "Seedy found part of a tie on the other side of the lilac bushes, Reilly, about twenty minutes ago."

Reilly said to the young officer, "See if you can find a necktie anywhere around here." To June he said, "Did Mr. Stone have any close friends at the bank?"

"Not that I ever noticed," she said. "Now, he *was* seeing someone, although I think they broke up. I saw them together at Rosie's Diner on two occasions, but it didn't seem like they were getting along all that well. Sometimes I run into the lady at lunchtime, so I'm going to say she works at one of the businesses on the square."

I had a feeling we'd found the bank's busybody.

"Do you know the woman's name?" Reilly asked.

"No, I'm afraid not. Oh, wait. I have overheard him on the phone with a Livvy on a number of occasions, and just between us, he wasn't very nice to her, which is why I said earlier that I think they broke up. So I'm going to go out on a limb and say Livvy is his girlfriend's name."

I had a sudden image of June as a plump brown squirrel sitting on a limb watching everything going on below.

"Can you give me her description?" Reilly asked.

"Well," June said, tapping her chin thoughtfully, "she's a tall woman, thin boned, with high cheekbones, kind of sunken cheeks, and bouffant brown hair. Not very attractive, if you ask me. Not the sort I'd expect Mr. Stone to go for at all. At. All." She raised her eyebrows to make sure we got the message.

Reilly paused. "Bouffant hair?"

"You know," June said, drawing an outline around her own head. "Out to here, eighties style."

The description fit the woman who'd almost collided with me at the deli. "Does she wear a black trench coat?" I asked.

"Yes," June said. "Have you seen her?"

"Just a little while ago," I said.

"You've got company," Marco said to Reilly, nodding toward the street where a news van had just pulled up.

"Terrific," Reilly said under his breath. "Okay, Ms. Griffin, thanks for your help. If you will go with this officer here, he'll take down your contact information."

"I don't have much time," June said to the other officer as they walked away. "My supervisor hates it when anyone's late. Not that she has any reason to complain about me."

"No sign of the tie, Sarge," the young cop reported.

"Then check to see if the lawn service was out this

morning, and if so, if they found any clothing." Reilly turned to me. "What did the tie look like?"

"Well," I said, and paused. All I truly remembered was that Tara had texted me and I had been in a hurry to get the food. "It was just the knot part of the tie, but I think it was a dark color."

"That's helpful," Reilly said dryly. "Dark as in black? Navy? Brown?"

I rubbed my temples. I really had to start paying more attention. "Maybe navy—or black."

"Victim is wearing a black suit," Marco said. "If he was a sharp dresser, the tie would have black in it."

"Was there any design on it," Reilly asked, "like stripes, diamonds, polka dots, little pink bunnies?"

For some reason diamonds triggered a vision of the bouffant hair woman stuffing something into her purse, but I couldn't get a clear image in my head. Two strikes against my memory in one morning. Oops. I'd forgotten the eggs, too. Make that three.

"I'm not sure, Reilly. Let's just go with a small pattern."

"Material?"

"I'm a florist, Reilly, not a seamstress."

Reilly pushed the bill of his hat back and gave me a disgruntled look.

"Lots of excitement on the square today, eh, Sergeant?" someone called.

I looked around as the *New Chapel News*'s crime reporter Connor MacKay joined our little group. Connor, who was Marco's age, was a handsome man with big blue eyes, light brown hair that he wore to his collar, a lanky build, and a flirtatious nature. He always dressed in cargo pants and a safari jacket with pockets that bulged with the tools of his trade.

"Looks like we have ourselves a gruesome scene, ligature marks and all," Connor said, practically salivating at the scoop he thought he'd get. "Are we calling it murder?"

"I don't have any information for you, MacKay," Reilly said. "You'll have to wait until the detectives and coroner get here."

"I'm assuming they are on their way?" Connor asked.

"Yeah, let's assume that together," Reilly said, then walked away.

"Gotcha, Sergeant," Connor called. He nodded at Marco and said with extreme politeness, "*Mr.* Salvare."

"MacKay," Marco said in a bored voice. He hadn't forgotten how Connor had played me to get information for several of the murder investigations we'd worked on before we were married, and for that reason, he was not a fan. And Connor knew it.

"*Mrs.* Salvare," Connor said with a devilish grin. "You're looking stupendous today. Any reason the two of you are here? Sniffing out a potential case perhaps?"

"I'm just taking breakfast to the shop," I said.

Ignoring Connor, Marco said to me, "You'd better get to Bloomers. Your bag is soaking up the butter."

More than that, my stomach was starting to eat itself, but I wasn't about to admit it. "Good call. And I have a client coming soon."

Marco put Seedy down and handed me the leash, and Seedy immediately began pulling me toward Franklin Street. "Keep me posted on what they find out," I said as I backed away. I turned toward the shop just as Grace opened the door to admit my new client.

And there went my breakfast time. Good thing I was *not* about to crash and burn.

Not that I needed to, but I pulled out a sandwich on

the spot and took a big bite, chewing hungrily as I crossed the street. Seedy hobbled ahead, straining on her leash in her eagerness to get to the shop, which surprised me since Jingles was nearby.

My next surprise was that it wasn't Bloomers she was aiming for. It was the window washer, who was now balanced on a ladder in front of the bay window on the far side of my yellow door. When Seedy paused to sniff the bucket, I scooped her up, fearing she might topple the ladder. Then, juggling the dog and the bag, which was about to disintegrate from the butter, I glanced up. "Good morning again, Jingles."

It wasn't Jingles. Though he was wearing a gray hooded sweatshirt and jeans similar to Jingles's, this man was young, maybe twenty, with a boyish face, fair complexion, and short brown hair.

"Sorry, I thought you were someone else. I'm Abby. I own Bloomers. And you are?"

"Robert." He returned to his work, apparently not interested in conversing. Seedy responded by wagging her tail and yipping as though trying to get his attention.

"Where's Jingles?" I asked.

Without missing a stroke, he replied, "I don't know. He didn't tell me where he was going."

"So he did *go* somewhere?"

"Since I'm here and he's not, that's rather obvious, isn't it?"

Well, that was rude. And there was Seedy wagging her tail as though she'd found a new playmate. "Do you know when Jingles will be back?"

"I don't know. He didn't tell me. I'm just filling in for him."

"So earlier when I said, 'Sorry, Jingles' . . ."

"You erred."

Apparently my bigger error was in trying to be polite.

"Abby, I don't mean to interrupt," Grace said, standing inside the door, "but your client is here and she's in a bit of a time crunch."

"I'm right behind you," I said, and followed her into the shop.

Grace took the white bag and handed me a cup of coffee to wash down the food. I had no clue how she knew to have it ready, but that was the mystery of Grace. "I put Miss Dugger in the parlor with a plate of blueberry scones and a pot of tea," she said.

"Thanks, Grace." I gave the cup and saucer back for her to hold while I let Seedy off her leash.

"What happened at the courthouse?"

So my client wouldn't hear, I said softly, "A banker was murdered and left on the side steps."

"Oh, good heavens," Grace whispered. "How dreadful."

"I'll tell you more later," I whispered back.

Laughter erupted from the coffee-and-tea parlor, a counterpoint to the drama I'd just witnessed across the street.

"Is Rosa in there?" I asked.

"Yes," Grace said. "She wanted to keep Miss Dugger company."

I started toward the parlor, then paused. "Did you see the young guy I was talking to outside? He's taking Jingles's place."

"Yes, I noticed him earlier."

"I've never seen anyone fill in for Jingles before. I don't think he's ever missed a day of work. I hope he's not ill."

"Didn't you see the article about Jingles in last Thursday's newspaper?"

"I don't get to read the newspaper anymore, Grace. Is Jingles okay?"

More laughter broke out in the adjacent room.

"You'd better get in there," Grace said. "I'll tell you about our poor window washer later."

Rosa Marisol Katarina Marin, my new employee, was a voluptuous thirtysomething Latina beauty with long legs, long, wavy dark brown hair, prominent cheekbones, pouty lips, and sparkling brown eyes. She wore clothing that hugged her curves and drew every male eye, and she liked it that way. She worked from eight o'clock until noon five days a week but always arrived by seven thirty right after she dropped off her eight-year-old son, Peter, at school.

A month and a half before, Rosa had come to Marco and me to find out who had killed her husband and had ended up lending a hand at the flower shop during a time when business was coming in faster than Lottie, Grace, and I could handle it. We'd soon discovered that Rosa was a natural at floral design and wonderful with people, but we never knew what was going to come out of her mouth; she didn't seem to have any discretion. And forget about a volume button.

I had balked at hiring her because of that, and because everything she did seemed to turn out beautifully with minimal effort on her part, whereas I'd always had to work hard to succeed. Even with extreme effort, I'd had two major failures, once when I was booted from law school, and the other when I was dumped by my fiancé because I'd been given the boot. Double whammy.

Eventually, however, I'd discovered that Rosa and I were a lot alike, so most of our issues had resolved themselves. But she still had no discretion.

Carrying my coffee cup, I went through the doorway into the parlor and headed for the white wrought-iron ice cream table in front of the bay window where the two women were looking through my floral wedding planner.

Rosa was wearing a bright pink V-necked silk blouse, with her trademark silver pendant in the shape of a lightning bolt, large hoop earrings, and a tight black skirt with high-heeled black boots, while my client, a thirty-five-year-old woman, was dressed modestly in a lime green jewel-necked sweater, gray slacks, and black flats.

"Hola," Rosa cried, beaming, as I pulled a chair up to the table. "Abby Knight Salvare, meet your new customer—Daffy Duck."

I glanced at Rosa in shock. "It's Taffi Dugger."

Rosa let out a tinkling laugh as she got up. "Sometimes I don't say things so well. I am so sorry for the mistake, Taffi. Have fun choosing your flowers."

"Thank you," Taffi said happily, smiling at Rosa as though she was the reason for her happiness.

As Rosa passed behind me, she leaned down to whisper, "I was close."

While Rosa swayed from the parlor on her very high heels, I gave my client an embarrassed smile. "I apologize about the name mix-up."

"No, that's okay, really," Taffi said. "I've never met anyone as lively and fun as Rosa. And she had some truly inspirational ideas for my wedding."

"Great," I said, forcing a smile. "Let's see what she came up with."

*   *   *

Half an hour later, I finished with Taffi and headed through the shop to the workroom to eat the rest of my sandwich. The appointment had gone well, even though Rosa had steered Taffi in a completely different direction than what she'd originally had in mind. Thinking Taffi might regret those choices later, I'd tried to guide her back, but she'd been adamant that Rosa's ideas were much better than hers.

In spite of my hunger, I paused outside the parlor to absorb the beauty of my shop. Bloomers had the original wood floors and tin ceiling of the three-story redbrick building circa 1900, with two big bay windows, one on the retail side and one in the parlor. A cash counter sat near the front door, an oak claw-footed table was the focal point in the center, and a glass-fronted refrigerated display case filled the back wall.

A wicker settee with a large dieffenbachia behind it occupied a back corner, and colorful wreaths filled the brick walls. A huge oak armoire on the inside wall displayed silk floral arrangements, ceramic décor, candlesticks, and other small items, and pots stocked with various kinds of green plants filled vacant spaces all around the shop. It was a wholly gratifying sight.

"Morning, sweetie," Lottie Dombowski said over her shoulder. She was filling the display case with fresh blossoms from the giant walk-in coolers in the back room. "I put your sandwich in the fridge."

"Sorry I forgot to buy eggs," I said.

"Don't worry about it," she said. "It all worked out."

Nothing fazed Lottie. She claimed it came from having raised her teenage quadruplet sons. Hailing from Kentucky, the tall, large-boned forty-seven-year-old had a proclivity for pink clothing, including pink barrettes to hold back her short, brassy curls. Lottie had owned Bloomers before I did, and in fact, I had worked as her delivery girl when I was home for summers between my college semesters.

But her husband's heart surgery and high insurance premiums had nearly bankrupted them, so Lottie had been forced to sell. Providence stepped in, because I had just been booted out of law school and had no future prospects at all. But I did have a small amount of trust money left from my grandpa's college fund, so Lottie and I traded places. I bought Bloomers, and she taught me everything she knew while working as my assistant and delivery person.

I had also worked with Grace previously. She had been attorney Dave Hammond's secretary when I clerked for him during my second semester of law school. About the time that Lottie was deciding whether to sell Bloomers and I was trying to find my path, Grace had retired, thinking she'd have time to do the things she'd always wanted to do. But two weeks into it, she was so bored that she accepted my meager offer of employment. For the past almost two years, the three of us had functioned like a well-oiled wheel.

"I just heard about the murder on the radio a few minutes ago," Lottie said, "but there weren't any details. Grace said you were at the scene. Do you know anything?"

"Only that the victim was a local banker," I said. "According to Reilly, he was killed at least a day ago but not at the courthouse. Someone took him there."

"Whatever would possess a person to do that?" Lottie asked.

"It would seem the murderer wanted to make a statement," Grace said, joining us.

"Like what?" Lottie asked. "'Look at me, I can kill and get away with it?'"

"One never knows what motive a mind will conjure," Grace said. She straightened her shoulders, locked her fingers together, and cleared her throat. It was her lecture pose, which meant a quote was forthcoming. *Good thing I'm not in a hurry to eat my egg sandwich, Mom.*

"As the Bard put it in his magnificent play *The Merchant of Venice*," Grace began, "'The devil can cite Scripture for his purpose.'"

"Good one, Gracie," Lottie said as we both clapped.

Grace gave a regal nod. She was a walking Wikipedia of quotations.

"With a whole day to get away, the killer must be long gone," Lottie said.

"Or is that certain he or she won't be caught," Grace added.

Normally the three of us would dissect an intriguing case for hours, but all I could think of now was the sandwich that would soon be moldering in its greasy bag, so I said, "I'll be in the kitchen," and stepped through the purple curtain into the workroom, where Rosa was putting together a floral arrangement, singing off-key to a song on the radio.

It hadn't been easy to allow a newcomer into my sacred space, but because Rosa's help was invaluable, I'd had to learn to share. The workroom was my personal paradise, a place of beauty and tranquillity, of floral scents and myriad colors. It had counters that ran around the room, with shelves above to hold our large assortment of vases and containers, and cabinets below to hold supplies. A built-in desk on the outside wall held my computer, printer, a calendar, framed photos, and the spindle for open orders. On the opposite wall sat two large walk-in coolers, one for fresh flowers and the other to hold completed arrangements waiting for delivery.

"What do you think of this?" Rosa asked as I passed the big, slate-covered table in the middle of the room. She turned her arrangement so I could see front and back.

"It's coming along," I said, and kept going.

"No, it's finished," she said.

"Then it looks great."

"You don't like it."

I paused to take a good look. Rosa had created a design of blue hydrangea, green hypericum berries, white ranunculus, and yellow cymbidium orchids, a combination that worked wonderfully together.

Of course it would.

Lottie, who had followed me in, paused for a look, too.

"I like it, Rosa," I said. "I'd just add a few more stems of ranunculus."

"Lottie, do you think so, too?" Rosa asked.

"I'm gonna have to agree with Abby."

"Then I will do it." Rosa smiled. If Lottie said it was okay, then that was the end of the discussion.

I'd had to learn to share Lottie, too.

I passed our small bathroom and entered the kitchen, a small galley-style space that ran along the back of the building. At the right end of the kitchen was the heavy security door that opened onto the alley and a staircase that led to the basement, a deep, dark, damp place where we stored large pots and supplies that wouldn't fit into the cabinets. It was also the graveyard for my mother's unsold art projects.

I opened the refrigerator and took out my sandwich, then sat on a stool at the small strip of counter nailed to the back wall to eat it, sighing as I chewed a bite. It was my first peaceful moment of the day.

"Want me to zap it in the microwave for you?" Lottie asked. She seemed to be tailing me.

"Nope. It's fine."

Lottie pulled out a stool beside me. "What's up, sweetie? You seem out of sorts today. Is it because of the murder?"

It was because of a lot of things, but I wasn't in a mood to discuss them. "I just want to finish my sandwich so I can get started on orders." I took another bite, hoping she'd take the hint.

"Here's a fresh cup of coffee for you," Grace said, gliding up behind me.

"Grace said you missed the article about Jingles last week," Lottie said.

I swallowed the bite and picked up the coffee cup. "I don't get to read the paper anymore. What happened to him?"

"He was in an altercation," Grace said, "and arrested."

I nearly spit out the coffee. "Jingles? *Our* Jingles?"

"Who is Jingles?" Rosa asked, squeezing into the small room with us.

"He cleans windows on the square," Lottie said. "Been doing it for twenty-five years. I'll pull the article up on the Internet and let you read it, Abby."

Now? I stifled a heavy sigh. All I wanted was ten minutes alone with my food.

"Why don't you see the newspaper anymore?" Grace asked, perching on the stool that Lottie had just vacated.

"My dad gets to it first," I said, chewing. "Then he reads articles out loud that he thinks will interest us."

"How sweet," Rosa said.

"No, it isn't," I said. "It's annoying."

Rosa looked at me in horror. "But he is your father."

"Can't fathers be annoying?" I asked. Assistants certainly could. I crumbled the paper bag my sandwich had been in and tossed it into the garbage can.

"Here it is, Abby," Lottie called from the workroom, so we trooped out en masse, me and my entourage.

"You can sit here to read it," Lottie said, starting to get up.

"No," Rosa said, pushing her back into the chair. "Read it out loud, Lottie. I want to hear it, too—unless that is too annoying for Abby." She winked at Grace and nudged me with her elbow.

I ignored her. "Go ahead, Lottie."

She read the article: "'A local man known only as Jingles the Window Washer was arrested Wednesday for threatening another man with a pocketknife.'"

Lottie paused to say, with a snort of derision, "Jingles? Threatening someone with a pocketknife? No way. The guy's lying through his teeth."

"I would have to agree with you, Lottie dear," Grace said.

As Lottie resumed reading, my gaze landed on the stack of orders on the spindle near the monitor, and I began doing a quick calculation of how long it would take to work through them.

"'Police received a nine-one-one emergency call from Dallas Stone, fifty, formerly of Springfield, Illinois, alleging that Jingles had threatened to kill him. According to Stone, 'This man isn't who you think he is.' Jingles surrendered the knife without incident and was taken to the county jail. Stone declined to press charges.'"

I estimated at least forty orders, and no telling how many had come in from the Internet overnight.

Lottie slapped her palm on the desk, startling me. "See what I mean? If that Dallas Stone was telling the truth, he'd have pressed charges."

Wait. What name had she just said?

"Perhaps Jingles has gone away for a few days in order to escape the inevitable bad publicity," Grace said.

I leaned in to see the computer screen.

"Why do you have the bug eyes?" Rosa asked me.

"Dallas Stone," I said. "That's the name of the murdered banker."

Rosa looked puzzled. "So the man who said that Jingles threatened to kill him has been killed?"

Wordlessly, all three of us nodded.

"Then maybe this Jingles did not go away to escape bad publicity," Rosa said. "Maybe he went away to escape. Period."

CHAPTER THREE

We gave Rosa such looks of dismay that she said, "What? Do I have egg in my teeth?"

"Jingles isn't a killer, sweetie," Lottie said. "He didn't murder anyone."

"Jingles is a gentle, compassionate soul," Grace said, putting her arm around Rosa's shoulders. "You'd have to know him to understand that he couldn't possibly have taken anyone's life."

One of Marco's tenets echoed in my mind: *Under the right circumstances, anyone can kill.* But I had to agree with Grace. Jingles wasn't the killer type. Still, why had he left town now?

"Holy cow, it's nine o'clock," Lottie said, and hurried off to unlock the door and turn over the OPEN sign.

"I need another cup of coffee," I said as Rosa plucked another order from the spindle. "Want me to bring you one, too?"

"Yes, please. And heavy on the cream."

Naturally. That was how I took it.

As I came through the curtain into the shop, I saw Seedy jump down from the window and hobble toward the workroom as though something had frightened her. I stepped up to the bay window and saw two policemen standing outside my front door talking to Jingles's replacement. One of them was Reilly, so I motioned for him to come inside when he was finished.

As I filled two yellow Flower Power mugs with Grace's gourmet coffee at the bar that ran along the back of the parlor, the bell over the door tinkled repeatedly and the white ice cream tables began to fill with people stopping by for a cup of java or tea and one of Grace's fresh scones. I paused to say hello to the regulars, then came out of the parlor just as Reilly entered Bloomers.

"Thanks," he said, taking the cup for Rosa from my hand and sipping it. He made a face and handed it back. "Too creamy. What's up?"

A pair of women were browsing nearby, so I moved in close to say, "I just wanted to know what was going on out there."

He acted as if he was going to tell me a secret, but all he whispered was, "Police business."

I whispered back, "If I were Marco, you'd tell me."

Reilly looked at me from beneath lowered eyebrows. "I was interviewing a potential witness."

"Did your potential witness see anything?"

"Nope."

"Did he tell you he was filling in for Jingles?"

"Yes." His mobile radio squawked, so he said, "Gotta go."

"Reilly," I said quietly, "you don't think Jingles is involved in the murder, do you?"

"You want my professional opinion?"

"Yes."

"Innocent until proven guilty."

"How about your personal opinion?"

"Ask me when I'm off duty."

"Oh, come on, Reilly. Just give me the upshot."

He hooked his thumbs in his thick black belt and leaned back, as though considering it. "I keep asking myself, why would Jingles pack a bag and take off now?"

"To see a sick relative perhaps? And how do you know he packed a bag?"

Reilly glanced around to make sure no one was close enough to hear, then said quietly, "This Robert Hall"— Reilly hitched his thumb over his shoulder to indicate the man washing windows— "rents a room at the old Y across the hall from Jingles. On Friday afternoon he saw Jingles packing a duffel bag and asked where he was going. Hall said Jingles was so stressed out that he left without answering."

"Jingles lives in the old YMCA?"

"Yeah. Didn't you know that?"

"Why would I know where Jingles lives?"

"Oh, right," Reilly said dryly. "You're new in town."

Obviously, I had to start paying more attention to gossip. What I did know was that after the YMCA had built a big new facility on the north end of town, it sold the old building located two blocks off the town square to the city, which had converted it into low-rent housing for men in need. An old motel had been turned into a similar facility for women.

"I've never considered that Jingles might be down on his luck," I said. In fact, I'd never really given much thought at all to the man. He was just always there. "Where did he live before the Y was converted?"

"He rented a room from an old man who lived near the square, but the man passed away four months ago." Reilly's police radio squawked again, so he pushed open the door and stepped outside to take the call, giving me a quick wave good-bye.

I looked out the window and saw that Robert had moved on to the windows of the real estate office one door down. The old Abby would have gone out and questioned him more about Jingles, but the new Abby had too much to do. The yin and yang of success.

Except for a ten-minute lunch break, Rosa and I worked nonstop for the rest of the day. Rosa was usually there only until noon, but her boss at her other place of employment had gone out of town for a conference and had given her the afternoon off. And because her son always went to his grandmother's house after school, she was able to stay until we closed. Still, even with Lottie slipping into the back room to help whenever she could, I knew we'd never finish by five o'clock.

"Today is Monday," Grace said when she brought us cups of tea for our midafternoon break, "and it's after three o'clock, so your mum should be popping in anytime now, Abby. What will she have in store for us, do you suppose? But you must know already, since you live with her."

I paused, a white rose in one hand and my floral knife in the other. What *had* Mom made? I remembered that she'd wanted my opinion on it, but that had been on Saturday afternoon and I'd been busy. Had she mentioned it again on Sunday?

"I'll just let her surprise you," I said, and continued working on the arrangement.

My mother had been a kindergarten teacher for most of her adult life, taking time off only when my brothers and I were very young. Several years ago, my father, looking for a unique Christmas gift, had bought her a pottery wheel, and that simple act of love had changed our lives forever. Now Mom was a weekend artist who showed up at Bloomers with her latest endeavor every Monday, expecting us to sell her so-called works of art. She thought she was helping us boost sales.

She had started out working with clay but had soon grown bored with that and begun switching to a new medium every few weeks. She'd made tea carts out of golf equipment, park benches out of skis and ski poles, a baby's crib mobile out of plastic bats (a "bat mobile"), sunglass frames out of sea glass (causing the worst headaches ever), and a baby bassinet that looked like a quilted sea bass caught in a net. We usually displayed her work until someone with a sense of humor bought it or, if it was really ugly, Lottie could sneak it down to the basement.

When the bell over the door tinkled five minutes later, I braced myself for my mom's newest project, only to have my fourteen-year-old niece, Tara, pop through the curtain.

"Hi, Auntie Amazing," she said, giving me a hug before dropping her purple-and-silver backpack on the floor and sliding onto a stool at the table. "*Hola,* Rosa."

Rosa, who never passed up a chance to give a hug, came around the table to embrace her. "*Hola*, Tara. You look so pretty in your flirty pink dress."

"Look," Tara said, holding out her leg. "Cool ankle boots, huh? Don't they remind you of a pair you have?"

"Yes, they do. Very cool," Rosa said.

"Tell me in Spanish," Tara said. She was fascinated by Rosa.

"*Son muy* cool," Rosa said.

"*Son muy* cool," Tara said, mimicking her accent.

The daughter of my younger brother Jordan and sister-in-law Kathy, Tara could have passed for my little sister.

We shared the same stature, hair and eye color, freckles, and, as Marco and I had discovered when Tara injected herself into one of our investigations, a proclivity for snooping. All Tara lacked to be my twin was fourteen years, twenty pounds, and a generous bust.

"I saw Seedy sleeping in the bay window," Tara said. "What a turnaround from that shy dog you first brought home."

Tara had adopted Seedy's adorable puppy Seedling when we'd adopted Seedy and had witnessed the remarkable transformation my little shelter mutt had made. But I didn't have a lot of time to chat. The spindle was still full and the afternoon was almost over. "So what's up, Tara?"

She sighed morosely and put her chin in her palm. "I need advice."

"What's the problem?"

"Okay, you remember my friend Jamie? Well, she likes this guy named Zeth, but I think Zeth likes me, and if I like him back, what will happen between Jamie and me?" She shrugged her shoulders. "I don't want to lose either one of them."

"We need more details," Rosa said. "Tell us about this Zett."

"Zeth," she corrected. "Okay, he's really hot and he's a good student—"

"I have to get some things from the cooler," I said. "Keep going."

Tara continued with her monologue while I pulled stems for the next order, prepped the container, put in the wet foam, and began to dethorn the roses, still keeping my eye on the clock. Mom hadn't stopped by yet, another demand on my time; I had promised to meet Marco after we closed at five; and when was I going to have time to call Nikki? My best friend, Nikki Hiduke, with whom I had lived after getting the boot from law school, had left two messages on my cell phone about wanting to get together, and I had yet to return her calls.

"So what should I do?" Tara asked, breaking into my thoughts.

My head snapped up. "What?"

"About Jamie and Zeth," Tara said.

"Umm."

"Here's what I would do," Rosa said, leaning on her elbows, totally engaged in the conversation.

For once I was glad for her interference. I finished the arrangement, wrapped and tagged it, and stored it in the cooler, then pulled another order.

"That's a great idea, Rosa," Tara said, and got up to give her a hug. "What do you think, Auntie A?"

Deer in the headlights moment number two. "I think that you should"—I had no clue what she was talking about—"run that past me again. I need a little more time to mull it over."

"Can't." Tara slung her backpack over one shoulder. "Have to go home and study for a test." She gave me a quick hug, then turned to Rosa and threw her arms around her. "You're the best, Rosa. *Muchas gracias.* I can't wait to try your suggestion."

After Tara left, we worked in silence for about thirty seconds; then Rosa said quietly as she snipped leaves, "What do *you* think of my suggestion?"

"Well," I said, then shrugged. "I guess it could work."

She gave me a skeptical glance. "Really?"

"Really."

She went back to snipping. "You have no idea what I'm talking about, do you?"

"None."

"You'd better be careful," Rosa said. "You don't want to push her away."

"How am I pushing her away?"

"By not paying attention. You think she didn't notice you giving her the bug eyes?"

"I was paying attention—part of the time."

"What was the name of her hot guy?"

"Jamie."

"*Dios mío,* Abby, that is her *girlfriend*'s name. The boy is called Zett. I know you are busy, but family is important, too. You have to give them some attention."

I did not appreciate receiving a lecture from my new employee. She had no idea of all the demands on my time. And wasn't his name Zeb?

"Yoo-hoo!" I heard from the other room.

With a heavy sigh, I rolled my shoulders. Mom had arrived.

"See?" Rosa said. "You're pushing away your mother before she even gets here."

"I give her lots of attention," I said, just as the curtain parted and Mom came in.

"You give lots of attention to whom?" Mom asked, coming over to press a kiss on my cheek.

"Tara," I said, darting a warning glance at Rosa. "She just stopped by."

"I know," Mom said. "I saw her out front. She really appreciated you taking time to talk to her, Rosa." This was said with a sidelong glance in my direction to see whether I caught it.

"*Gracias*, Maureen," Rosa said, coming around the table to give her a hug and an air kiss. "You look so nice in turquoise."

"Thank you," Mom said. "You're very sweet to say so."

Now that she mentioned it, my mom did look good in her turquoise top and dark brown slacks. The colors accentuated her light brown hair and peaches-and-cream skin. For someone in her fifties, Mom looked great.

"I agree," I said as she hung her navy jacket over one of the stools and set her tote bag down by her feet. Whatever new art was inside, it wasn't very big.

"Love that sweater, Mom."

"You should. You bought it for me last Christmas." Mom cocked one eyebrow. "Remember?"

"Well, of course I remember." Did not remember at all.

Rosa rubbed her hands together, her eyes sparkling with anticipation. "What did you bring us today?"

"Didn't Abby tell you?" Mom asked.

"Tell us what?" Lottie asked, stepping through the curtain.

"About my latest artistic endeavor," Mom said.

"You know," I said, "we've been so busy today that it slipped my mind. Why don't you show them?"

Mom gave me a questioning glance. "Okay." Turning to face the women, which now included Grace, she said, "I've decided to go in a completely new direction — writing children's mysteries."

She reached into her bag and pulled out a bound manuscript with a card stock cover showing a crayon sketch of Bloomers. In front of the flower shop sat a brown-and-white dog wearing a plaid Sherlock Holmes cap standing beside a potted yew. A gun and what appeared to be shards of metal lay on the sidewalk nearby.

That was what she'd wanted me to see on Saturday?

"This is just a prototype, of course, but you get the idea."

Rosa read the title out loud. "*Shrubs and Shrapnel.*"

It was all I could do not to groan. Shrapnel in a children's book? By the expression on Lottie's face, I could see she was fighting a laugh. Grace looked appalled.

Rosa was confused. "I don't get the idea, Maureen. I thought shrapnel were sharp metal pieces from a bomb explosion."

"Usually, yes," Grace said quietly, clearly embarrassed for my mom.

Rosa, never one to squelch any thought that came into her head, looked at my mom. "So a bomb explodes in a children's book? Do all the children die?"

"Heavens no!" Mom said. "I just thought the title had a nice ring to it."

Probably not the kind that was going to come from a cash register.

At our silence, Mom said, "I'll keep looking."

Trying to make her feel better, Lottie said, "Look at your name, Maureen. You're an author!"

"Muy excelente," Rosa said. "But why did you draw the dog with three legs?"

Mom glanced at me again. "I was sure Abby would have mentioned this. All of the books will be about Seeky, a three-legged dog detective that lives at Bloomingvales Flower Shop and seeks clues. Seeky. Get it?"

Rosa clapped her hands together and laughed. "I love it. How clever."

"And you're all in the story," Mom said.

I hoped she hadn't called me Flabby.

"I'll give you all a complimentary copy once it's published. First I need Abby to proofread it for me. I wanted her to read it Saturday, but she didn't have time."

Rosa glanced at me and raised her eyebrows.

"I was really busy," I mumbled.

"Will your books be sold in the bookstore in town?" Lottie asked.

"I'm going to put them up for sale right here at Bloomers," Mom announced, beaming with pride. "Truly, can you think of a better place?"

Not that I could say out loud.

"Once my manuscript is polished, I can have books printed and delivered by the end of next week," Mom said. "So let's look around for a place to display them."

"Who's your publisher?" Grace asked.

"I suppose you could say me," Mom said lightly. "I'm paying to have them printed. It was expensive, but with all of you helping me sell them, I'm positive I'll recoup my money and have extra to put in your cash drawer besides."

"What will you sell them for?" Lottie asked.

"Twenty-four dollars and ninety-five cents," Mom said. "Before tax."

For a skinny little book by an unknown writer? This was a bad situation. If no one was interested in buying them, Mom would be crushed. And if we pushed them onto our regular customers, we risked angering them, especially if the book stunk.

Rosa put her arm around Mom's shoulders. "We will do a good job for you, Maureen. Now let's go find a place for them."

As they walked arm in arm toward the curtain, Mom asked, "Are you enjoying working here, Rosa?"

"I am," Rosa replied, "but I must confess I'm a little worried because of the murder that happened right across the street."

Mom came to a dead stop and swung around to stare at me in alarm.

"Don't panic," I said. "The murder didn't take place there."

"That's supposed to be comforting?" Mom asked. "Another killing in our quiet little town?"

"It's not so little or quiet anymore, Maureen," Lottie said. "We're getting more urbanized each day, and with urbanization comes urban problems."

"When I was a child," Mom said, "we didn't even lock our front doors at night. Now I need an alarm system."

Grace cleared her throat and squared her shoulders, folding her hands in front of her waist. "Quoting the famous Roman leader Marcus Aurelius Antoninus, 'Everything is in a state of metamorphosis. Thou thyself art in everlasting change and in corruption to correspond; so is the whole universe.'"

"I don't understand," Rosa said.

"It means we can't stop progress," Lottie said.

And yet there we stood not getting any work done.

I stayed at the shop until six thirty that evening; then Seedy and I headed up the street to meet Marco for dinner. Down the Hatch was packed when we arrived, and there was no sign of my husband, but his brother Rafe was pouring beer behind the bar.

Raphael Salvare was ten years younger than Marco, a little leaner and greener than his big brother but equally as sexy with his Mediterranean good looks. After Rafe dropped out of college a semester before graduation, his mom sent him to Marco to be straightened out. It had been a struggle, but finally Rafe was on a good path, learning how to manage the bar so Marco could devote more time to his private detective business and, more important, to me. I was still waiting for that last part to happen.

"Hey, hot stuff," Rafe called over the noise. "You're late tonight."

I wasn't up to yelling back, so I just gave him a wave, picked up my shivering Seedy, and shouldered my way through the crowd standing three deep at the bar.

Stepping into Down the Hatch Bar and Grill was a trip back in time, to when orange, avocado, and dark walnut paneling were all the rage. It was the oldest standing bar in New Chapel and the favorite watering hole for attorneys, judges, and businesspeople in town, as well as the college students from New Chapel University, which was located just half a mile from the town square.

I'd been urging Marco to redo it since he became the owner two years earlier, but he always claimed he was afraid of a customer revolt. I understood his desire to keep his clients happy, yet every time I glanced up at the wall over the row of orange booths and saw the giant blue plastic carp hanging there, my insides screamed, *Renovate!*

"Your honey's in the back," Gert the waitress said to me in her gravelly smoker's voice. "Want me to get him for you?"

"No, thanks. I'll surprise him."

A diminutive but spunky senior citizen, Gert had worked at the bar since the 1960s, which was the last time the interior had been updated. She was also a mom for all the young employees who often went to her for advice.

"Is Abby treating you well?" she asked Seedy, who wagged her tail and gave a little yip. "You must be doing something right, doll," she said to me. "This little peanut is really coming out of her shell."

Because there wasn't an open table in the house, Marco and I ended up eating in his office, with Seedy curled up in Marco's big desk chair. Seated in the black leather slingback chairs facing his ebony metal desk with our feet propped on the desktop and our food in our laps, we took turns filling each other in on the events of the day. When it was my turn, I told him about the newspaper article on Jingles, my subsequent conversation with Reilly, and the information that Robert Hall had provided.

"I agree that Jingles being stressed out, packing a bag, and leaving suddenly sounds bad," I said, "but I refuse to believe he's a killer on the run. For all we know, he received a call from a relative in distress and had to take off."

Marco put his plate on the desk. "The key words there are 'for all we know.'"

"What do you mean?"

"What do we really know about the window washer, babe? He has a name besides Jingles, but no one knows it. Do you ever see him with friends? Does he have a family? You didn't even know he was living at the Y."

"And you did?"

"Working at a bar? Are you kidding?"

"Still, Marco, you can't judge Jingles based on bar gossip. He's been washing windows on the square for a long time. Someone has to know more about him."

"But see, that's what I mean. With all the gossip I hear at the bar, the only thing I know is where he lives. Why doesn't he use his real name? Is he hiding something?"

"So, based on a nickname, you're saying Jingles might be the murderer?"

"I'm playing devil's advocate, sweetheart. Just because who you see every day is a quiet, hardworking older man, that doesn't mean he can't also have committed a crime. Everyone has a breaking point, and no one truly knows what makes another person tick."

In a sudden change of mood, Marco gave me his sexy half smile, where one side of his mouth curved up impishly. "That is, unless he shares that person's childhood bedroom with her."

That sounded like an invitation to me. I put my plate next to his, then sat in his lap, my arms around his neck, my legs dangling over the arm of the chair. "So what makes me tick, Salvare?"

"This, for one thing." He kissed me for a long, luxurious moment, his firm lips on mine, sending tingles of pleasure coursing through my body. In a sexy murmur he added, "And this," and began nibbling my earlobe and down my neck.

Delicious sensations rippled through my body. "You didn't learn those things from my childhood bedroom."

"Mmm," he said, which meant my words weren't registering. Marco's brain had become disengaged. "Want to see what else I learned?" he whispered.

"Wait. I'll lock the door."

"Not necessary." Marco began unbuttoning my white shirt. "No one's going to come in unless I say they can."

I caught his hands. Men may get caught up in the heat of the moment, but women will always be pragmatic. "Not true. Jillian would come in. And so would—"

A loud knock at the door made me jump.

"What is it?" Marco snapped.

"I'm giving you a heads-up," Rafe called. "Mom is here."

With a heavy sigh, I finished, "—your mother."

CHAPTER FOUR

Francesca Salvare was an imposing presence. In her midfifties she had the energy, hourglass shape, and smooth olive skin of a much younger woman. Her eyes were dark brown and crinkled at the corners like Marco's, with dark brown arched brows and thick black lashes. Her gloriously full-bodied dark hair waved around her face and onto the tops of her shoulders. Her white silk shirt, paired with multiple silver chains and flowing black slacks, was impeccably clean. If Hollywood ever held a young Sophia Loren look-alike contest, Francesca would win it.

As though we were doing something wrong, I sprang to my feet and turned my back to quickly button my shirt. As Marco stood up, I gave him a look that said, *Well? Did the closed door stop* her?

Francesca paused in the doorway to evaluate the situation. Then, choosing to ignore our obviously private moment, she held out her arms. "Marco, my son." She kissed both cheeks, then turned to me with arms wide. "Bella Abby, how are you, my darling? Is my son treating you right?"

"Your son," I said, giving Marco a smile, "spoils me rotten."

"Then I did a good job of raising him," she said, running a critical eye over me. "Are you feeling well? Sleeping okay?"

"Yes, I'm fine."

"Hungrier than usual?" she questioned. "Any queasiness when you wake up?"

"Mamma," Marco said sharply, using the Italian inflection. "Stop."

She gave him a baffled look that was worthy of an Oscar. "Stop what?"

"We have enough on our plates without you putting pressure on us," he said. "You have grandchildren already. Dote on *them*."

She looked chagrined. "I'm sorry, Marco, but these things can sneak up on you when you least expect them." She shrugged eloquently. "I love being a grandmother. I cannot hide my feelings. Being my son, you of all people should know that."

"We'll let you know when we're ready to start a family," I said.

She crossed her hands over her heart. "That is all I ask."

"What brings you here, Mom?" Marco asked.

"I was shopping at the deli and heard the news about the murder, and of course my first concern was for your safety." She took my hand between hers. "Bella, promise me that you will not leave your little shop in the evening unless Marco comes for you."

"I've got her covered," Marco said, ushering Francesca toward the door. "Go home and stop worrying."

"I am a *mother*," she said from the hallway. "It's my duty to worry." In a whisper that carried all the way to my ears, she said, "Make sure Bella eats well. You want your future *bambini* to be healthy."

"Bye, Francesca," I called.

Marco came back in and sat down. "Sorry."

"I understand she means well," I said, "but I'm glad you told her to stop it. There's too much going on to even think about thinking about starting a family."

"I know," he said in a comforting tone, taking my hand and pulling me toward him. "Now where were we?"

Rafe stuck his head in the doorway. "Marco, if you're done eating, we could use another hand at the bar. A big group of college dudes just came in."

Heaving a frustrated sigh, Marco asked him, "Can you give me ten minutes?"

"Sure," Rafe said, and shut the door.

Ten whole minutes. Couldn't get much more romantic than that.

"Go tend to your customers," I said, giving Marco a nudge. "I need to take Seedy home and unwind. It's been a stressful day."

Marco pointed at me. "You. Me. Later."

His words were brief but his message stirred all kinds of yumminess inside me. "It's a date."

Back at my parents' house, I walked Seedy around outside for five minutes so she could take care of her business; then we went into the house through the back door. As she hobbled up the hallway toward the front staircase, I opened a bottle of Cabernet Sauvignon that I'd picked up at the Old World Deli weeks before and pulled a goblet from the cabinet, visions of relaxing in a hot bath with a glass of wine and a good book dancing in my head. My mom, however, had other ideas.

"Abigail, come look at some cover sketches I drew for the next two books," she said, walking up behind me.

"Now?" I was pouring wine. It was clearly a sign that I needed some downtime. Didn't she see that?

"Bring your glass with you. In fact, I'll have some, too." She got out another goblet and set it beside mine. "We can sip Cabernet and brainstorm together. Oh, and remind me to give you a copy of the first book so you can take it to bed with you."

That wasn't what I wanted in bed with me. I put the bottle down on the counter with a *thunk*. "Mom, I'm tired. I've had a long, hectic day. I'll look at your covers tomorrow." Maybe . . . If I was in a better mood.

I picked up my glass and started for the door.

"Okay," she said in a hurt voice. "That's fine."

When Mom said, "That's fine," nothing was fine. But I was wound too tightly to turn back. I had feelings, too. Didn't anyone notice that?

I sulked in the tub until the water chilled, feeling both angry and guilty. I crawled into bed to read and fell asleep so soundly, I didn't even hear Marco come in.

Tuesday

"Morning, Sunshine," Marco said as I sat up and stretched. "Here's your coffee."

"Thank you." With my eyes half shut and still in those first few seconds before reality set in, I savored the mellow brew with a happy sigh. Then I opened my eyes all the way and saw a giant faded movie poster of *The Wizard of Oz* staring at me from across the room. The Cowardly Lion seemed to be mocking me.

"Why the frown?" Marco asked.

I put my coffee on the nightstand and threw back the covers. "That silly old poster is coming down. And so are those ridiculous attendance certificates." I marched across the carpet and began to take down everything on the wall.

"Come on, Seedy," Marco called, snapping his fingers, "or we might be next."

"I'm sorry," I said. "I don't want to be in a bad mood already, but these things"—I placed the stack of framed certificates on the floor and gave them a shove with my foot—"just remind me that I'm trapped in my parents' house. Do you know that I was all set for a relaxing bath last night when Mom ambushed me? And then she was hurt when I didn't want to spend the rest of my evening with her."

Marco put his arm around me, letting me nestle under his chin as he rubbed my back. "I knew something was wrong when I found you sleeping with your paperback clenched in your hands and your teeth grinding together. I'm sorry, sweetheart. I wish I could hurry up the building process. But just think. One day you'll look back and see how short our stay here actually was. Come on, let's get some breakfast in you. That always makes you feel better."

I wrapped my robe around me and followed him to the kitchen, where Dad was already reading the paper aloud to Mom, and she was stirring something in a pot on the stove, getting ready to pour it into the four bowls stacked nearby. I wanted to grab the car keys and run.

"Morning, kids," Dad said jovially.

"Morning," I said in a grumpy voice. When Mom didn't answer, I figured she hadn't heard me, so I said louder, "Morning, Mom."

She kept her back to me and said in a stiff voice, "Good morning, Abigail."

And there we had it. Mom had gone from hurt to angry; Dad was clearing his voice to begin the article again; Marco was checking the time; and I had already pulled out my phone to read e-mails. Tuesday was off to a fine start.

Bloomers buzzed with activity all day. The coffee-and-tea parlor had customers from the time we opened until the time we closed; orders came in steadily; shoppers browsed and bought ready-made arrangements; and I worked nonstop until our afternoon break, when I had to take Seedy outside. Then I sat down at my desk to give my legs a rest, shook out my cramped hands, and relaxed with the cup of chamomile tea Grace had brought me.

"I have to drop a deposit at the bank before I deliver this last batch of flowers," Lottie said, pulling out large funeral arrangements from one of the walk-in coolers. "Too much cash in the till makes me nervous. Can you cover the shop, Gracie? I need to get these arrangements over to Happy Dreams before four o'clock."

"I'll do my best," she said, putting a hand to her forehead.

"Are you okay, Grace?" I asked.

"I'm feeling a little light-headed, but I'm sure it will pass."

"Did you eat lunch?" I asked.

"I nibbled on a scone."

Hearing the word "scone," Seedy came out from beneath the table to wag her tail at Grace. Clearly there was some precedent for this action.

"It's not for you, Seedy," I said. She tilted her head at me. Then, apparently figuring it out, she went back underneath to her doggy bed to chew on a toy.

"You need some protein, Gracie," Lottie said. "I try to grab a handful of peanuts when I can. There's a jar in the kitchen. Go get some."

The bell over the door jingled and the three of us glanced at one another. Lottie had a topiary in one arm and a funeral wreath in the other, and I was snipping long-stemmed roses.

"I'll see to it," Grace said, and, straightening her shoulders, marched out.

"Abby," Lottie said, "we need someone to help out in the afternoons. As New Chapel grows and Bloomers gets busier, we're gonna be run ragged, and Grace isn't as young as we are. This pace is already taking a toll on her."

"I know," I said with a sigh.

"Why don't you ask Rosa to work full-time?"

"Rosa would need health benefits, and I can't afford that," I said.

"Are you sure she wouldn't be covered under Sergio's old policy? Seems like I've heard that widows can get some kind of coverage. Anyway, it wouldn't hurt to ask."

"I thought I'd just put an ad online for another part-time person."

"Asking Rosa would be simpler," Lottie said in that singsong voice mothers use when they want to make a point without adding *you fool* to it.

"I guess," I said, when I really wanted to say, *Sorry, but no.* I felt a frisson of annoyance with Lottie for adding extra pressure to my day, but then that little voice of conscience inside reared up at the thought that I could be annoyed with the woman who had rescued me from flunk-out oblivion.

Grace stuck her head through the curtain and said quietly, "Abby, your cousin is headed this way. I saw her from the window."

Just what I needed to make my afternoon perfect: a visit from the diva. I went back to the worktable and picked up my clippers. It always helped me keep calm if I was working.

"Maybe Jillian can lend a hand up front until I get back," Lottie said, zipping up her jacket. "She knows how to schmooze the customers."

As Lottie left through the back door, a double baby stroller came crashing and bumping its way into the workroom from the front, sending Seedy scampering for safety into the kitchen as fast as her three legs could carry her. Inside one stroller lay a tiny girl wrapped in frilly aqua-and-pink bunting. Inside the other sat Princess, a young black-and-white Boston terrier wearing a gold collar and aqua sweater. Whimpers were coming from both strollers.

Steering the contraption was my über-fashionable and very spoiled cousin Jillian, dressed in a gold leather swing coat and short aqua leather boots, and carrying a huge aqua plaid diaper bag. Her copper hair hung in a silken sheet down her back. Her big eyes were lined in aqua eyeliner and her lips were tinted coral. Everything about her was perfection—except her mood.

"Why did I do this to myself?" she asked, flopping down in my desk chair and swiveling to face me. "Why did I think this would be fun?"

Obviously we'd get no assistance from Jillian today. "Are you talking about having a baby?"

"No one told me being a mother would be this hard." She saw her terrier ready to jump out and grabbed the dog before she could leap. "And it's your fault I have Princess. If you hadn't taken me to the animal shelter, I never would have seen her."

"You love that dog, Jillian."

Placing Princess back in the stroller, she pointed her index finger and said, "Stay."

When the dog prepared to jump again, she said, "Oh, whatever. You don't listen to me anyway."

"How about we fasten her leash to the stroller handle?" I asked. Princess had been known to create havoc wherever she went, and I wasn't in the mood to have my work space torn up.

"Don't ever have a baby, Abs," Jillian said as she secured the dog's leash. "It will turn you into a sleepless, irritable monster, because that's what I am, a sleep-deprived, grouchy, failure-of-a-mother *monster*." She put her hands over her face and sobbed, causing the whimpers from baby and dog to escalate. "I'm so terrible, you won't return my phone calls. And did you even hear what I told you yesterday morning when I called?"

"Of course I *heard*," I said slowly, while I tried to recall her end of the conversation. "It was about Harper and the wonderful thing she did."

Jillian lowered her hands to stare at me in horror. "Wonderful? She cried all night! Is that what you're calling wonderful these days?"

As Jillian began to sob anew, I looked at the stack of orders and felt the muscles in my shoulders tighten. Lottie was gone, Grace was woozy, no one was manning the shop, and I was up to my eyeballs in stress. But what could I do? Ignore Jillian? Apparently, I'd already done that.

I grabbed a doggy treat from Seedy's supply and stuck it in the dog's mouth, reinserted the dropped plug into the baby's mouth, then put my arms around my cousin and held her while she poured out her troubles.

Jillian Ophelia Knight Osborne was my first cousin on my father's side. At twenty-six, she was a head taller and a year younger than me—unless you went by maturity, in which case she was twelve—had a mere dusting of freckles, and was a whole lot thinner, even after having had a baby.

When Jillian was little, she had severe scoliosis, resulting in a lot of parental pampering until she was old enough to undergo treatments. Her crooked back also resulted in her being bullied at school, which even at a young age I wouldn't tolerate. So I stepped in to protect her and had been her guardian ever since.

After college, Jillian had opened a personal shopping service called Chez Jillian, which she ran from her home. She'd also run through myriad fiancés before finally settling on Claymore Osborne, a successful CPA and the younger brother of Pryce Osborne II, the man I'd nearly married.

As it turned out, the universe had something better in mind for me. Just a few months after I thought my life was ruined, I took a big leap of faith and bought Bloomers and then met the man of my dreams. Funny how things worked out when you were able to look back at them.

But right now I couldn't keep my eyes off the clock. *Tick-tock*. Why did Jillian have to pick today to have a meltdown?

The bell over the door jingled. I knew customers were in the shop. I had to get my cousin out the door as quickly as I could so I could tend to business.

"What triggered this reaction, Jillian? You've always been so self-confident."

She raised her head, and I noticed the purple bags under her eyes. "I'm sleep deprived, Abs. I might have slept two hours last night. I can't function on two hours. You know I need at least seven."

It was one of the few ways in which Jillian and I were alike.

"You have a nanny. You have a caring husband. What's keeping you awake?"

"Do you know what it's like having the Osbornes for in-laws? They judge me all the time. I can see them assessing Harper every time they come over. Is she getting adequate milk? Did she gain enough weight? Any rashes from being left in wet diapers? Will that pearl halo cause brain tumors?

"And that's another thing. They're always dropping by. I never know when they'll ring the doorbell. Morning, afternoon, evening—it could be anytime. I don't dare nap, and I've lost five pounds from worrying about having everything perfect for them. The pressure is getting to me, Abs. I don't know what to do."

I could've told her a thing or two about pressure, but as she had resumed sobbing, now did not seem like the right time.

"Jillian, you need to have a serious talk with Claymore. Let him work on his parents. That's his responsibility."

The bell over the door jingled again.

"I tried to explain my feelings to him," Jillian said, "but he thinks his parents are wonderful. Abby, you have to help me."

"I'm sorry, Jillian," I said, backing toward the door, "but I have to go up front to wait on customers. Lottie is out on deliveries and Grace is busy in the parlor."

"But you didn't answer me. What should I do?"

"I'll call you this evening and we can discuss it then, okay? Great. Take care now."

I slipped through the curtain and hurried to the cash counter, where an impatient man was holding a black ceramic vase filled with white roses that he'd plucked from

the display case. He tapped his credit card on the countertop as I rang up his purchase, then scowled at me when I
offered to wrap the flowers.

"Don't you always wrap flowers?" he snarled. "It should
be an automatic yes."

He almost ran into Jillian's stroller when he turned to
go, then cast me a blaming glance as though I had caused
his near collision.

There was one less customer I'd have to worry about.

Jillian gave me a sad-eyed frown as she waited for
him to open the door for her, clearly an attempt to make
me feel guilty.

"I'll call," I said. "I promise."

Now I had two phone calls to return. I hoped my BFF
Nikki was still speaking to me.

The other customers I'd heard come in had either
headed into the parlor or left the shop, so I checked on
Grace, who gave me a nod to let me know she was holding
up, and went back to my haven behind the curtain. But
even then, what with running up front to wait on shoppers, hurrying to the back to work on orders, and answering the phone, I had a hard time finding any Zen moments.

Seedy and I didn't get to Down the Hatch until after
six thirty p.m. for the second night in a row, when it was
too late to nab a table, so once again we ate a quick meal
at Marco's desk.

After listening to my litany of complaints, Marco said,
"Lottie's right. You need more help. Why don't you want
to offer the job to Rosa?"

"Because Rosa needs benefits, and I can't afford them."

"How do you know she needs them unless you ask
her? She should be covered under her late husband's insurance policy for eighteen months after his death. By

then, if your business continues to grow, you might be able to offer health benefits to all three women. You know what Lottie is always telling you. Think positive."

Who had time to think?

"Is this a private party or can anyone join?" I heard.

Sergeant Reilly stepped into Marco's office. He was wearing jeans and a pale green shirt, obviously off duty.

"Come in," Marco said, standing. "Take my chair. I'll sit at my desk."

"Thanks," Reilly said as he eased himself down beside me. "I have news about Jingles I thought you needed to hear. Oh, by the way, I ordered a sandwich. Okay if I eat with you guys?"

I was so irritable, even the word "guys" grated on my nerves. "Since the only other guy in the room is my husband, it looks like Marco will have to field that question."

"*Someone's* in a bad mood," Reilly said, raising his eyebrows.

First he called me a guy, then a mere someone. My day was complete.

CHAPTER FIVE

"I'll tell Rafe to send your food back here," Marco said to Reilly, picking up his desk phone.

"What's the news about Jingles?" I asked Reilly.

"There's a warrant out to bring him in. Detectives want to question him about the murder."

Marco hung up the phone. "Jingles? Why?"

Reilly glanced over his shoulders as though someone might be listening in. Must have been the other guy he'd referred to earlier. "Seems there's a connection between our murder victim Dallas Stone and our local window washer. Apparently, they knew each other a long time ago, when Jingles was going by his real name, Samuel Atkins."

I tried to picture Jingles as a Samuel, but the name sounded too proper. Sam, maybe. "So what if they knew each other years ago?"

"By itself, you're right," Reilly said. "But here's the catch. Detectives found a gold money clip in Stone's pocket with the initials *S.A.* on it—I'm talking real gold, not gold plate—along with a letter from Samuel Atkins's son dated one week ago in which he expresses dismay that his father has been working all these years as a window washer and calling himself Jingles. The last thing he wrote was to please let him know how to contact his dad.

Then—*bingo*. Stone ends up dead. That's why they want to talk to Jingles."

"Right off the bat, I'll question the gold money clip belonging to Jingles," Marco said. "This is a senior citizen who rents a room at the Y, hardly the type to use a gold money clip. And if the clip is Jingles's, how would it end up in a banker's pocket? Are you sure you've got the right guy? Maybe Stone's maternal grandfather's initials were S.A."

"They're contacting Samuel Atkins's son as we speak," Reilly said. "He should be able to identify Jingles and tell us about the clip. As far as it ending up in the banker's pocket, one of the detectives has a couple working theories. One is that Jingles used the gold clip to pay him for something. The other is that Stone stole it from him."

"Which detectives are assigned to the case?" I asked.

"Lead detective is Al Corbison," Reilly said, and at my groan, he added, "I know you're not a fan of Corbison, but—"

"You think?" I asked. "After he tried to railroad me into confessing to a murder he knew I didn't commit but was too lazy to look for anyone else?"

"You're touching a raw nerve, Sean," Marco warned. "Tread lightly, my friend."

"Seriously, Reilly," I said, "what single fact has come to light that would lead Corbison to surmise that our window washer used a valuable money clip to barter with a banker? Or that this banker slipped into the Y, found Jingles's room, rummaged through his belongings, and stole it? Is there any history of Jingles bartering with people? Or of Dallas Stone stealing?"

"Look, Abby," Reilly said, "I don't know what evidence the detectives have and I'm not defending Corbison, but he's not totally off the wall here. There's another connection between the two men. Dallas Stone took a room at the former Y just a couple of weeks ago."

Oops. I stood corrected. It *wasn't* completely out of bounds to think that Stone might have stolen something from Jingles's room.

Despite my exhaustion and general crabby disposition, at that bit of interesting info my brain woke up and shook itself a few times. "Interesting," I said. "I wonder how easy it is to break into someone's room."

"I don't know," Reilly said. "I've never been on a call there."

"Have they located the primary murder scene?" Marco asked.

"Not yet," Reilly said, "but because the ground is soft from all the spring rain, they were able to spot tracks made by a wheeled cart of some sort. They lead from the side of the courthouse to the curb at Franklin and then pick up at the mouth of the alley that runs between Bloomers and the realty business next door. Since that short stretch of alley connects to the longer alley that runs behind Franklin, they're searching that entire area."

"Have you heard what was used to strangle Stone?" Marco asked.

"The forensics expert is coming at the end of the week," Reilly said. "Right now the coroner's best guess is something soft. Definitely not rope. I'd bet it's the missing necktie."

And Seedy had been sniffing it, or part of it at least. If only I'd known. "The groundskeepers didn't find it?"

Reilly shook his head.

"Maybe someone tossed it in the nearest trash bin," I said.

"We searched them," Reilly said.

I felt a flicker of a memory. Had I seen the tie some-where else? Maybe when Seedy and I made our return trip across the courthouse lawn?

"Time of the murder?" Marco asked.

"Early estimate is Friday between two and eight p.m.," Reilly said. "Then we have a witness who saw Jingles packing a bag around four o'clock."

"Is your witness Robert Hall?" Marco asked.

"Correct," Reilly said.

"I still don't see the need for a warrant," I said. "All they have to go on is the victim and Jingles knowing each other in the past and living in the same building now, a gold clip that may or may not have belonged to Jingles—oh, and a letter from a son who's trying to contact his dad. They can't place Jingles at the murder scene because they don't have one, and they can't tie him to the weapon, which they also don't have."

Reilly leaned forward. "This is why I'm telling you guys—sorry, I mean both of you. It's all circumstantial at this point, but you know how that can go. The DA needs to find someone quickly to pin the crime to so he can reassure the public that they're safe."

"And in the process make himself look like a hero," I said.

"Another raw nerve," Marco told Reilly.

"There are three connections between Jingles and the victim," Reilly said. "Tenuous maybe, but if the DA sets his sights on Jingles as his prime suspect—well, you know how that goes. So I thought you might want to look into it on the QT."

Marco glanced at me as he answered, "I'm sympathetic to Jingles's predicament, but we'll have to take a pass, Sean. We have a little too much going on right now."

"Way too much," I said, even though part of my brain was jumping up and down at the thought of a new case.

Brain to Abby: *Puzzle to solve! Whoopee! When can we start?*

Given my mental fatigue, this was clearly unacceptable and, frankly, shocking behavior.

Abby to brain: *Back off, buster. Don't make me come up there.*

"Just wait until Jingles comes back to town, Reilly," I said. "I'll bet he'll be able to clear this up in five minutes."

Wednesday

Sometimes my naïveté shocked even me. Why had I thought things would go well for Jingles when District Attorney Melvin Darnell was involved? Just over a year before, DA Darnell, working hand in hand with Detective Al Corbison, had tried to indict me for the murder of my former law professor because I'd delivered an arrangement to the professor's office prior to his being killed there. It had been a horrific experience. I still had nightmares.

And I wasn't alone in that. Marco, too, had had a similar experience with Darnell. It was another reason why we accepted cases like Jingles's. Too many people had been sent to prison wrongly because of overeager prosecutors who were willing to suppress or overlook evidence in order to get the conviction they wanted.

I didn't learn about Jingles's fate until noon, when

Marco came down to Bloomers to bring sandwiches for the four of us, a little surprise that made me love him even more.

"Dave dropped by to see me this morning," Marco said, feeding me the sandwich while I continued to work. "Reilly was right. Jingles is in trouble. He's being held in the county jail on suspicion of murder, awaiting his bond hearing."

I was appalled. "Poor Jingles! But surely Dave can get him out."

Dave Hammond was the attorney I'd clerked for while in law school. He had an office above Bingstrom's Jewelry Shop on Lincoln where he took on private cases as well as criminal matters. Whenever a legal problem arose, Dave was my go-to guy. They didn't come any more upstanding than him.

"Not until the judge determines whether he qualifies for a bond. Dave wouldn't give me any more information than that, but he did say that Jingles was going to need allies." Marco held out the sandwich so I could take another bite. "What do you think?"

"Delicious, but you know I always like turkey and Swiss cheese."

"I mean about getting involved."

I swallowed hard. "Marco, how can we? *When* can we? I haven't even been out to see our new house in over a week."

"I'm taking care of that, babe."

"I know! You take care of everything—grocery shopping, laundry, paying bills—and that makes me feel guilty."

"Abby, would you relax? I can handle it." He held up the sandwich. "Finish it off. There you go."

"And now you're even feeding me," I said with my mouth full.

Marco cupped my chin and looked into my eyes. "You take care of Bloomers and leave the rest to me, okay? As far as Jingles is concerned, let's wait to see what happens. Maybe the detectives will come up with evidence to point them in another direction."

"There has to be more evidence somewhere. Jingles wouldn't have come back to town if he was guilty."

"I could debate that, but not now. Come on, Seedy. Let's go for a walk."

Curled up in her bed, Seedy raised her head, wagged her tail, and stood up for a stretch before following Marco to the curtain.

"Hey," I called, and went to put my arms around him. "How did I get so lucky?"

"I could ask the same thing."

"Shall we try date night again tonight?"

"You've got it, babe." He gave me a kiss, then crouched down to fasten the leash to Seedy's collar, and left.

"That was nice of Marco," Lottie said, coming into the room to restock the display case. We'd had so many walk-in customers, she could hardly keep it filled.

"I finished my sandwich," I told her, "so take a break and have yours."

"I'll let Grace go first," Lottie said. "She hasn't stopped moving all morning. She sold out of her scones. I told her to order some pastries from the bakery, but she hasn't had a chance to get away."

"I'm leaving now," Rosa said, sticking her head through the curtain. She held up a paper bag. "I'm taking my sandwich with me. I'll eat it at my next job. That was so sweet of Marco to bring them down. Is there anything I can do for you before I go?"

I shook my head. "No. See you tomorrow."

Lottie gave me a chiding look before stepping inside the walk-in cooler.

I knew she wanted me to ask Rosa about working full-time, but even if I discounted the health insurance issue, I still had serious reservations about Rosa being with me all day.

Pros:
We were in desperate need of help in the afternoons.
Rosa did a good job for us.
Cons:
I couldn't give her health insurance.
She made everything she undertook seem like a piece of cake.

That would seemingly be a pro, but since I'd had to struggle for each and every success, I shifted it to the con side.

She acted like a know-it-all when it came to my family.
Lottie and Grace viewed her as a sort of Wonder Woman.

Two pros to four cons. End of debate. No Rosa.

Out in the shop, the bell over the door kept jingling, a reminder that my business was flourishing, and suddenly I felt small and petty. What was wrong with me? Why was I being churlish about a woman who my assistants thought was perfect for the job?

I slid the "piece of cake" comment back to the pro side and stepped to the curtain. "Rosa, would you come back here, please?"

"Yes?" Rosa asked.

"Do you have health insurance?"

"Yes, through my second job. Why?"

I was about to say, *It's nothing; I was just wondering*, because obviously she wouldn't want to quit that job to take one with no health insurance. But then Lottie stepped back out with her arms loaded with flowers and gave me a look that said, *It won't hurt to ask.*

So I said, "Because we need someone here in the afternoons. The thing is, I can't afford to carry health insurance for my employees, so I wouldn't be able to offer you—"

"I'll take it!" she cried.

"But what about insurance?" I asked.

"It's not a problem," she said. "I can get a COBRA policy through Sergio's former employer."

"Sweetie," Lottie said, "if memory serves, that coverage would only be good for eighteen months. Then what will you do?"

Tears of joy welling in her big, expressive eyes, Rosa waved away the concern. "That's a year and a half from now. I will put it in God's hands and something will come along."

She came toward me with open arms and practically lifted me off the ground hugging me. "*Gracias, gracias,* Abby. Every night I pray that I can work here full-time, and now my prayer has been answered."

"All of our prayers," Lottie amended.

I looked at her in surprise. She hadn't shared that with me.

Rosa walked to the curtain, thinking out loud. "I will talk to my boss today to see how long it will take to replace me. With any luck I can start in two weeks."

I knew I should have put up an ad online. We needed help now.

Rosa checked her watch. "*Dios mío*, I will be late. I'll see you tomorrow."

Lottie turned to me with a smile. "Was that so hard?"

I had another surprise visit from Marco at five o'clock. This time he wasn't bearing food, but he was bringing a request.

"We've been invited to a meeting of the downtown merchants tonight at seven at Big Red Quick Print," he said. "They want to discuss Jingles's predicament."

I felt my shoulders tighten at the thought of one more thing to do. "I was hoping we could go out and see the new house before I went home and collapsed. Do we have to go?"

"Yeah, pretty much. We're the guests of honor."

I had just enough time for a bowl of chicken stew before we headed to the printshop on Lincoln Avenue, the main street that ran through town. Inside the shop's reception area, a space about the size of a small bedroom that was outfitted with orange plastic chairs and a long counter along the back wall, I saw lots of familiar faces: Greg, the owner of Bingstrom's Jewelry; Donna from Windows on the Square Women's Boutique; Rob and Bonnie from Quick Print; Kathy, Olive Tree Day Spa's owner; Jennifer from Old World Deli; and a dozen more.

"We're so glad you could make it," Bonnie said, waving us up to the counter so we could stand in front of everyone. "We're all sick about what's happening to Jingles."

"You know he's in jail?" I asked.

"A friend of mine is a police dispatch operator," Jennifer said. "She contacted me because she's outraged, too."

"We feel he's being targeted unfairly," Greg said.

"I can vouch for that happening," I said, and several of them chuckled, remembering my experience, which had made the newspaper.

"Obviously the police don't know the man at all," Kathy said. "Anyone who really knew Jingles would realize he's not a killer."

The door opened and Connor MacKay stepped inside, waving his notebook in the air. "I'm here. You didn't start without me, did you?"

"Just getting started," Rob from the printshop called out.

I glanced at Marco and saw his expression harden. "What is MacKay doing here?" he growled.

Greg Bingstrom heard the comment and said to us quietly, "We asked Connor to come. We want to stir up the public against this injustice, so we figured we'd try for some free publicity."

Connor made his way to the counter, acting shocked when he saw us. "Well, look who we have here. New Chapel's favorite private eyes."

"We're just here to listen," I said.

Donna from the women's boutique said, "I'm sure most of you are aware of the volunteer work Jingles does, but for our reporter's sake, let's list them. I'll go first. He's at the Alzheimer's Care Center every Sunday afternoon, reading and playing checkers with the residents. My mother is one of those residents, by the way."

"Jingles visits patients at the VNA hospice center two evenings a week," a woman named Lou said. "I know because I'm a nurse there. Anyone who's ever had a loved one in hospice knows that it takes a special kind of person to be a volunteer there."

"Jingles takes my elderly neighbor to her dialysis appointment every Saturday morning," Jennifer from the deli said. "The woman doesn't have any family around to help."

"Wait," Connor said, scribbling notes. "What's the connection between the dialysis patient and Jingles?"

"She used to work at Buck's Shoe Shop here on the square," Jennifer said. "Every morning for over ten years she brought Jingles a bagel and a cup of coffee. I suppose he wanted to repay her kindness."

"Okay," Connor said, nodding as he finished writing. "Got it. What else?"

"*What else* is that we can't figure out why the police are being so tough on him," Rob said. "Most of the cops know Jingles, so what's going on really?"

"I'll tell you what's going on," I said, warming up to the subject of injustice. "It's all about—"

"Protocol," Marco said, cutting me off. He shot me a warning glance. "The detectives are just following standard police procedure."

"Whatever they're following," Greg said, "it sucks."

"Can I quote you on that?" Connor asked.

"I'd rather you didn't," Greg said quietly. "I need the police to keep their eye on my store."

"Okay," Connor said. "'An anonymous shop owner' is how I'll write it up."

"So we've pooled our resources," Jennifer said to Connor, "in order to hire Marco and Abby to conduct an investigation that will clear Jingles's name."

"We're counting on you," Bonnie said to us, taking my hand. "Please say you'll help."

All eyes were on us now, waiting for an answer they weren't going to like. I scanned their hopeful faces, ending with Connor, who grinned as if to say, *I knew you'd get involved.*

I glanced at Marco with wide eyes, asking silently, *How do we handle this?* Fortunately, Marco and I had become quite adept at reading each other's facial signals, which was especially beneficial in touchy situations like this one.

"No problem," he told the crowd. "We'll handle the investigation."

No, Marco. How *do we handle it? How! You missed the first word!*

Now my dear husband had put us in another bind, and I was not pleased. My brain, on the other hand, was doing cartwheels.

Brain to Abby: *You know you want this. Go with the flow, Abby. Just go with the flow.*

CHAPTER SIX

"You're quiet, Sunshine. What's up?"

We were on our way home, Marco driving my 'Vette through the dark streets, the radio tuned in to a local news station with the volume on low. I wasn't talking because I was focused on making a mental list of all the things I liked about him. It was done primarily to counter the other list I'd made right after the meeting. Right now, the other list was longer.

"I'm tired," I said finally.

"And?"

"And nothing."

"Yeah, right." He turned the corner onto my parents' street. "I can tell when you're angry."

"Really? Can you also tell when I want to get out of doing something? Because you seemed to have missed that message at the meeting."

"*I'm* going to take the case, Abby. Me. Alone. I just didn't want to say that in front of everyone because they would've wondered why. I didn't think you'd want to explain how stressed out you are."

So Marco had been protecting me? Now I felt guilty again. "Then I'm sorry I snapped at you."

He pulled the car up in front of the house and killed

the motor, then reached for my hand. "There's no need to stress out, babe. I've got everything covered."

Marco didn't seem to understand that his covering everything was its own kind of stress.

He put his hand on the back of my head and leaned toward me, his soulful, loving gaze searching mine until I had no choice but to melt inside. "Am I forgiven?"

I ran my hand along his strong jawline. "How could I stay mad at you, Marco?"

I gave him a kiss that was interrupted by a rap on the window. I looked around and saw my dad outside the car in his wheelchair.

With a sigh, I rolled down my window. "What are you doing, Dad?"

"Your mother and I just got back from the store. I saw you pull up and thought I'd give you a hard time, like I used to do when you were in high school and I caught you necking in the backseat of a car."

Clearly my dad was mistaking me for my brothers, because I didn't have any dates in high school. It wasn't until I went away to college that I attracted boys. However, I didn't want Marco to know that embarrassing fact.

"Okay, Dad," I said wearily. "We're coming inside now."

"Great. Your mom has an idea for a book title she wants to run past you, and I found an article on the Internet about Jingles that I thought you'd want to hear."

That was how I could stay mad at Marco.

In the end, I couldn't stay angry long. I simply loved my husband too much. On top of that, he was a very good persuader. All it took was a steamy sideways glance to let me know what was on his mind, and I turned into a big lump of Play-Doh. The words to an old favorite song of my mom's came to mind: *Bend me, shape me, anyway you want me.* All the stress of the day? In Marco's arms— gone.

Thursday

My morning started much too early. Five a.m., to be exact, two hours before I had to crawl out from the covers and face the new day. And why? Because my brain had gone into investigator mode, laying out a course of action that it mistakenly believed I'd be following.

"Not going to happen," I muttered, pulling the blanket over my head.

"What's not going to happen?" Marco mumbled, turning toward me.

I uncovered my face to whisper, "I was dreaming. Go back to sleep."

To relax my mind, I focused on taking slow, deep breaths. *In, count to five. Out, count to five. In, count to . . .*

Step one: Go see Jingles in jail. Find out if he is, in fact, Samuel Atkins.

Step two: If no, case closed. If yes, ask Jingles if he owned a gold money clip.

"Stop it!"

Marco rolled onto his back. "Was I snoring?"

"No. You're fine. Go back to sleep."

I decided to try another mental exercise. I closed my eyes and began to recite silently: *A for anemone. B for baby's breath. C for clematis. D for daisy. E for . . .*

Step three: Ask Jingles how he knew Dallas Stone. Also whether the man who wrote the letter in Dallas Stone's pocket is Jingles's son.

Step four: Find out whether Dallas had criminal history. Any enemies?

I clapped my hands over my ears, as though that would drown out my thoughts. Why was this happening? I didn't have time for an investigation.

I gave up and slid quietly out of bed. The room was pitch-black but I knew it by heart, so I made my way across the carpet, grabbed my robe from the hook on the back of the door, and let myself out. Before I could close the door, Seedy hobbled through, wagging her tail as though she'd found a playmate.

We went downstairs to the kitchen, where I sat at the table and wrote out the list in my head. Once it was on paper, I felt an enormous relief. There. That was all I needed: a list for Marco. Then Seedy and I curled up on the sofa in the family room under a thick, fake fur afghan and fell sound asleep.

When I opened my eyes, both parents were gazing down at me in concern.

"Did you and Marco have a fight?" Mom asked.

"No, I couldn't sleep," I said. "I didn't want to wake him up."

Dad held up my list. "Looks like you're working on the murder case."

"Not me," I said, sitting up. "That's for Marco. The downtown merchants asked us to work on Jingles's behalf, but I'm too busy, so Marco is going to take the job."

"You're too busy to snoop?" Dad glanced at Mom and they both laughed.

I folded the blanket and put it on the sofa. Another morning off to a galloping start.

*   *   *

"Thanks for the list," Marco said as the three of us headed toward town. It was ten minutes to eight o'clock, and as usual he was driving and Seedy was in my lap watching the scenery glide past.

"It's nice to see a plan on paper," Marco said. "I'll be meeting Dave at the jail to talk to Jingles in half an hour, so if you change your mind, I'd love to have you with me."

·   And a part of me wanted badly to be there with him, but the thought of all the orders waiting at the shop killed that feeling. It was the price of success, I supposed.

My phone rang, so I checked the screen and saw Nikki's name on it.

"Hi, Nik," I said cheerfully. "How are you?"

"Like you care," she said only half jokingly. "I thought we were going to have a girls' night out—when was that, three weeks ago?"

"I'm sorry, Nikki. I've been swamped at work. But I haven't forgotten about you."

"Really?"

I sensed the tone. She was angry.

Nikki and I had been best friends since third grade, when she'd skated by my house, fallen and skinned her knee, and had to be bandaged up by my mom. We'd been as close as sisters, sharing first dates, first kisses, first periods, and first true loves. After I was kicked out of law school, and with my marriage plans in tatters, rather than return home in shame, I'd moved into Nikki's apartment, and we'd resided quite happily together until Marco and I got married.

That had been the game changer. My promises to stay close had gotten lost in the shuffle of wedded bliss, family angst, and business stress.

"Let's set a date right now," I said. "Tell me when you're free and I will be there."

"You know when I'm free, Abby."

Yes, I did. I knew she worked afternoons at the county hospital as an X-ray technician and was off on weekends. But this coming weekend was Marco's weekend off, and did I want to miss out on an opportunity to be with him? We had so little quality time together.

Brain to Abby: *Working on Jingles's case together would solve that.*

Abby to brain: *Is your short-term memory not working? Orders! We have orders!*

I started scrolling through the calendar on my phone, hoping to spot a clearing. "There has to be something here," I muttered.

I heard a heavy sigh. "Whatever. Let me know when you find something."

"That didn't go well," I told Marco, slipping my phone in my purse. "Nikki's feelings are hurt."

"Looks like trouble ahead," Marco said.

"That's what I'm afraid of. I really need to set a firm date with her and stick to it."

"No, I mean actual trouble ahead."

I glanced up and saw fire engines blocking Lincoln Avenue, the main drag through town. Traffic was being diverted onto a side street, so Marco tried to get to Franklin by going around to Indiana Street on the south side of the square. That was blocked, too.

"What's happening?" Marco asked a policeman who was standing guard at one of the roadblocks.

"Gas line break," the cop said. "The square has been evacuated."

"Can I get to my bar?" Marco asked.

"Not if it's on the square."

My phone rang, and I saw Lottie's name on the screen. "Hey, Lottie, I can't get to Bloomers."

"I know. We tried, too. Gracie, Rosa, and I are at the Daily Grind Coffee Shop if you want to join us. We're going to wait here until they let us back in."

I covered the phone and whispered to Marco, "Are you still going to see Jingles?"

At his nod, I said, "I've got something else to do first, Lottie. Let me know if there are any updates in the situation."

Brain to Abby: *Wheeeeeee! Let's roll.*

Visiting an inmate at the county jail is neither easy nor pleasant. Of course, *being* an inmate isn't exactly a party, either. I know because I was once arrested and thrown in lockup in a case of mistaken—or rather stolen—identity.

We left Seedy with Marco's brother Rafe, who was renting Marco's former apartment, then met Dave Hammond in front of the county jail building located three blocks east of the square. We had to surrender our possessions, undergo a search, and be buzzed through a security door into another chamber before finally being taken to an interview room, a process that ate up fifteen minutes. Then, when I walked into the room, which was about the size of a closet, my claustrophobia reared its ugly head. With a thick steel door, no windows, and only a rectangular table and four hard chairs to break up the space, the gray block walls seemed to be coming in at me.

"Deep breaths, Sunshine," Marco said. "Focus on helping Jingles."

We waited for ten agonizingly long minutes until a guard

brought poor Jingles into the cramped room. He was wearing an orange jumpsuit, black rubber flip-flops, and the saddest expression I'd ever seen. He had a crown of white hair around a balding pate that was usually covered with a baseball cap, wrinkles around his light brown eyes, scraggly white eyebrows, deep grooves on either side of his down-turned mouth, and a sagging jawline and throat.

I'd never actually studied Jingles's face—he was just a pleasant older guy I'd wave to—but as I examined him now I could tell that he'd had a lot of misery in his life. I would have placed him in his eighties rather than his early seventies.

"I brought some friends to see you," Dave said as Jingles sat down across from Marco and me. "These are the Salvares—Marco and Abby. I'm sure you know their faces."

Jingles reached across and shook hands with each of us.

"As you've no doubt heard," Dave said, "Marco and Abby are private investigators, and they're going to look into the case the police seem to be building against you."

Jingles gazed at his hands, clasped on top of the table in prayer pose, and heaved a heavy sigh.

"We need to ask you some questions to get started," Marco said.

I opened the notebook and uncapped the pen I'd been allowed to bring with me.

"First of all," Marco said, "are you Samuel Atkins?"

Jingles waited a moment before giving a single nod. I quickly noted the question and answer in the notebook. On to step two.

"Do you own a gold money clip engraved with the initials *S.A.*?" Marco asked.

There was another hesitation; then Jingles nodded again.

Damn.

"Did you know Dallas Stone before coming to New Chapel?" Marco asked.

Again a hesitation followed by a nod. Jingles wouldn't look at us, which I'd always believed to mean that the person was lying. This time, however, I got the feeling that he was ashamed.

"You knew Dallas in what regard?" Marco asked.

Jingles tapped his thumbs together, as though pondering the question. Then he leaned closer to Dave, shoulder to shoulder with him, and said in a quiet voice, "I can't do this, Mr. Hammond. It's a bad idea. I suggest we take our chances with the judicial system. Innocent until proven guilty, and all that."

Shock number one: Jingles's naïveté when it came to the courts.

Shock number two: Jingles's cultured manner of speaking. He sounded more like my high school English teacher than an old window washer who rattled coins when he talked and shuffled slightly when he walked.

Shock number three: my bias. Why couldn't an elderly window washer sound cultured?

"Samuel," Dave began.

"Jingles," the window washer said quickly. "Not Samuel. Please."

"Jingles," Dave said, "if I felt comfortable with that option, I wouldn't have brought these folks in to see you. The police can only hold you here another six hours before they either have to charge you with something or let you go. In the meantime, Marco and Abby can be working on your behalf to make sure there's nothing to charge you with."

Not Marco and Abby, I wanted to say. *Just Marco.* But I didn't want to intrude on their conversation.

When the window washer didn't reply, Dave said, "The Salvares will be invaluable to us, trust me. We need them on our team, and rest assured that anything we say in this room goes no further. You don't have to worry about any confidential information getting out."

"It will get out," Jingles said emphatically. "It can't help but get out if they start investigating."

The man had a stubborn set to his mouth and still wouldn't look at us, so I reached across and put my hand on his wrist. "Marco and I were both very close to being charged with murder once. We understand how you feel. But if you think it's embarrassing to tell *us* the details of your life, imagine having your face splashed all over the TV news channels, along with your location, your occupation, and any rumors that are spreading about you. Talk about information getting out. And *that*, I can promise you, *will* happen when you're officially charged."

He gazed at me for the first time, his eyes filling with tears. "But you see, I never wanted—" He broke off and turned his face away, his chin trembling. He used his sleeve to wipe his eyes, then cleared his throat and looked up at the ceiling, as though trying to regain control. Finally he drew in a breath and started over, his voice a hoarse whisper. "I never wanted my boys to know what became of me."

"There's no shame in being a window washer," I said.

"It's not—" He paused, shook his head, and started again. "It was just better for them to think I died."

"Why? What did you do?" I asked.

He rubbed his hands over his face and said in a voice

that sounded as if he'd already given up hope, "What does it matter? It's done."

"Did you kill someone?" Marco asked.

His bluntness seemed to shake Jingles out of his despair. "No!" He glanced at Marco in shock.

"Did you murder Dallas Stone?" Marco continued quickly, keeping him off balance.

"Of course not!"

With barely a beat between questions, Marco asked, "Did you give him your money clip?"

"No!"

"Did you take his necktie?"

"His *necktie*? No, of course not."

"Did you have a run-in with him in the past?"

At that, Jingles stopped and looked away. We waited several moments for him to resume. Then Marco said, "Please answer the question, sir."

Jingles rubbed his face again but wouldn't respond. Dave gave us a shrug as though to say, *There's nothing you can do if he doesn't want to cooperate.*

I glanced at my watch, growing antsy. I'd kept my claustrophobia under control so far, but I didn't want to push it. Had the gas leak been fixed yet? Would I be able to get into Bloomers?

Marco noticed me checking the time and in a firm voice said, "Sir, my wife and I are busy people with businesses to run. We're not going to waste our time or yours if you're not interested in helping your cause."

"I'm sorry," Jingles muttered, glancing briefly at Marco before bowing his head. "It wasn't my idea to ask you here. It's probably for the best if we call it quits now before you lose any more valuable time."

Dave shook his head in disbelief. "Then I guess we're done here. Marco, Abby, thanks for coming in."

Before Marco and I could rise, the door opened and a sheriff's deputy stuck his head in. "Dave, a word, please?"

"Sure." He glanced at us with a concerned expression, then stepped out of the room. A cop wouldn't interrupt a lawyer's visit unless it was pertinent to that case. What was up?

Jingles stared at the closed door for a moment, then turned back to us. "Is that normal? Interrupting a lawyer-client session?"

"No," Marco said.

Jingles gazed at him without blinking, as though trying to read more into Marco's reply, but my husband remained silent.

Taking pity on Jingles, I said, "It must be some news on the case."

Jingles glanced at me, the fear in his eyes raw and strong and surprising. For just a moment, I wondered whether it was possible that Jingles *had* murdered Dallas Stone.

CHAPTER SEVEN

When Dave came back into the room, he was frowning.

Jingles had twisted around to see him and now rose halfway from his chair, clearly alarmed. "What is it?"

"The detectives have identified the primary murder site," Dave said. "It's the storage shed in the alley where you keep your window washing supplies."

Jingles's Adam's apple bobbed as he swallowed hard. "My *shed*?"

Dave nodded. "They're ready to bring a murder charge against you."

The color drained from the old man's face. He sat down hard. "But I wasn't even in town when the murder happened."

"How do you know when the murder happened?" Marco asked.

"Robert told me when I got back Tuesday," he replied.

"Is that Robert Hall?" I asked.

Jingles nodded.

"What did Robert tell you?" Marco asked.

"That Dallas's body had been found and the police were looking for me."

"So, as far as you knew, Dallas was murdered on Monday morning?" I asked.

"Correct," Jingles said.

"No, that's not correct," Dave said. "When you came to see me yesterday, I told you the coroner estimated the death as occurring on Friday afternoon. The timing of your departure is one of the reasons for my concern."

Jingles gazed at him blankly. "I don't recall that, Mr. Hammond. I must have been still reeling from the shock."

"What shocked you?" Marco asked. The way he was focusing a laserlike gaze on Jingles, I knew Marco still considered him a viable suspect.

"What shocked me?" Jingles repeated, as though surprised by the question, which was exactly Marco's intention. "That a man I knew had been killed, and the police were looking for me."

"Where did you go Friday?" Marco asked.

"To the Indiana Dunes State Park," Jingles said.

"Can you verify that?" Marco asked as I wrote it down. "Did you meet any other campers?"

Jingles shook his head. "Not on Friday. I camped in an isolated area so I would be alone."

"Is there anyone who can verify that you were in the Dunes area?" Marco asked. "Did you stop for gas? Buy groceries at a local store? Run into a friend?"

Jingles shook his head slowly, staring at Marco with terrified eyes, as though it had begun to dawn on him how serious his circumstances were. "I spoke with a park ranger on Saturday. Will that help?"

Marco shook his head. "We need someone who saw you Friday."

No alibi witnesses, I wrote. Not good, considering that

they'd identified the murder scene as his storage shed. No wonder the detectives were all over him.

"Jingles," Dave said, "do you understand now why I brought these people in? I suggest you let Marco and Abby do their job and find the guilty party, because right now everything the police have is pointing to you."

Jingles sank back into his chair; his hands were trembling hard.

"I'm going to suggest this," Marco said. "Let's get all the facts down on paper and then you can decide whether you want us to investigate on your behalf. Okay?"

Jingles nodded.

"Going back to my previous question," Marco said, "did you have a run-in with Dallas Stone in the past?"

The old man sighed heavily. "You could say that."

"Would you explain?" Marco asked.

Jingles rubbed his eyes. "I owned a brokerage firm in my former life. Dallas was vice president of accounting. One day my CFO came to me with the suspicion that Dallas had been hiding money and transferring it to his own bank account. I had an outside audit performed, hired an investigator, and when it proved true, fired Dallas."

Shock number four: Jingles as the CEO of an investment firm. I couldn't picture it.

"How much did he steal?" I asked.

"In the vicinity of two hundred thousand."

It was an amount that would pay for most of our new house, yet Jingles shrugged as though it was small change. It made me wonder how much money Jingles made back then. And why he lived such a frugal life now.

"Was there any threat of retaliation after you fired him?" Marco asked.

"No threats, but Dallas fought hard to pin the blame on someone else. I had to have him removed from the premises."

"Did you file criminal charges against him?"

"No."

"Why not?" Marco asked. "He broke the law."

"I decided to let it go," Jingles replied. "It was easier that way."

"Easier than what?" I asked.

"Having to go to court. I was extremely busy at the time. And I did feel some pity for him."

Jingles was being much too cavalier about the loss, and that wasn't sitting well with me. "How did Dallas trace you to New Chapel?"

"Happenstance," Jingles said. "I saw him walking to the bank one morning. I didn't think he recognized me since I look quite a bit different now, but I could see him studying me. Then he moved into the old YMCA building a few weeks back and soon after he must have searched through my things because I could tell someone had been in my room. I had no idea it was Dallas until he told me he knew who I was.

"I denied it, of course, thinking there wasn't any way he could prove it. I own nothing from my old life, save the money clip. Yet he was able to track down one of my sons and write to him. Dallas showed me my son's letter last week and said he would write back and let him know where I was unless I paid him a significant sum of money."

"Did you pay him?" Marco asked.

"I don't have any money," Jingles said. "I tried to explain that to Dallas, but he wouldn't believe me. He kept claiming I'd stashed a fortune somewhere."

"Why would he think that?" I asked.

Jingles's gaze drifted off as though viewing the past. "Because at one time I did have a good deal of money."

I wanted to ask what had happened to it but felt it would be too intrusive unless it became pertinent to the case. Still, I couldn't help wondering what had prompted his escape into the austere life he lived now. "Where did you live before?"

"Springfield, Illinois."

"After Dallas showed you the letter," Marco said, "is that when you got into an altercation with him?"

Jingles sighed heavily. "I only tried to grab the letter out of his hand. Then he shoved me so hard I fell through the doorway into the hall. Robert heard the commotion and came out of his room to see what was happening, then ran back and got his army knife. Robert is quite protective of me, you see."

"Why did the police find *you* holding Robert's knife?" I asked.

"When I saw him return with that blade out, I feared for Robert's safety. He's young and inexperienced, no match for Dallas. So I stepped between them, assured Robert I was fine, and finally convinced him to give me his knife. What I didn't know was that Dallas had already called the police and told them I was threatening to kill him. And of course when the police arrived, weapons drawn, there I was holding the knife."

"Describe the whole scene for me as the cops saw it," Marco said.

Jingles shook his head as though the memory pained him. "It was pandemonium. Dallas was on his knees covering his head with his arms as though I'd attacked him, and Robert, who had been trying to pull me into his room to save me, ran into his room and slammed the door. I tried to explain to the cops what was going on, but they said that because I had threatened to kill Dallas, they had to arrest me."

"And Dallas just stood there and let them arrest you?" I asked.

"It was what he wanted," Jingles said. "With me in jail, he had free access to my room."

"We'll need to get a witness statement from Robert," Marco said to me. "Jingles, do you have any idea why Robert ran when he heard the cops?"

"I never felt it was my business to pry," Jingles said, "but he's scared to death of them. Ask him. He'll tell you all about it."

"What happened after you were taken to jail?" Marco asked.

"They released me," Jingles said. "Dallas had declined to press charges."

So Dallas had gotten his jollies and then eased up on the old man. The more I heard about Dallas Stone, the less I liked him. Clearly someone else had felt an even stronger dislike for him. But how strong did it have to be to resort to murder?

"Did you give Dallas your gold clip so he wouldn't write back to your son?" I asked.

"No," Jingles said sternly. "That money clip belonged to my father. It's the only thing I have that was his. I would never give it away under any circumstances. I thought it was well hidden, but obviously Dallas found my hiding place."

"Were you aware it was missing?" Marco asked.

"I never thought to check. I was shocked when Dave told me it was found in Dallas's pocket."

"After the altercation on Thursday, when was the next time you saw Dallas?"

"I never saw him again," Jingles said. "I was so upset over him writing to my son, and then my arrest, that I packed a bag and left."

"The altercation was on Thursday," Marco said, "yet you didn't leave until Friday afternoon."

"I tried to put the whole incident out of my mind—I didn't want to let my customers down—but I couldn't think straight. I can't express to you how deeply disturbing it was to learn that my boys know I'm alive. So I finished my work on Friday and then left."

I couldn't help but wonder what circumstances had caused Jingles to feel that way about his sons. I tried to imagine my father vanishing one day, preferring to let my brothers and me think he was dead. But he would never do that. However, I could remember times when I wished he would disappear . . . Like this morning. With Mom.

"What were your plans?" Marco asked. "Just head for the Dunes State Park?"

"Yes, sir. It's where I go when I need to recharge, so all I kept thinking was, Get to the Dunes, figure out what to do. So I packed a few supplies and headed there. I didn't think it would matter if I was absent for a few days."

"Did you make arrangements with Robert to cover for you on Monday?"

Jingles shook his head, looking chagrined. "No, but I should have. He's covered for me before and he was quite worried about me. I just didn't think I'd be away so long."

"For someone who doesn't like to disappoint his customers," Marco said, "you acted irresponsibly."

Jingles sighed forlornly, his shoulders rounding even further.

"Marco," I said quietly, "that's a bit harsh."

"No, Abby, Marco's right," Dave said. "And here's what the prosecutor is going to claim, Jingles. You were upset that Dallas had contacted your son, that he'd demanded money to keep quiet, that he called the cops on you, that you were cuffed and taken to jail because he lied to the police, so you murdered him. Then you packed a bag and ran. You didn't even tell your friend where you were going because you were in so much of a hurry to get out of town."

Jingles stared at Dave, then at Marco, his Adam's apple bobbing as he swallowed.

"But he did come back," I said. "That has to help his cause."

"It should," Dave said, "but the prosecutor will ignore it to make his case."

"How long were you away?" Marco asked.

Jingles counted silently on shaking fingers. "Three and a half days. I returned Tuesday morning."

"What did you take with you?" Marco asked.

"A sleeping bag, underwear, a box of protein bars"— he paused to think—"and a few bottles of water. I believe that's it."

"That's all you had from Friday until Tuesday morning?" I asked. My stomach was growling. I'd barely eaten a thing at breakfast, too irritated by my parents' presence to have much of an appetite, so food was on my mind.

"It doesn't take much to fuel these bones," Jingles said ruefully.

"Describe how you heard the news from Robert," Marco asked.

"I walked to the square to let him know I was back. He was washing windows at the bank and immediately told me about Dallas. So I went right over to Mr. Hammond's office to find out what to do."

"You went to see Dave last week, too, right?" I asked.

"Yes, ma'am," Jingles said.

"May we know what that was about?" I asked.

Jingles glanced at Dave, who said, "That's your call."

"I wanted to find out how to stop Dallas's harassment," Jingles said.

Another strike against the window washer. His motive kept growing stronger.

"By harassment, are you referring to him replying to your son's letter?" Marco asked.

"No, this was before Dallas received a reply from my boy," Jingles said. "He'd started threatening me a week prior that if I didn't give him money, he'd contact them. I called his bluff, told him he could try, but that it wouldn't do any good. I didn't think he'd actually write to them. In the meantime, I talked to Dave about him."

"And your advice, Dave?" Marco asked.

"I counseled him on how to handle the threats," Dave said.

"How did Dallas find your son?" I asked.

Jingles shrugged. "People can find anybody these days, I suppose."

"What do you know about Dallas Stone?" Marco asked.

"Not much. I didn't fraternize with my employees. But I can tell you that, while at my firm, he divorced and remarried. I also heard talk of a gambling addiction."

"Do you know why Dallas moved into the old Y?" Marco asked.

"I can only guess he was down on his luck again," Jingles said.

I stopped writing. "Again?"

"I'm fairly certain the reason he stole from my firm was to pay off a gambling debt."

So it was more than mere greed. Dallas needed the money. But how had he ended up in New Chapel? Was it happenstance, as Jingles believed, or had he been on the man's trail, hoping to blackmail him?

No doubt about it, Dallas Stone would be an interesting person to investigate—if I was going to work on this case, which I was not. Today was a mere . . . aberration.

Brain to Abby: *Yeah, right. More like an appetizer.*

At the thought of food, my stomach began to growl. I was about to hide it with a cough when I heard a ding on my phone. I dug it out, glanced at the screen, and saw a text from my mom.

What do you think about this for a title: Crime Doesn't Carrot All.

It was so bad I didn't know how to respond, so I just typed quickly, *No.*

"Just a few more questions," Marco said, glancing my way to be sure I was ready. "What did the letter from your son say?"

"I didn't get to read it," Jingles said. "All Dallas would tell me is that my boy wanted to know where I was and how to get in touch with me."

"Do you know whether Dallas replied to him?" Marco asked.

Jingles shook his head, and I could see worry mixed with exhaustion in his face. The interview was wearing him down.

"Which son wrote the letter?" Marco asked.

"My oldest boy," Jingles said, head bowing again. "Sammy." Then he looked at Marco in alarm. "You're not going to contact him, are you?"

"Only if I have to," Marco said.

Jingles turned to Dave. "Am I going to be released from jail?"

"I'll do everything in my power to make that happen," Dave said. "And so will Marco and Abby, if you agree to their taking the case."

Marco, I wanted to say again. *Just Marco!*

"Are you okay with that arrangement?" Marco asked Jingles. "Would you rather wait to see a write-up of the notes Abby took today?"

"I don't need to see the notes," Jingles said, "but the truth is, I have no money to pay for your services, and I wouldn't expect you to work for free."

"It's taken care of," Dave said. "The downtown merchants set up a fund for you."

Jingles stared at him in amazement.

"It's true, Jingles," I said. "Everyone wants to help."

Tears came to his eyes. He looked down, as though ashamed, and said in a hoarse voice, "I don't know what to say."

"Say yes," I said.

He was quiet for a moment. Then he glanced up at me.

"I've known your dad for all the years I've lived here, Abby, and I watched him raise you into a good woman. I don't know your husband well, but you wouldn't have married him if he wasn't a good person as well, and I can tell by that determined look on your faces that you'll do everything you can to help me."

Okay, *this* would be the time to explain that I wouldn't be in on the investigation, that the look on my face was actually panic at the thought of adding anything else to my workload. But before I could speak, Jingles continued.

"So if the two of you are ready to find the real killer, I'd be a fool to say no."

"I—I—" I glanced at Marco for help.

Marco slid his hand over mine and gave it a light squeeze. "Abby's so excited to get started, she's speechless."

Dave patted Jingles on the back. "Wise move. Congratulations."

Marco reached over and shook his hand. "We'll let the other merchants on the square know," he said. "They'll be relieved."

"Thank you," Jingles said.

Brain to Abby: *Now for the main course.*

Abby to brain: *Shut up.*

CHAPTER EIGHT

"Marco, you spoke for both of us again before checking with me," I said as we left the jail building.

"Don't you remember our signal? The hand squeeze? Meaning, 'Go along with what I say'?"

Oh, my God. How had I forgotten that? We used to use that signal all the time. There had to be something wrong with my memory.

"I told you I'd handle the investigation," Marco said. "No worries, okay? I want you to concentrate on your business."

"Thanks, Marco."

He put his hand on my back and rubbed it. "Feel better now?"

I nodded.

"Good." He leaned close and kissed my cheek. "I want you to be happy."

Marco was taking the case, and I was off the hook. So why had I just lied to him? I didn't feel better at all. I felt—disappointed. Frustrated. And guilty. And now I had a sharp pain in my neck, too.

"I sure would like to know why Jingles has been hiding from his sons all these years," I said, rubbing my neck as we headed to the parking lot where we'd left the 'Vette.

"It'll come out during the investigation. What was your impression of Jingles?"

"That he's innocent," I said. "How about yours?"

"I'm reserving judgment."

"Really?"

"Come on, Abby. Put your Sherlock Holmes cap on and tell me why Jingles is a viable suspect."

I thought a moment, then ticked off the reasons on my fingers. "He has a strong motive. He disappeared right after the murder. He has no alibi witnesses. His money clip was in Dallas's pocket. The murder happened in his storage shed."

"Yep."

"But that last one is also why it can't be him, Marco. It's too obvious."

"Sunshine, unless this was premeditated, a spontaneous act of aggression is more likely to happen on the killer's turf. Maybe Dallas tracked Jingles down at his shed to tell him he had the money clip. You heard how adamant Jingles was about keeping that clip. It could be that he was so outraged, he grabbed a rag or towel or something from the shed and wrapped it around Dallas's throat before the man could walk away. A crime of passion."

"I can't see Jingles subduing a man some twenty years younger, Marco."

"Do you know how strong Jingles is?"

"No."

"He carries buckets of soapy water and a ladder around town and works with his arms for hours every day. He's a lot stronger than you think."

"Marco, he shuffles when he walks."

"He pushes his bucket on its dolly, Abby. I've seen him walking from the Y to the town square. He doesn't shuffle."

"I guess I've never really paid much attention to him. But if forensics finds out that the murder weapon is Dallas's tie, how did Jingles get it?"

Marco thought for a second. "The murder happened on Friday afternoon, so if Dallas tracked Jingles down at the shed, he might have come directly from the bank still wearing his tie. Then it would be just a matter of grabbing and tightening it."

"Why would Jingles leave his gold clip in Dallas's pocket?"

"Maybe he didn't know Dallas had it on him or he simply panicked and ran."

"I'm sorry, Marco, but I still don't believe Jingles is the murderer."

"Sweetheart, we've seen people who've been pushed past their breaking points, men and women, even children who've committed crimes of passion. There was only one logical reason for Dallas to go to that shed, and that was to find Jingles."

"Okay, let's say Jingles strangled him in a moment of anger, but to store the body for three days and then carry it to a public place? Why?"

"It's possible Jingles didn't know what to do. Maybe in his panic he locked his shed and headed to the Dunes to figure it out. We have only his word that he came back on Tuesday. What if he actually returned in the middle of the night Sunday or early Monday morning? He lives alone. Who would know?"

"Does posing a body on the steps sound like something an old man would do?"

"You know my rule. Everyone is a suspect until we cross them out."

I mulled it over and decided that I had to go with my

gut instinct, which was still telling me that Jingles was not the killer. It was also telling me I'd better eat before the redheaded beast made her appearance.

Just as we slid into the car, Marco's phone rang. He put it to his ear and said, "Hey, Sean, what's happening?" He listened, then said, "For how long? Seriously? I can't even get in the back way? Unbelievable. Okay. Sure. Thanks."

He dropped the phone into his lap and started the engine. "Well, we've got a free morning."

"How long before the gas leak is fixed?"

"Hours. They're not sure how bad it is yet. They've got earthmovers on the scene digging under the pavement. Reilly said he'd let me know when we could get back in."

I could only imagine the backlog of orders that had come in since yesterday, and the hours it would take to catch up. Just the thought of it caused my shoulders to tense and the pain in my neck to sharpen. I rubbed my neck, rolled my shoulders, and sighed, silently cursing the fates for working against me. Yet a part of me was doing cartwheels.

"I'm going to look for Robert Hall," Marco said. "Want to come with me, or should I drop you at the Daily Grind so you can wait with Lottie and Grace?"

Brain to Abby: *That's an easy one. The chef is in the kitchen. Let's start cooking.*

Abby to brain: *Must you use food terms?*

"How about if we stop for breakfast somewhere and then go find Robert?" I asked.

By the way Marco smiled at me, I knew he was pleased that I was joining him.

We detoured around the square to Rosie's Diner, located one block off the square on the west side, where we were lucky to find an open booth.

Named after the original owner's daughter, Rosie's had been in operation since the early 1970s, and up until a few months ago, looked it. But the yellow Formica tables, avocado plastic chairs and booths, and dark paneling were gone, replaced by light wood tables with cane-backed chairs, rich wood floors, aqua walls, and white accents. Even the menu had gone through a renovation, now offering fresh, farm-to-table food, grass-fed hormone-free beef and chicken entrées, and a nice selection of vegetarian meals.

"The diner looks great now, doesn't it?" I asked, hoping Marco would get the hint and schedule a makeover for Down the Hatch.

"Mmm-hmm." His head was behind the menu.

"I wonder who did the renovation. Maybe you could get his name."

No response.

"Marco?"

"Not going to happen, Abby."

I was surprised when Rosie herself came to take our order. The short, plump, tough-talking, middle-aged restaurateur spent most of her time working the cash register or schmoozing with customers. Rarely did she put her waitress apron on.

"Yeah, we're running shorthanded," Rosie said, chomping her gum as she filled our cups with steaming hot coffee. "One of our waitresses had a vacation day scheduled, and our new gal has called in sick all week."

"You finally hired someone," I said. "Good for you. I just did that, too. Business is blooming all over the square—no pun intended."

"To tell you the truth, I wasn't gonna hire anyone," Rosie said, running her fingers through her short gray curls, "but this gal really needed the work. She's new in town and kinda down on her luck, so I took pity on her. What the hey, you know? Everyone needs a hand up once in a while. Her husband really stiffed her, poor thing—and then *he* got stiffed." Rosie snorted. "Sorry. I couldn't resist that one."

"He got stiffed?" I repeated.

Rosie shrugged. "I was making a joke. He's the guy who got murdered. Shame on me, I know."

I glanced at Marco, who had stopped perusing his menu and was now listening attentively. As I reached for my pen and the notebook, Marco asked, "What's the waitress's name?"

"Lavinia," Rosie said, "but sometimes she goes by Livvy. Last name is Stone."

Marco and I looked at each other. Livvy was the name of the woman the bank teller thought Dallas had been seeing.

"And this waitress called in sick Monday?" he asked.

"No, I sent her home Monday right after the lunch rush because she told me she wasn't feeling well. I thought it was because she'd heard about the murder, but she said she felt like she was coming down with something. I can't have her spreading germs to my customers, so what can I say but go home until you're better?"

"Have you talked to Lavinia since then?" Marco asked.

"She called Tuesday morning to say she had a doctor's appointment. But I swear she was at the airport. It sounded like flight announcements in the background."

"Did she work last Friday?" Marco asked.

"Sure did," Rosie said. "Until two p.m."

"What did you mean when you said Lavinia got stiffed?" I asked.

"You know, bamboozled. Hoodwinked," Rosie said. "Lavinia told me that when she and Mr. Stone got married, he bragged about having money, but it turned out he was taking her for a ride, and it wasn't in a Mercedes-Benz. By the time she filed for divorce, he'd drained her bank account and left her with a big fat nothin.'"

"So they're divorced?" I asked.

"Nope. He didn't stick around long enough to sign the papers," Rosie said.

"Did she say where they lived at the time?" Marco asked.

"She moved here from Springfield, Illinois, so I guess that's where they were living," Rosie said.

Lavinia Stone, I wrote. *From Springfield, Illinois. Married to Dallas Stone, who stole her savings. Was off work during time of murder. Began calling in sick Tuesday morning. Might have called from airport.*

"Do you have her address?" Marco asked.

"In the back," Rosie said. "I almost asked why you needed it, but I did hear that you're working the murder case. I couldn't make it to the meeting, but I did contribute to Jingles's fund. Isn't it nice the way everyone is rallying behind him? That's what makes our town so great." She put one hand on my shoulder. "You're adorable, you two, working together on your cases. Not too many husbands and wives could do that. Let me take your orders and then I'll get that address for you."

I reached for the little pitcher of cream as she bustled away.

"Why are you scrunching your nose?" Marco asked.

Wow, did that sound attractive. I tried to rearrange my expression into something more pleasant as I poured cream in my coffee. "I can't help but feel bad that people think we're working the investigation together. You're doing all the work and I'm getting half the credit."

"Forget about it. You can't let it bother you, babe."

Well, that made it all better. I stirred my coffee in silence. Why did men think they could solve women's problems with a simple statement? But in the interest of love and harmony, I let it pass. "Quite a coincidence that Lavinia was off work on Friday afternoon and got sick on Monday after the body was discovered, isn't it?"

"It'll be more of a coincidence if she skipped town."

I began to list on my fingers: "Dallas drains her bank account; she follows him here; he ends up dead . . . I do believe we've found another suspect, Mr. Salvare."

"We?"

"You! I meant to say you."

Marco smiled as he raised his coffee cup to his lips.

After a satisfying meal we hopped back into the car, circled around the square, and parked on Taylor Street, half a block up from the Hampton Arms Apartments, where Lavinia Stone resided. Fifty years ago the five-story brown-brick building had been a showplace, but a lax owner had let it fall into a sorry state of disrepair. Now it was inhabited mostly by transients and a few senior citizens who'd been living there since the early days.

The building held a special significance for Marco and me. It was where we'd first come together to work on a murder investigation, another time when trouble had bumped into me—literally, when someone crashed into my 'Vette in a hit-and-run accident. Marco had just bought the bar, and I was one month into owning Bloomers. He'd seen the damage on my car and offered to help me find the perpetrator. That investigation had led straight into the Billy Ryan murder case.

"Remember this place?" I asked, slipping my hand into Marco's as we approached the front door.

"Yep. The birthplace of Team Salvare."

"Once I convinced you to let me help you."

"As I recall, it didn't take much convincing."

Amazing what a little flirting could do. I smiled and squeezed his hand, remembering the first stakeout I'd gone on with him. Sitting for hours in the dark with nothing to eat or drink hadn't been a basket of fun. Sitting in the dark with the hottest guy in town *had* been. And back then, I'd had plenty of time to help him investigate.

Inside the front door, we checked the row of mailboxes until we found Lavinia's name under apartment 6A, then rang the buzzer. We waited a few seconds before ringing again, but there was no response. I checked the names and spotted one that I remembered: Betty Summers.

"Marco, here's the woman who gave me information in the Ryan case. Let's see if she knows anything about Lavinia."

"I'll let you handle her," he said.

This time, my ringing got a response. Through the intercom, I introduced myself, and we were buzzed through the security door into a dingy gray hallway that smelled of musty carpet and odors I didn't want to identify. Betty's apartment was in the middle of the hallway, and as we approached, she stepped out of her doorway to greet us.

The tiny, shriveled, gray-haired woman with the hump in her back and head jutting forward like a turtle's smiled broadly when she saw me. "Abby Knight, how are you, dearie? My, my, hasn't the time flown since you were here last? I've been following your exploits in the newspaper, you know. But how do you manage doing this and running your flower shop?"

"It isn't easy," I said, rubbing my neck, which had immediately started to tighten again.

"And this fine-looking gentleman must be your husband."

"Marco Salvare," my fine-looking gentleman said.

"What can I do for you, dearies?" Betty asked.

"Do you know a woman named Lavinia Stone?" I asked. "She lives just up the hallway in 6A."

"Sure," Betty said. "I know Mrs. Stone. I see her in the laundry room sometimes."

"Mrs. Stone called off sick this week," I said. "Her boss is concerned about her, so we're doing a wellness check."

Betty looked puzzled. "That's odd. I thought she left on vacation."

"What makes you think that?" I asked.

"Because of the suitcase she was rolling up the hallway," Betty said. "And the cab waiting outside."

Yep, that would do it. "When was this?" I asked, pulling out my notebook.

Betty tapped her chin. "Was it Tuesday? Yes. I go to therapy on Tuesday mornings. That's when I saw her leave. I had a knee replacement a few months ago. It got so I couldn't walk from the bedroom to the kitchen . . . Oh, my. You're taking notes. I'm not going to get Lavinia in trouble, am I?"

"Don't worry about that, Betty," I said. "This is just a memory aid. So what kind of neighbor would you say Mrs. Stone is?"

"A very nice one," Betty said. "Always willing to help a neighbor out. Do you know that once she carried two twenty-pound bags of salt for my water softener all the way up here? She had one on each shoulder. Imagine that! And another time, I happened to mention that I thought there was a mouse in the laundry room. Wouldn't you know, she took care of it the next day?"

"How?" Marco asked.

"Rat poison," Betty said. "She must have had a problem before, because she said anytime I had a pest complaint to let her know because she had an arsenal in her pantry."

An arsenal of poison. Interesting.

"Why don't you come inside?" Betty asked, glancing over her shoulder into her apartment. "I've got my kettle heating. I can make you nice cups of tea."

I thanked her but had to turn down her offer or we might never get away. "Just a few more questions, Betty, and then we have to go. Was Mrs. Stone having problems with her husband?"

"Isn't it funny that you should ask?" Betty said with a chuckle. "I made the mistake of asking Mrs. Stone if she was a widow. 'Not yet,' she said. 'Not yet.' Then she laughed. Well, she could see right off that I was shocked, so she waved her hand in the air like she was batting a balloon and said, 'Never mind what I said. My husband screwed me over badly, so I keep hoping the jack—' Well, I won't mention the word she used in polite company, so let's just say she used the word *mule.* 'I keep hoping the jack *mule* will kick the bucket, but so far it ain't happening.'

"She talked like that, you know. *Ain't,* and *warshing* machine, and *rastle.* My granny was from southern Indiana and she talked like that. My, how we would tease her about it. Why, one time—"

"Did Mrs. Stone say whether she'd had any contact with her husband?" Marco asked.

"Oh, heavens," Betty said. "She never confided about personal things. But once I did hear her talking to him on the phone. Now, it's not that I eavesdrop, you understand, but when things are said in a strident voice, how can a body help but hear?"

"I understand," I said, nodding, trying to get her to move her story along. "Were they arguing?"

"That's how it sounded to me," Betty said. "Poor Mrs. Stone just couldn't seem to get him to understand how desperately she needed money. 'You'd let me starve to death,' she kept saying. 'You'd leave me to die like you did your first wife so you could buy your fancy clothes and go out with your fancy girlfriend.'" Betty paused to whisper, "I caught that he was stepping out with someone named Candy Cane."

An ex-wife, an estranged wife, and a girlfriend named Candy Cane. Dallas Stone had been quite a player.

"How did you know she was speaking to her husband?" Marco asked.

"She mentioned their divorce papers and how he was hurting them both by not signing them. 'There are penalties for what you're doing, Dal,' she said. 'You'll see. You can wish me dead all you want, but—'" Betty stopped and put her fingers over her lips. "Oh, I don't want to repeat what poor Mrs. Stone said next. My mama taught me never to talk unkindly about anyone."

"I'll bet your mama also told you to be honest," Marco said.

"That's true, yes," she said, looking up at Marco with appraising eyes.

"Did Mrs. Stone threaten her husband?" he asked.

Betty hesitated, looking unsure of herself. "I'm not certain I'd call it a threat."

"What did she say?" I asked.

"I don't want to get it wrong." Betty paused. "Mrs.

Stone has enough hardship as it is. I wouldn't want to add to her trouble."

"It might keep her out of trouble," I said.

After a moment to consider, Betty said with a firm nod, "All right, then. These were her exact words: 'We'll just see who dies first, won't we?'"

That was definitely *not* going to keep Lavinia Stone out of trouble.

CHAPTER NINE

"My teakettle is whistling," Betty said, glancing nervously behind her. "I wouldn't want to start a fire. If my husband would only wear his hearing aids, it wouldn't be a problem. Why, once—"

I reached into my bag and pulled out one of our business cards. "Betty, I'm sorry to cut you off, but we have to get back to work. My cell phone number is at the bottom. If you see that Lavinia has returned, would you call me?"

Betty gazed at me with her watery blue eyes and gave my cheek a pinch. "Well, certainly I will, dearie. Such a cute little thing you are."

Marco was already striding toward the door, so I walked backward, calling, "Thanks, Betty. Good luck with your knee therapy."

"Rosie's hunch was right," Marco said as we left the building. "Lavinia must have been at the airport."

"If Lavinia killed Dallas," I said, "she might have fled the country. My question, though, is, why would she pose her husband on the courthouse steps?"

"We'd have to know her better to answer that." Marco checked the time. "It's not quite noon. Do you want to call it quits or come with me to see if we can find Robert?"

Was that even a fair question? "I'm sticking with you, Salvare. Let's pick up Seedy on our way. I'm sure she misses us."

When we pulled up in front of the old two-story house where Marco's former apartment and Rafe's current one was located, Rafe was waiting outside with Seedy, who was straining on her leash to get to our car.

"She was great," he said as I opened the passenger door to let her in. "We played and took a walk, and she slept while I worked on the computer."

"That's my girl," I said as Seedy wiggled in my arms, licking my chin to show her happiness.

"Thanks, bro," Marco called.

"Any word on when the gas leak will be fixed?" Rafe asked, leaning his arms on the window.

"A couple of hours, according to Reilly," Marco said. "I'll let you know as soon as I hear something."

"No rush," Rafe said. "I'm enjoying a free afternoon."

"Us, too," I said.

I still couldn't believe my good fortune. A day to help Marco work on the case *and* I'd managed to shake off feelings of guilt about not getting my work done. It was almost like old times. And my shoulders didn't even tense when I thought of the orders piling up. I was enjoying myself too much.

But what did that mean? I loved my job. I'd never give up the bliss I felt when I worked with flowers. What I didn't enjoy were all the other demands on my time, and those came primarily from my family. Mom, Dad, Tara, Jillian, gatherings with Marco's family, more gatherings with mine—even trying to meet up with Nikki felt like a burden. I wanted to concentrate on my work at

Bloomers and with Marco—and that was it. If everyone else would just leave me alone, even for one day, I'd be happy.

Now my shoulders were tense.

Because the square had been shut down, we decided to try Robert's residence first at the former YMCA building, a block-long, three-story brown-brick building nestled into an old neighborhood just north of the town square. It had multiple entrances, some with wheelchair-accessible ramps, and a big banner over the main doors that read: NEW CHAPEL MEN'S LIFE CENTER.

With Seedy on her leash, we entered through the main doors into a spacious, high-ceilinged lobby. It had floor-to-ceiling windows along the street-facing wall, with long benches beneath upholstered in a red, tan, and blue tweed fabric, and four blue plastic tub chairs at a round coffee table in the far corner. The lobby had once been a bustling information hub for the various activities available throughout the building. Now our footsteps echoed on the gray-and-white tile floor as we headed for an L-shaped information booth along the back wall staffed by two older men. They were perched on stools watching a small TV on the countertop that was set at full volume. No one else was around.

Spotting the men, Seedy jerked to a halt, planted her feet, and refused to budge.

A tall, skinny man lowered the glasses on his nose and rose on his stool to peer over the counter at the dog. "May we help you?"

I scooped Seedy up and followed Marco to the counter. "We're looking for Robert Hall," he said.

The tall man had a ring of white hair, bright blue eyes behind slender rectangular glasses, long, thin arms, and the longest fingers I'd ever seen. A brass name tag over his shirt pocket read *Chester*.

Chester turned to the other man. "Did Robert come back yet?"

His coworker was a stubby guy with a round, wrinkled face, upturned nose, and dark gray receding hairline. His badge read *Sol*, but I wouldn't have been surprised if it had read *Pug*. He squinted at us through puffy eyes and his heavy jowls jiggled when he spoke. "He's upstairs." Sol turned down the volume on the TV and added, "If you want to visit him, you'll have to sign in, but pets aren't allowed inside."

"Would it be okay if we visited with Robert here in the lobby?" I asked. "Our dog is very well behaved. She won't be a problem."

Miss Well Behaved tucked her head beneath my arm and wouldn't look at them.

"Sure. Fine." Sol aimed a scowl at Chester. "Why should they listen to us? No one else does."

After Marco signed the guest book, Chester swiveled it to see our names. "Mr. and Mrs. Marco Salvare," he read loudly, then studied us, tilting his head the way Seedy did when she was puzzled. "Are you the private eye team I read about in the newspapers?"

"Turn up your hearing aid," Sol grumbled, giving him a nudge in the ribs. "You're shouting again."

"What?" Chester asked, fumbling with his earpiece.

"Yes, we're private investigators," my handsome PI said politely.

"I thought I recognized you," Chester said with a delighted smile. "Your photos have been in the newspaper a couple of times."

"Sixteen," I said. Not that I'd counted them. Okay, I

had. And glued them in a scrapbook. With star stickers all around them.

"Phooey," Sol said. "I've never once had my name in that blasted newspaper, and I was a decorated hero in the Korean War."

Chester gazed at Sol, chuckling. "Not *four*, Sol. She said sixteen." He turned to us. "And he says *I'm* deaf."

"War, you idiot," Sol cried. "War!"

"Anyway," Chester said, "I heard that the downtown merchants have asked you to help Jingles clear his name, and I think that's just wonderful. Jingles is one of the kindest men to walk this planet. Isn't that right, Sol?"

"Since I don't know everyone who walks the planet," Sol said crossly, "I wouldn't know."

"Says one of the *meanest* men to walk the planet," Chester said in a loud whisper.

Clearly they spent too much time together.

"Would you mind answering a few questions about Jingles?" Marco asked.

"We'd love to." After a glance in Sol's direction, Chester amended it. "I would, anyway."

"Ever have any problems with Jingles getting along with the other residents?" Marco asked.

Before Chester could reply, Sol blurted, "Nope. Never."

"Well," Chester said in a singsong voice, "not until recently."

"What happened recently?" Marco asked.

"There was a little dustup with one of the other men," Chester said in almost a whisper, "but it wasn't Jingles's fault really."

"Then why did you mention it?" Sol snapped.

"Because it might be important," Chester said.

"Are you referring to the incident with Dallas Stone?"

I asked, then remembered I wasn't supposed to use leading questions. It was one of Marco's main interview rules.

But when they both nodded, Marco got into the act, so I put Seedy on the floor, pulled out my notebook and pen, and prepared to write.

"What can you tell us about Dallas?" Marco asked.

After an exchange of glances and a long pause, Chester said, "I don't really like to speak ill of the dead."

"Understandable," Marco said. "Just whatever you feel like sharing."

"Mr. Stone didn't live here very long," Chester said, "so maybe we're wrong about him, but he seemed, well . . ." He shrugged.

"Phooey," Sol said. "He was underhanded."

"How so?" Marco asked as I jotted down *underhanded*.

"How so?" Sol's jowls shook with irritation. "How much time do you have? I caught him trying to slip his girlfriend out of the building early one morning, and that's just the latest incident."

"Overnight guests are prohibited," Chester said. "Mr. Stone received a warning about it. Another time, one of our residents complained that he saw Mr. Stone coming out of someone else's room when that person was at work. The building supervisor questioned Mr. Stone, but he denied it."

"Was this Jingles's room?" I asked.

"No," Sol said. "Different floor."

"Was anything reported missing?" Marco asked.

"Not from the resident's room," Chester said. "But we've had equipment go missing from the workout area. So we were told to keep our eye on Mr. Stone."

"What kind of equipment was taken?" Marco asked.

"Weights, barbells," Sol said. "Even a workout bench."

"Was Dallas's room checked to see if the equipment was there?" I asked.

"Not while he was alive," Chester said, "but when the detectives went in, I did take a peek from the doorway. I saw nothing in the way of equipment, and I'm sure he couldn't have stashed an entire bench and a set of barbells in his closet."

"So my question is, then, how would someone sneak large workout equipment out of here?" Marco asked.

"There are several entrances," Chester said. "In the middle of the night, no one can get inside, but residents can leave whenever they want."

"Do you know his girlfriend's name?" Marco asked.

The men glanced at each other. "Kelli, with an *i*, wasn't it?" Chester asked.

"No, it was some kind of hippie name, like Cookie," Sol said.

Tick-tock, guys. Once that gas leak was fixed, I had to get back to Bloomers, and I didn't want to miss out on talking to Robert Hall. "Could it have been Candi with an *i*?" I asked. *Oops.* Broke the rule again.

Chester snapped his fingers. "Kandi! That was it. Kandi with a *K* and an *i*. She had on a name tag like this one" — Chester tapped his brass badge — "but bigger and fancier. It had colored crystals all around it. She was quite a bit younger than Mr. Stone was, too. Quite. A. Bit." He put his hand to the side of his mouth and whispered, "Try thirty years' age difference."

That *was* a big difference. That put Kandi at around twenty-four.

"She looked like a hooker," Sol blurted.

In his lilting voice Chester replied, "Let's not go there."

"Anything else about Dallas that you remember?" Marco asked.

Chester turned toward his partner and said in a loud whisper, "Should I mention that Mr. Stone had a stalker?"

Sol shook his head in disbelief. "You just *did* mention it."

"When?" Chester asked.

Sol just shook his head.

"You saw someone stalking Dallas Stone?" I asked.

Chester nodded. "For the last three weeks or so. She would lurk in the shrubs outside the doors after dark and follow him when he left here."

"She *lurked*?" Sol asked.

"That's what people do when they hang out in a shrub, Sol," Chester said. "They *lurk*."

"Would you describe the woman?" I asked.

"It was hard to see her because she was, well, you know"—Chester darted a glance at his counter-mate—"lurking, so all I can really tell you is that she had a horrible hairstyle."

My antennae began to rise.

Sol clapped his hand to his forehead. "That's all you saw? A bad hairdo?"

"Well, obviously it's more than you saw. Besides, she was crouching. All I could see was a black coat and that hairdo. Who wears a beehive these days?"

The antennae were up and waving. "Would you say she had bouffant hair?" I asked.

Chester pointed at me. "Bingo."

CHAPTER TEN

"**D**id you tell the police about this woman?" Marco asked Chester as I wrote: *Was Lavinia stalking Dallas?*

"The detective didn't ask us questions about Mr. Stone," Chester said. "He only wanted to hear about Jingles."

"That figures," I grumbled.

Marco moved on. "Did you tell Dallas about the stalker?"

"Of course," Chester said. "Mr. Stone said not to worry about her."

"What he said," Sol amended, "was that if you didn't feed it, it would go away."

How callous to equate the woman to an animal. Dallas was a real piece of work.

"When was the last time you saw this woman?" Marco asked.

Chester tapped his chin. "Last week sometime."

"Okay, that's very helpful. Now, what can you tell us about Robert Hall?"

"Quiet, keeps to himself," Sol said. "Doesn't seem to have any friends."

"That's not fair," Chester said. "Just because we never

see anyone come here doesn't mean he's friendless. And you're forgetting Jingles. He's his friend."

"I stand corrected, then," Sol said, glowering at his partner.

"Ever had any trouble between Robert and Dallas other than when the police arrested Jingles?" Marco asked.

His question surprised me. I hadn't thought to count Robert among our suspects, but obviously Marco wasn't discounting him, either.

"Not that I'm aware of," Chester said. "Right, Sol? Robert avoids trouble. In fact, he's rather antisocial."

"And you criticize *me* for saying he's friendless?"

Chester sniffed. "All I mean is, he's an introvert as opposed to an extrovert." Giving us an apologetic glance, he said, "It would be best if you just asked Robert."

"It would be best if you went and got him," Sol said.

"Well, excuse me," Chester snapped back. "We wouldn't want *you* to strain yourself."

"Wouldn't it be easier to call his room?" I asked.

"He doesn't have a phone," Chester said. "He can't afford one."

"Does he have regular employment?" Marco asked.

"He does, yes, but he makes very little money," Chester said.

Sol huffed grumpily. "And what he does make he uses to buy comic books."

Chester sighed. "Give him a break, Sol. He's a young man."

Before the two men started a new argument, Marco handed each of them a business card. "If you remember anything else about Dallas Stone or anything pertaining to the murder, I'd appreciate a call."

While Chester went to get Robert, Marco pulled one of

the tub chairs to face the end bench; then he and I sat down to wait. Seedy sat on the floor by the window, watching a pair of squirrels playing in the huge oak tree out front.

My phone rang and I saw my mom's name on the screen. With an exasperated huff, I showed Marco the name, then, with forced cheer, said, "Hi, Mom. What's up?"

"Are you all right? I just heard about the gas leak by Bloomers, and you know how I worry."

"Worry about what? That I'm passed out on the street, with people stepping over me? If something happened, Marco would call you."

"You don't have to get snippy with me, Abigail. I'm concerned, that's all."

"The time to be concerned is when you get a call saying that I'm in the hospit—"

Marco put his palm over my phone. "Why are you arguing with her? Just assure her you're well, thank her for being concerned, and hang up."

"Hang up? That would really tick her off."

"You know what I'm saying. Be nice. She loves you."

"Abigail? Are you there? Hello?"

"I'm fine, Mom. I'm nowhere near the gas leak. Why aren't you teaching?"

"My class is at recess," she said impatiently. "The news about the town square evacuation is all over the teachers' lounge. Do you know what caused it?"

"I haven't heard, but they're supposed to have it fixed soon."

"Promise you won't go near Bloomers unless there's absolutely no danger."

"Mom, you know I—" At a warning look from Marco, I sighed and said, "Okay, I promise."

"While I've got you on the phone," she said, "put this

Saturday at five o'clock on your calendar. Jonathan and Portia are hosting a family dinner at the country club. They want to make an announcement."

"About what?"

"They're being secretive. We'll just have to wait and see."

It couldn't be that Portia was expecting. As a former model, my sister-in-law prided herself on being as thin as humanly possible without blowing away on a strong gust of wind. She had vowed to never ruin her figure, or what there was of one, with a pregnancy.

And it was no surprise that Jonathan, my oldest brother, a heart surgeon, had chosen the club for the occasion. Since Portia didn't know the first thing about cooking, they ate most meals there. I wasn't sure whether she even knew where her kitchen was.

But the thought of another family get-together at the New Chapel Country Club made me feel crabby again. I wasn't a "club" person. I was a bar and grill girl. The only reason my parents were able to join it was because both of my brothers were members there, giving them a family discount. My mother loved it; growing up on a farm, she'd always dreamed of belonging to something besides 4-H. Dad, not so much.

"I hear someone coming, Abby," Marco said quietly.

"It's on my calendar, Mom. Gotta go. Bye." I hung up before she could say anything more.

"What was that about?" Marco asked.

"Jon and Portia are hosting a dinner at the country club this Saturday to make a surprise announcement." Seeing Marco about to comment, I added, "And no, it can't be that she's pregnant."

"I was going to say that we promised my sister we'd come to her house for dinner on Saturday."

I wasn't sure which stressed me out more—the thought of dinner at the country club or dinner with Mamma Salvare and Marco's boisterous family. But we'd already accepted his mom's offer, so that trumped my family's invitation. "I didn't want to go to the country club anyway."

"I appreciate the sacrifice," Marco said dryly, "but it sounds like this is going to be a special occasion. My mother will understand."

As the men came out of an elevator on the far side of the lobby, I reached behind my chair to stroke Seedy's head. "Be a good girl," I told her. "Nothing to fear here."

She looked up at me, wagged her bushy tail, and gave a little yip as we rose to greet the two men. But then Seedy spotted them walking toward us and immediately ducked under the bench.

Seeing Robert Hall again, I was struck by how young he looked. He was slender, wearing a colorful, tight-fitting T-shirt with some kind of logo on it, and vintage plaid dress pants with gray felt sneakers. Impeccably groomed, he had short, dark brown hair framing a narrow face, a short nose, and a boyish chin, and he carried himself with the air of one who was practicing royal etiquette.

"Robert," Chester said, "this is Mr. and Mrs. Salvare."

"Hi, Robert," Marco said, offering his hand. "I'm Marco. This is Abby."

He shook Marco's hand but merely nodded at me. With his head held stiffly upright, only his gaze moved as he peered at Seedy cowering behind me. "And this is?"

Strangely, Seedy's tail began to thump on the floor. I crouched beside Seedy and ran my hand down her back. It was supposed to keep her calm, but for once it didn't seem necessary. "Her name is Seedy. You saw her Monday morning in front of Bloomers."

"Of course," he said. "Unfortunately, I must inform you that there are no dogs allowed in this shelter. You did see the sign upon entering the building, the one that says 'No Dogs Allowed,' didn't you?"

I'd forgotten how rude Robert was. Before I could answer, Seedy rolled over onto her back, her three paws in the air, wagging her tail as though she wanted a tummy rub.

"She has three legs," Robert said, as though this was something he felt obliged to point out.

"Seedy was badly abused before we rescued her," Marco said.

"A rescue dog." He turned the phrase over as though examining it from all angles.

"This is amazing," I said, petting her. "Seedy is never like this around people she doesn't know. You must have a special ability with dogs, Robert."

As though he found my statement ponderable, Robert studied my happy mutt. Then he got down on one knee and placed the fingertips of his right hand on Seedy's belly, gently scratching the fur as though he'd never done such a thing before. Seedy's tail wagged faster.

"A special ability," he repeated slowly, getting up. "Perhaps an exception to the rule could be made this one time, since dogs are traditionally privileged with four legs, and this dog clearly has three. Moreover, I am inclined to allow in any such animal who senses my special abilities."

I glanced at Marco with a look that said, *He's "inclined to allow in"?*

Marco returned my look with one of his own: *His "special abilities"?*

"I think *we* can safely bend the rules this once," Chester said, no doubt a reminder as to who was in charge.

Robert rubbed his chin as though weighing the situation. "Then let it be noted that, although the rule states clearly that no dogs are allowed inside, we have come to an agreement that a onetime exception shall be made. You may want to write that down, Chester, for future reference. Now, then." With his hands folded together, Robert gazed from Marco to me as a doctor might to his patients. "How may I be of assistance?"

Once again, Chester put his hand to the side of his mouth, whispering, "I told Robert you needed his help. I didn't say for what."

"Oh, yes, one more thing," Robert said. "I must forewarn you that if, in fact, you require me to answer any questions that involve my whereabouts or activities outside of this facility, I will require a private space in which to speak. This is due to a certain burly, cantankerous caretaker who has a proclivity to perpetuate the belief that I am some sort of simpering idiot, which I can assure you I am not. Are we in accord?"

Robert gazed from Marco to me, waiting for our answers. But all I could do was stand there with my mouth open. I glanced at Marco. He was speechless, too.

Chester cleared his throat, looking embarrassed, and said quietly, "Robert doesn't care for Sol."

"The feeling's mutual," Sol blurted without looking up from the TV.

Chester gave us an apologetic shrug, then patted Robert's shoulder. "Why don't you take them to the lounge? No one is using it, so you'll have all the privacy you need."

"Very well." Robert turned and marched toward a hallway on the far side of the lobby. "Follow me."

I changed my mind about Robert. He was rude *and* strange.

* * *

"What does the logo on your shirt stand for?" I asked Robert.

"Hawkeye," Robert said, tracking someone walking past the door.

We were seated across from him at a table in the residents' lounge, which at one time had been the basketball court and still retained the smell of sweaty bodies. Seedy was under my chair, crunching a doggy treat.

Around us were half a dozen more round tables with chairs for dining or playing games. At the far end was the media center, filled with ten mismatched recliners facing a huge rear-projection TV. A beverage dispenser sat against a side wall, with cabinets and a counter next to it. The door behind me had tempered-glass panels on either side, which was where Robert's attention was focused.

"Who's Hawkeye?" I asked, looking at Marco.

Robert glanced at me then, his eyes dancing with enthusiasm. "Hawkeye is one of my top five Avengers. I bought a life-sized poster of him at CC last year."

"CC?" I glanced at my husband again in the hope that I wasn't the only one in the room who didn't have a clue what Robert was talking about.

"Comic Con," Marco explained. "It's a huge comic book convention that takes place in all the major cities in the U.S."

Apparently I *was* the only clueless one in the room.

Robert looked at Marco with new respect. "That's right. And while you are correct in stating that Comic Con does take place in most major cities, a true comic book aficionado would know that the only convention truly worth attending is the San Diego convention. Unfortunately, I lack the resources to attend this year. I will, however, be attending the convention in Chicago."

He aimed his index finger at me and said, "You should come. You would be the perfect Scarlet Witch."

"Excuse me?" I asked.

"Scarlet Witch," Robert repeated slowly, as though I had lost my hearing.

Besides feeling clueless, I was now annoyed, too. A witch indeed. "Never heard of her."

"One of the Avengers?" Robert asked, as though prodding my flawed memory bank.

I glanced at Marco for help.

"Marvel comic book heroes," Marco said quietly.

In an animated voice, Robert said, "Scarlet Witch is a sorceress endowed with the energy to cause people to spontaneously combust. With your red hair and your"—he pointed to my bust—"you would be perfect. Perhaps a little on the short side, but with five-inch spike heels and—"

"Okay," Marco cut in. "How about if we get down to business?"

I took out the notebook and pen, then studied my fingertips. Spontaneous combustion. Interesting. Would it work on Mom's art projects?

Losing that sudden spark of enthusiasm, Robert repositioned himself back into perfect posture, placing his folded hands on his lap. "What may I do for you? And keep in mind that I will be resuming my window washing duties just as soon as the downtown opens up."

"We're here for our friend Jingles," Marco began.

"I'm glad someone is finally doing *something* to help him," Robert said, looking indignant. "Unlike the members of the New Chapel police force, who would rather pick on the weak and innocent of the world." He reached across the table to tap my notebook. "You may quote me on that." He sat back, then leaned forward again. "It's *R-O-B-E-R-T*." He waited a beat. "*H-A-L-L*."

"Got it," I said.

"Sounds like you've had a run-in with the cops," Marco said.

"Not me. Some acquaintances I was rooming with at the time," Robert said. "So whatever you do, do not trust them. They will break down your door, riffle your house, destroy your prized possessions, then announce that they *somehow* got the wrong address and leave. No offer to pay for the destruction, no apology, just gone." He shook his head.

"This actually happened to friends of yours?" Marco asked.

"Yes, but you won't see it in any newspaper," Robert said. "You know, a conspiracy of silence." He watched me for a moment, then leaned forward again. "Make sure you note that they were acquaintances, not friends."

I wrote it down and he sat back with a satisfied smile.

"I understand your concern," Marco said, "and I agree that the police were in the wrong, but right now we're working on a tight timeline. So can you shed some light on the skirmish between Jingles and Dallas Stone that happened last week?"

"Well, of course I *can*. What you should ask is whether I *will*. But since we are on a time constraint, I will proceed. The skirmish was the perfect example of what I had just stated about the police force. The manner in which they treated Jingles was abysmal. I only wish I had made a video of it to distribute via YouTube so that everyone would understand exactly the kind of bullying behavior they are wont to exhibit."

"Did you get all that?" Marco asked me as I scribbled furiously. I gave him a look that said, *Are you serious?*

Marco paused to let me catch up. "How did the skirmish between Dallas and Jingles start?"

"You'd have to ask him. All I know is that I heard loud arguing, so I went out to see what was happening. That was when I heard the man I now know as Dallas Stone calling Jingles names and threatening him. I ran back to my room to grab my WOMP and then returned to the hall to protect my friend."

"Wait," I said, still writing frantically. "What's a 'womp'?"

"Weapon of Mass Protection," Robert said again in a tone that implied I should know.

"Describe it," Marco said.

"I can do better than that." Robert reached into his back jean pocket and pulled out a thick, multitooled pocket knife with a shiny black handle.

Ah, the knife Jingles had described.

Robert leaned over to see what I'd written. "You have to capitalize the letters in WOMP. It's W-O-M-P."

"Is that a comic book term?" I asked.

"It's a Robert Hall term," he said with the tiniest of smiles, straightening his shoulders. "I drew my inspiration for it from the Marvel heroes."

"So you ran to the hallway with your WOMP," Marco said. "What happened next?"

Robert pinched the bridge of his nose as he imagined the scene. "Mr. Stone was holding a piece of paper above Jingles's head, dangling it just beyond his reach and taunting him, 'Come and get it, old man.' Just like that. When Jingles reached for it, Mr. Stone pushed Jingles so hard, he hit the door frame and slid down. That was when I ordered Mr. Stone to back away or I'd use my WOMP.

"Mr. Stone immediately put his hands in the air and backed up, obviously intimidated by my threat, which was what I intended. I helped Jingles get to his feet and he dusted himself off. He assured me that he was okay, but I knew he wasn't. The poor man was trembling all over. His explanation was that my WOMP made him nervous because it was so powerful, so I let him hold it so he could see that in the right hands it was safe."

"What was Dallas doing during this time?" Marco asked.

"I couldn't see him. He was inside Jingles's apartment."

"So you and Jingles were in the hallway, with Jingles holding your knife," Marco said, "while Dallas was inside Jingles's apartment. What happened next?"

I heard loud sirens. And then heavy boots pounding up the stairs. I knew what that meant. The enemy had invaded. I tried my hardest to bring Jingles into my apartment, but he refused my assistance, so I ran inside and barricaded the door."

"But then you realized it was only the cops," I said.

"*Only* the cops?" Robert leaned forward in his chair, his hands on his knees, like a father explaining something to a child. "Mrs. Salvare, the cops *are* the enemy."

CHAPTER ELEVEN

I was about to tell Robert that my father had been a cop, and a darned good one, too, but Marco stepped in. "Prior to that occurrence, did you ever hear Dallas and Jingles argue?"

Robert leaned back, folded his arms across his chest, and said in his deadpan manner, "Not an actual argument, no, but I did hear a conversation between Mr. Stone and Jingles about two weeks ago that became rather heated."

"Where did this conversation take place?" Marco asked.

"In the hallway outside Jingles's apartment. The walls are thin. One cannot help but overhear."

"What did you overhear?" Marco asked.

"Mr. Stone asked Jingles to help him out because he was broke. Jingles said no, he had no money. Then Mr. Stone retaliated by saying that Jingles of all people should understand how situations can get out of hand."

I wrote all that down, then added: *Why Jingles of all people?*

"On a sidenote," Robert said, "I'll bet Jingles would have helped him out if he'd had the money, because that's the kind of generous individual he is."

"Did Dallas say what his situation was?" Marco asked.

"No, but I assumed by the rest of their conversation that Jingles knew."

"What was the rest of the conversation?" Marco asked.

"Let's see. First there was the demand for money, then the refusal, then the plea for understanding . . . Ah. I remember. The accusation. Mr. Stone accused Jingles of lying. His exact words were, 'You've got money, old man. You're always helping others. How about helping me?' Poor Jingles just kept asking him to leave, but his words had no effect, so I pounded on the door and told him to beat it."

"Did that work?" I asked.

Robert looked away, tapping his chin thoughtfully. "Did that work? Well, after my command to leave, it grew quiet. Then Jingles said, 'It's okay, Robert. Dallas is just leaving.' And then he did. So, yes, I'd say it worked."

"Did you hear any more arguments between them?" Marco asked.

Robert thought a moment. "No, those were the only ones I heard."

"Do you have any theories on who killed Dallas?" Marco asked.

"A theory," Robert said, turning it over. "A theory is a proposed explanation whose status is conjectural, so I suppose I could offer several conjectures, but rather than waste any more of my valuable time on hypothetical contemplation, I'd rather skip to the outcome, which is that whoever it was did the town a favor."

"Do you believe Jingles could be the killer?" Marco asked.

Robert's gaze once again tracked someone moving outside the room. "I'd have to say not *the* killer—but possibly *a* killer."

"What do you mean?" Marco asked.

"Jingles refuses to talk about his past. People who won't talk about their pasts are hiding from it. And before you ask, I'll offer two conjectures as to why. One is that the person is carrying too many painful memories. The other is that the person is hiding too much guilt. Of course, there is a third possibility, which is a combination of the first two. Therefore, Jingles could have killed someone and either finds it too painful to discuss or feels too guilty to admit to it, or both."

"How do you know all this?" I asked.

He tapped his head. "I read a lot."

"Comic books?" I asked.

"Nothing but."

"And you got all that from comic books?" I asked.

He looked down his nose at me. "You obviously don't read them." His gaze drifted back to the door. "If you ever want to see my collection, let me know."

"Just a few more questions," Marco said. "How old are you?"

"Twenty-two and one quarter."

"Did you go to college?"

"I went, yes, until I realized that I was already more intelligent than most of the people in my classes, and then I decided to self-educate. It turns out I liked the professor better." He snickered at his own joke.

"Where do you come from?"

He pointed toward the ceiling. I halfway expected him to say *outer space*, but he said, "North of here in Sawyer, Michigan."

"I've been to Sawyer," I said. "I love the big market—"

"I lived on a farm," Robert said in a bored voice. "We grew our own food."

"Are your parents still there?" I asked.

"Mother is. Dad passed on."

"Are you employed?" Marco asked.

"Most definitely. I work at the hobby shop, although at present my employer is giving me time off to fill in for Jingles."

"Gem's Hobby Shop on the square?" Marco asked.

"Yes." He glanced at the big clock over the door. "Will there be anything else?"

"Just a few more questions," Marco said. "Where were you Friday afternoon?"

Robert gave Marco a quizzical, almost excited look. "That's the type of question detectives ask suspects. Am I to take it I'm a suspect?"

"You're to take it that I am curious about your whereabouts Friday afternoon," Marco said.

"Shall I assume you will also need to fingerprint me?" He examined his fingertips. "I've never been fingerprinted before."

"That's not my job," Marco said. "Just your whereabouts will do."

"Very well. I went to the farm Friday afternoon. You may validate that with my mother."

"Would you provide your mom's phone number and address?" I asked.

"I will," Robert said, and rattled it off as I wrote rapidly. He leaned forward to check it, pointing out that I'd left out the periods in *PO Box*. "You might want to visit her rather than call as she is usually outside working the farm. Plus, reception is quite poor between here and Sawyer. I can't tell you how many dropped calls—well, actually I can tell you. I have a log upstairs if you'd care to see it."

"Not necessary," Marco said. "What time Friday did you head for Sawyer?"

"I can't give you the exact time as I'm not in the habit of wearing a watch, but it was after Jingles left. I made it there in time for supper."

"Would you go over what happened Friday afternoon with Jingles?" Marco asked.

Robert's eyes fluttered shut. Like a machine replaying a tape, he said, "I was on my way to my room and saw Jingles's door open. I could hear him muttering to himself in an unhappy tone, so my conjecture was that something was wrong. I stuck my head in and saw him packing, so I said, 'If you're going to be away, would you like me to take over for you?'"

"You didn't ask him what was wrong?" I asked.

"It was none of my business," Robert said, as though shocked I would even suggest it.

"What was Jingles's response?" Marco asked.

"He had no response at all. In fact, Jingles looked at me as though he didn't recognize me. He zipped up his bag and said he had to get out of there. Then he pushed past me and left. I called after him, 'So do you want me to wash windows while you're gone?' But he just kept going, so I shut his door and went to my room."

"What was he putting in his bag?" I asked.

Robert listed on his fingers. "Three pairs of underwear, three pairs of socks, a box of peanut-flavored snack bars, a matchbook, a pair of gloves, and a six-pack of water."

"What about a sleeping bag?" I asked.

"You asked what he was putting *in* his bag. The sleeping bag was next to it."

"Describe the gloves," Marco said.

"Two identical pieces of material designed for keeping the individual fingers covered as well as the palm up to the wrist."

Marco's jaw twitched. I could tell Robert was trying his patience, so I quickly scribbled, *Be specific*, in the notebook so he could read it.

"Would you describe these particular gloves in detail?" Marco asked.

"Black leather, five fingers apiece. I wasn't able to see if they had a lining, but they looked quite nice."

His list matched everything Jingles had mentioned and more. Fleetingly, I thought how fortunate it was that Jingles had kept those supplies on hand, ready at a moment's notice. But . . . why?

I shook my head. No doubts allowed.

"Was Jingles back the next day?" Marco asked.

"I couldn't tell you. I was at my mother's. She makes pot roast on Saturdays. I didn't want to miss that."

"Did you see Jingles on Sunday?" Marco asked.

"No, I spend Sundays at the university library." With a proud smile, he said, "They know me there. Sometimes they let me shelve books."

"Did you see Jingles on Monday?" Marco asked. Questioning Robert was like leading a child by the hand.

"I did not, so I checked with Chester and Sol, and they hadn't, either. That was when I knew I had to take over for him."

"Were you alarmed by Jingles's disappearance?" I asked.

With that expressionless look, he asked, "Why would I be alarmed?"

"You might be worried over why he left," I suggested, "or worried that something had happened to him."

"Oh, you're asking for conjectures again," Robert said.

"Did you see Jingles at all on Monday?" Marco asked.

"No, I did not."

"When did you see Jingles next?"

"On Tuesday afternoon while I was washing the bank windows on Indiana Street. He came to say thank you for handling things, so I informed him that Mr. Stone was dead, the police were looking for him, and that given my acquaintance's experience, he'd better talk to a lawyer."

"What was Jingles's reaction?"

"As I recall, he put his right hand over his mouth and took a step backward."

"What did he say?"

"He expressed shock over the above items."

"And by expressing shock you mean . . . ?"

"He said, 'I'm in shock.'"

I had to hide my smile. Marco was not finding this amusing.

"Did Jingles ask you for any details on the murder?" Marco asked.

"No. He merely thanked me for filling in for him and asked if I would continue until he knew what was going on. So I did."

"Were you inside Jingles's shed on Monday morning?"

Robert gave him a puzzled glance. "Of course. How could I wash windows without the proper equipment?"

"Had you ever been to his shed before Monday?"

"Yes. I filled in for him on two other occasions."

"Did you see anything unusual inside the shed on Monday? This could be important, so please think hard."

Robert tapped his lips, gazing upward for a moment. "I do have something to report, although you may not find it unusual, since it was a storage shed and one stores things in storage sheds. But I did notice a very old Nike shoe box."

When he didn't continue, Marco asked, "Did you look inside?"

"It was wrong of me to pry, I know, but I expected to see vintage Nike shoes. Instead I found letters addressed to Samuel Atkins along with a photo of a man I believe to be a younger Jingles with an attractive woman and two boys standing beside a silver Ferrari. My guess is that they're his family, yet he lives alone in a men's shelter and doesn't own a car. So although you might say it's interesting, I'd call it unusual."

I knew that wasn't what Marco was aiming for. *Be more specific,* I wrote in the notebook again. He gave a nod.

"*Other* than the shoe box, while you were inside the shed gathering the window washing equipment, did anything strike you as out of place *for* a shed?"

"There was no dead body, if that's what you mean."

"Okay," Marco said slowly. "And once again, as you were inside the shed, did you see any black material, such as a scarf, necktie, rope perhaps?"

Robert pondered briefly. "I don't believe I've ever seen black rope. But the answer to your question is no."

"What time were you there to pick up the equipment?"

"As I stated before, I don't wear a watch, but I left my room at seven o'clock and it takes three thousand five hundred twenty-two steps to reach the hobby shop downtown. The shed is another block and a half away, so I'll have to account for that."

"Can you give me a rough estimate?" Marco asked.

Robert glanced my way. "What time did you see me washing your window?"

"Eight o'clock the first time."

Robert turned toward Marco. "Then a rough estimate would be seven thirty."

"Was the shed locked?"

"No."

"Does Jingles ever lock it?"

"I don't know. You'd have to ask him that."

"Did it look as though anyone else had been inside the shed?"

Robert cocked his head, thinking. "No."

"Okay," Marco said, clearly wanting to wrap it up.

"Not inside."

I could see Marco's jaw twitching again. "Did it look as though anyone else had been outside, near, under, or on top of the shed?"

"Yes. There was a woman's necklace lying on the ground outside."

My ears pricked up. A woman had been there?

"Why didn't you mention that when I asked if you had seen anything unusual?" Marco was near the snarling point.

"Because you asked if I'd seen anything unusual *inside* the shed. I had not."

Marco looked at me. "Do you want to take over here?"

I patted his arm. "Sure. Robert, did you pick the necklace up?"

"Why would I pick it up? It didn't belong to me."

"Would you describe the necklace?"

Robert closed his eyes as though conjuring an image. "It was a blue gemstone surrounded by small clear stones that may or may not have been diamonds. It was set in gold dangling from a thin gold chain, though whether it was solid gold or merely gold plated I couldn't tell you."

"Did you inform the police of its existence?"

"So they could accuse me of theft and give them a reason to storm my apartment? I think not."

I glanced at my notes. "I think that will do it, unless you can think of anything else we need to know."

"There is one thing." Robert pointed toward the door. "It's only conjecture, mind you, but I believe your dog is about to urinate."

I twisted around and saw Seedy sniffing the doorjamb. "Seedy, no!" I cried and ran to get her, clutching the notepad and pen against me. I opened the door and Seedy scooted out, heading straight through the big lobby to the double glass doors and then hobbling to the nearest tree to do her duty. We were on our way to the car when Marco came out of the Y checking his phone.

"No news from Reilly. Downtown must still be closed."

"It's after one o'clock," I said. "How about grabbing a bite and going over the notes while we eat?"

Marco opened the car door. "Do I dare go against the Scarlet Witch's desires?"

As soon as we were settled in the car, I turned so I could see him. "Speaking of that, Captain America, when did you learn so much about comic books?"

Marco, with his manly scruff and square jaw, blushed. It was something he rarely did. "When I was a boy."

"You were a comic book fan? I wouldn't have guessed that about you."

"Then you'll really find this hard to believe. I had hundreds of comic books. I wanted to be a superhero when I grew up. I even had a costume. It seems a little nerdy now, but back then I was obsessed."

How adorable was that? I reached over to hold his hand. "My nerdy little Superman."

"Actually, I never got into Superman. I was a Batman kind of guy."

"The Caped Crusader?"

"The Dark Knight." The corner of his mouth curved up. "And the world's greatest detective."

"Ah. Now it all makes sense. Well, you don't wear a cape, and the only dark knight in your life is me when the lights are off"—I gave his hand a squeeze—"but you *are* the world's greatest detective to me, and you will always be my superhero."

Marco leaned over and kissed me—a deep, meaningful, lasting kiss that took my breath away and left me wanting more.

"Watch it, Salvare," I said, kissing him again, "or I'll make you spontaneously combust."

"Baby, you've done that many times."

We parked the 'Vette on a side street near It's A Wrap, a popular local restaurant on the main drag east of the town square and a few blocks up from New Chapel University, where lighter fare was offered. As we rounded the corner, Seedy leading the way, Grace Bingham came striding up the sidewalk toward us. She was wearing a black pencil skirt and a light blue sweater set, but she'd exchanged her usual pumps for a pair of sneakers.

"Halloo," she called. "Stopping for a bite, are we?"

"You know it," I said. "Did you get tired of sitting at the coffee shop?"

Grace bent over to pet Seedy, who was wagging her tail in delight at seeing one of her favorite humans. "I can't sit for more than an hour, so I shopped a bit and now I'm out for a brisk walk. Any idea when the leak will be repaired?"

"I'm waiting for a call from Reilly," Marco said. "I'll text when I hear something."

"I would appreciate it, Marco. Thank you." She straightened. "If you're going to eat, shall I take Seedy with me? I'd love the company."

"That'd be great," I said. "Seedy, want to go with Grace?" She wagged her tail and gave a little yip.

"Text me when you're almost finished, and I'll bring her back," Grace called as the two set off.

"Grace's timing was perfect," Marco said, peering through the restaurant's large plate-glass window. "The place is packed. Seedy would've been a nervous wreck."

"I think Grace is psychic," I said as he opened the door for me. "She always shows up at exactly the right moment. She does this all the time at Bloomers."

"She isn't psychic, Sunshine. She works for you. It's her job to be there at the right time. And she just happened to be out for a walk."

We headed for the only empty table in the restaurant, smack-dab in the middle of the room. Set in a former furniture store, the big, boxy It's A Wrap had original brown-brick walls, a high open ceiling crisscrossed with heat ducts painted black, square wooden tables set close together, and a counter across the back where diners could sit and watch the chefs at work in the open kitchen.

A waitress appeared within minutes, weaving herself between the crammed diners to deliver our menus and glasses of water. It made me appreciate my coffee-and-tea parlor, where people weren't so close that they were practically in one another's laps.

After perusing the selection of wraps, panini, and salads, I ordered a turkey-spinach-feta wrap with a bottle of their special ginger beer, then took out my notes while Marco ordered.

"What did you think of Robert?" I asked when the waitress was gone.

"I've never wanted to choke a witness before."

"Seriously."

"I am being serious. The guy is literal to a fault. What was your impression? Reliable witness, flake, or suspect?"

"You left out mild-mannered supergenius. But suspect? Really?"

"You know the rule. We can't discount Robert until we verify his alibi. He never did give us a direct answer about who he thought killed Dallas. All he said was that the person did the town a favor. The other thing that bothered me is how quick he was to wield that army knife. It made me wonder whether he would've stabbed Dallas if Jingles hadn't talked him down."

After the waitress delivered our drinks, I asked, "What would his motive be?"

"I'd say it's that he didn't like the way Dallas treated Jingles."

I put a straw in my ginger beer. "So the question becomes, would Robert set him up as the murderer?"

"And the answer is that it's always better to question everything so we don't miss an important detail."

"You know, Marco, everything Robert told us matches Jingles's own accounts, so in my mind it proves that Jingles isn't lying."

"Unfortunately, it also strengthens his motive."

I really didn't want to hear that, but I couldn't argue, either. And I didn't even bring up my question about why Jingles kept emergency supplies so readily at hand. No sense stirring the pot.

"Anything else in your notes?"

"Yes, the blue necklace. Obviously it belongs to a woman, and we know of two women, Lavinia and Kandi. So who would have dropped it and when?"

"Don't limit your thinking, babe. Dallas could have been carrying it on him, a gift for his girlfriend maybe." He pulled out his cell phone and typed in a reminder. "I'll ask Reilly to check the evidence list when I hear from him. If the detectives found it, they've probably sent it in for DNA testing."

Marco took a drink of his root beer. "Let's talk about Lavinia."

Reading from my notes, I said, "According to what Lavinia told Betty, Dallas drained her bank account and left Springfield without signing the divorce papers. From Rosie we know she was sent home sick the day Dallas was murdered and has been absent all week. Betty saw her leave with a suitcase Tuesday via cab. She's physically strong and has an arsenal of poisons in her apartment. She was seen stalking Dallas.

"And in answer to Betty's question about whether she was a widow, Lavinia said, and I'm quoting Betty, 'Not yet. Not yet. I keep hoping the jack *mule* will kick the bucket, but so far it ain't happening.' She was heard saying to Dallas, 'We'll just see who dies first, won't we?'"

"Definitely a solid suspect."

"Between Robert and Lavinia, she has the stronger motive, hands down, Marco."

"Our problem is that Jingles has the most compelling motive of all, in addition to the circumstantial evidence the cops have on him. And then there's the black leather dress gloves. That's not the sort of thing you'd take to camp out. Work gloves maybe. I'll have to ask Jingles where they are now. They'll need to be tested. I also want to ask him why he keeps emergency supplies on hand."

I had a feeling Jingles would wonder whose side we were on.

The waitress brought our orders, so I waited until she left to say, "I know Jingles didn't do it, Marco."

"No, you *hope* he didn't do it. Don't lose sight of that." Marco squirted mustard into his roast beef, cheddar cheese, and jalapeño pepper panini. "The day you let your guard down, it'll come back to bite you."

I couldn't imagine Jingles as a killer, even if I did let my guard down, but I knew Marco was right. "We have another potential suspect to investigate — Kandi Cane — and why am I thinking stripper?"

Marco wiped his mouth with a napkin. "The only two strip clubs around here are about thirty miles northwest of town. I'll contact the managers to see if I can find her, but if Chester was right about her being a hooker, there's no way to check that out without going undercover."

I was about to take a bite, but that stopped me. "The only undercover work *you're* doing, Salvare, is in bed with me." I reached across the table to tap my fingertips on his arm. "Remember, I can make you combust."

Marco's gaze became hooded as he watched me sip my drink through the straw. He ran his thumb along my cheek and said in a husky voice, "I'd like to see you try."

"That sounds like an invitation."

Marco smiled lazily. "Why don't we finish up here and take off? I have a plan in mind for us, Scarlet."

Tingles of excitement raced up my spine as I gazed at

my husband, his body still chiseled from his Army Ranger days. With his formfitting gray T-shirt, trim waist, and tight black jeans, how could I not be excited? My romantic hubby was an expert planner. I couldn't wait to see what he had in mind.

But then his cell phone rang. He glanced at his screen and said, "Hold that thought. It's Reilly. I'll make this quick."

He put the phone to his ear. "Are we back in business?" He listened a moment, shook his head at me, then said, "No kidding. So another hour, then? Okay, thanks, man."

Marco put his phone away and reached across the table to trace a design on the back of my hand. "You heard?"

I smiled. "Yes, I did."

His voice dropped to a husky whisper. "We have a whole hour to do whatever we want." He ran his fingers up my arm. "And you know what I want."

The tingles were coming on strong now. "Go on."

"I suggest we grab a bottle of bubbly—"

"Yes?"

"Slip back to the house—"

Whatever words he said after "the house" were drowned out by the siren going off in my head. House, as in my parents' domicile? *Tingles gone.*

"Why are you frowning?" he asked.

I sighed and rested my chin in my palm. "You want us to go back to my parents' house—with my dad roaming around just waiting for company?"

"That isn't what I had in mind, but I'm sure he'd get the picture when we shut our bedroom door."

"Eww. I don't want Dad imagining us—you know. *Eww.*"

"What do you think he imagines every night when we shut our door?"

"Us sleeping. And do not change the picture in my head, okay?"

"Fine." Marco pondered for a moment; then one corner of his mouth curved up impishly. "Okay, then how about this? You haven't been to see our new house in over a week."

"Use our free hour to check on the building progress? That isn't what *I* had in mind."

"You didn't let me finish. Let's grab a blanket and the bubbly, go out to the new house, and find a cozy corner—"

A commotion at the front of the restaurant made us both turn to see what was happening. And there was Jillian with her twin stroller banging her way through the tables to reach us.

"That isn't what I had in mind, either," I said.

CHAPTER TWELVE

People were scooting chairs out of the way, even moving tables, to let Jillian through as she made her way toward us. The baby wailed on one side of the stroller and the dog barked on the other, its paws on the side, pausing every few seconds to sniff the air for potential food offerings.

Marco started to get up, and I knew he was about to make an escape, which was what he usually did when Jillian happened onto the scene, but this time I was faster. I clamped my hand over his wrist. "No you don't. We're on team time, Salvare."

Marco did a two-second internal debate, saw the panic in my eyes, and sat back into the wooden chair. "You're right."

"I'll get us out of here as fast as I can," I said.

"Ha!" Jillian said over the noise from the strollers' occupants as she brought her double-wide to a halt. "Thought you could elude me, didn't you?"

She yanked out a chair and sat down, then carefully arranged her long patchwork skirt and brushed back her silky copper locks, tossing her head like a show horse. She seemed completely unaware of the disgruntled looks from the diners all around us. "It's extremely sad when I have to hunt you down like a wild animal in order to talk to you. Hello, Marco."

"Jillian," he muttered.

"Stop that, Princess!" Jillian swatted the barking terrier's nose, and Princess pulled back into the stroller. Then my cousin reached into the other stroller, unfastened Harper's safety belt, and lifted her out. "Here," she said, handing me the screaming pink-and-purple bundle. "Watch her while I go get a cup of coffee."

"I'll get it for you," Marco said, and shot out of his chair before I could catch him.

I put the baby over my shoulder and began to bounce. I wasn't sure why I bounced, but it seemed the right thing to do because Harper quieted instantly. I glanced at the four middle-aged women seated at a table to my right and shrugged apologetically. They gave me understanding smiles in return.

"Why did you have to hunt me down?" I asked quietly. "What's the problem now?"

"What's the problem *now*?" She shook her head in disbelief and said, loud enough to be heard three tables away, "I poured my heart out to you the other day, and what did you do? Ran away from me with a promise to call. Have you called, Abby? Have you?"

I hugged the baby against me as I leaned toward her to say quietly, "I wasn't running away. I was short-handed at the shop when you dropped by and I had to go up front to wait on customers. How did you find me here?"

"Your 'Vette is parked around the corner, and Grace is walking Seedy down Lincoln. Knowing all the shops on the square are closed, I checked the time and deduced that you were having a late lunch here."

Of all the times for Jillian to be clever. "You're not the only one who's been stressed out lately, Jillian. I've got more business than three people can handle, and yet everyone keeps demanding pieces of my time. Plus, my dream home is being built, and I don't even know what it looks like. And you know I'm living at my parents' home. At their *home*, Jillian. Can you imagine the strain of living in your old bedroom under your parents' roof?"

I had stopped bouncing to deliver my retort, and now Harper was whimpering, so I started again.

Jillian thought about it, then shook her head. "And what can you do? Your house won't be ready for months. You have no money to rent a place . . ." She gasped and sat up straight. "I know! Stay with us. We have a third bedroom that no one is using."

I was so stunned all I could think to say was, "But the baby."

"Exactly! You can help me with her, and Marco and Claymore can hang out in front of the TV on the weekends and watch those sporty events. It'll be fun."

If I knew Marco, he'd be hanging out at Down the Hatch instead. Permanently.

Marco arrived with her coffee at that moment, so Jillian turned to him with a wide smile. "Thank you, Marco." She took the cup, held up her index finger so he'd wait while she took a sip, then said, "*Mmm.* Perfect. And now thank *me.*"

Marco took a seat to my right. "Thank you for what?"

Jillian's big golden eyes sparkled with excitement. "You're going to come live with Claymore and me."

Marco glanced at me, one eyebrow raised, and asked dryly, "Am I being evicted?"

Jillian giggled. "I don't mean just you, silly. You *and* Abs."

Marco's other eyebrow joined its partner. "What?"

I had to nip Jillian's idea in the bud before my husband burst a blood vessel in his forehead. Holding the baby in the crook of my left elbow, I slid my free hand into Marco's hand beneath the table and gave it a quick squeeze. "Jillian, we are just bowled over by your generosity—and I'm sure my parents will be, too, eventually, after they've forgiven you."

Jillian's radiant smile turned to a puzzled frown. "Forgiven me for what?"

"My parents see these months with us as their last chance to bond, Jill, and they're not going to let go of that lightly because, let's face it, they're getting *old.*"

"But they're only in their fifties," she said. "That's not old."

I noticed that the fiftysomething ladies at the next table had gone silent, and when I glanced over, they were scowling at me.

I leaned closer to my cousin. "Still, they won't be around forever. Shouldn't we allow our parents whatever small pleasures they can grab from life while they're still here? Do you want to be the one they blame for taking away the small slice of joy we bring to their lives?"

This time Marco squeezed my hand. "I'm going to the restroom."

I squeezed back and let go, hoping that meant he was going to find a way to rescue us, then realized I'd stopped bouncing again.

"I'm confused," Jillian said. "You just told me your parents were driving you up the wall, and now you want to stay there?"

Seeing as how the ladies beside us were straining to catch every word, I leaned even closer. "They *are* driving me up the wall, Jillian, but I'm not driving *them* up the wall. They consider us a bonus to their dull existence. How can I deny them that?"

She picked up her coffee and took a sip, thinking about it. "Well, fine," she said at last. "Stay with them and suffer. I was just trying to help you, unlike *you*, who would rather run away than help with *my* problems."

Well, that did it. Now the ladies were muttering and making huffing sounds. I was afraid to glance at them.

"I tried to help," I said for their benefit. "I told you to talk to Claymore about your in-laws."

"And I told *you* he was part of the problem."

"Who's Claymore?" one of the women whispered to another.

"Her husband, no doubt," the other woman whispered back, and from the corner of my eye, I saw the others nod knowingly.

"Yes, he *is* my husband," Jillian said, swiveling to talk to them, "and before my beautiful baby was born"—she held out her arms to me so I could hand Harper to her—"he was the perfect spouse."

"Isn't that always the way?" one of the women asked, sighing.

Jillian pulled back the top of the baby blanket so she could kiss Harper's forehead. "But then you were born, weren't you, my angel?" Turning back to the women, she said dramatically, "And suddenly my devoted husband became Claymore the obedient son of P. J. and Evelyn Osborne."

"Oh, he's an *Osborne*," one of the women said, and again the others nodded. Everyone in town knew who the scions of New Chapel were, and P.J. and Evelyn were a part of that elite group.

"Jillian," I said, trying to draw her attention back to me, "if you want to change the situation, you have to make Claymore see your side of it."

"Good luck with that," one of the women said with a snicker.

"I know!" Jillian said to her. "And then there's Abby, the one person I count on to help me. But where is she in my darkest hour?"

"Who is Abby?" one of the women whispered.

"She must be the nanny," her friend answered.

"No!" Jillian gestured toward me. "Abby Knight. The florist. From Bloomers? Anyway, I tried to explain to Abby that I've lost control, that my in-laws have invaded my house and are trying to run my life, but she doesn't get it."

"I get it, Jill," I snapped.

Princess chose that moment to leap from the stroller and begin scrounging on the floor for scraps.

"And Claymore refuses to stick up for me," Jillian continued, ignoring me to play to her audience. "If they could, P.J. and Evelyn would kidnap my precious little angel so they could raise her according to their standards."

Indignant murmurs came from a table to my right. I glanced around and saw two young couples listening now.

"Get this," Jillian said, turning toward her new audience. "My mother-in-law stops by *at least* once a day—*unannounced*—to tell me I'm doing everything wrong. I don't feed Harper enough; I don't change her enough; I don't burp her enough . . ." Tears welled in Jillian's eyes and rolled down her cheeks as she said on a sob, "Nothing I do is ever enough for that woman."

Meryl Streep, move over.

"Oh, honey, that's awful," one of the middle-aged women from the first table said. She was about to say more when Princess jumped into her lap and began sniffing her face.

"I had a mother-in-law just like that," her friend said. "That woman made my life miserable."

"If your mother ever treats me like that," one of the young women at the second table said to her spouse, "I will divorce you."

Jillian held Harper out to them. "Does this child look mistreated to you?"

As if on cue, Harper began to wail.

"Not at all," one of the younger women said, then repeated, louder, "Not at all."

Jillian turned toward the first table and repeated the gesture.

"She's a beautiful, healthy baby," one of them called. "Quite a set of lungs."

"You're doing a great job of mothering her, honey," another called, trying to keep Princess from jumping onto the table.

"I *am* doing a great job," Jillian said, sniffling. At that moment Princess escaped the woman's clutches and leaped onto the table, stepping into her plate of food. Jillian grabbed a chunk of bread Marco had left on his plate, shoved it in the dog's mouth, and put her back into the stroller. "I'm a *good* mother!"

"Can I hold that precious bundle?" yet another woman asked.

"Oh, please do!" Jillian handed her the wailing infant, then sank back into her chair as though completely spent. In the next instant she was turning her chair toward their table and wedging herself in. "So you understand my predicament?"

"You bet we do," the woman holding Harper said, bouncing a finally happy child.

"And *we're* here to help," another one said, giving me the stink-eye.

"Your in-laws sound more like outlaws to me," yet another said, and three tables of diners in the vicinity broke into laughter.

Jillian had become the entertainment.

My cousin, happy now that she was the center of attention, reached for a handful of grapes off their fruit plate appetizer. "What do you think I should do?" she asked, munching.

I realized Marco hadn't returned and I looked around to find him standing at the coffee counter, sipping his java from a cardboard cup. He nodded toward the door.

I turned back to find Jillian listening intently to all their advice, so I grabbed my purse from the floor and, moving at a crouch, made my way toward the entrance and out onto the sidewalk, where Marco was already waiting.

There, strolling toward us, were Grace and Seedy.

"See what I mean?" I said to Marco. "I forgot to text

Grace, and yet here she comes. I'm telling you, Marco, she's psychic."

"I texted her five minutes ago, Sunshine."

"How did you know five minutes ago that we'd be leaving now?"

Marco glanced around as though afraid of being over-heard, then said quietly, "I didn't want to tell you this before, but I'm the one who's psychic."

I laughed, but then, upon further thought, I said, "Wait a minute. You were going to leave me with Jillian, weren't you?"

"*You* were about to move us into her guest room."

"I may evict you after all."

"Your dad would never go for it. I *listen* when he reads the newspaper."

"Have a nice luncheon, did we?" Grace asked, hand-ing the leash to me.

"Lunch was great," Marco said.

"Until Jillian showed up," I grumbled.

Grace shook her head sadly. "When I saw her pushing her pram up the street, I had a strong feeling that she was looking for you."

I glanced at Marco and mouthed, *Psychic.*

With Seedy present, we gave up on any romantic notions and drove to the development where our house was be-ing built. I was surprised to see the frame up and the roof joists on, since the last time I'd been there we'd had only a foundation.

We walked around the inside, where I tried to get an idea of furniture placement, using the wall studs that outlined the rooms as my guides. Workers had built tem-porary steps to the basement that I wasn't about to attempt, so I stayed on the main floor with Seedy while Marco went down to inspect.

"Everything looks good down there," Marco said when he came up. "What do you think of the upstairs?"

"I keep trying to imagine what my kitchen will look like, but it's hard when there's nothing to see."

Marco's cell phone beeped to signal a text message. "'Gas leak fixed,'" he read. "'Downtown should be open in half an hour.'" He glanced at his watch. "That will make it around three o'clock. I'd better let Rafe know so he can meet me at the bar."

"And that will give me a few hours to work before supper."

We both paused at that, and then I stepped into Marco's open arms and laid my head against his shoulder. "Today was fun, Marco, like old times. I wish it wasn't over so soon."

Stroking my back, he murmured in my ear, "I hear you, sweetheart. I always prefer having you at my side. But things will ease up when Rosa comes on full-time."

"I know, but two weeks seems like such a long way off."

I felt a tap on my leg and glanced down to see Seedy gazing up at us as though to say, *Hey! I want a hug, too!*

My cell phone rang, so while Marco crouched down to pet the dog, I pulled out my mobile and saw Betty Summers's name on the screen. Putting her on speakerphone, I said, "Hi, Betty. Is everything okay?"

"I thought you'd want to know that Mrs. Stone is back. I spoke with her a few minutes ago. I wouldn't have known who she was if I hadn't watched her let herself into her apartment."

"Why is that, Betty?"

"She had on a black straw hat with a wide floppy brim that hid most of her face. I told her she looked like a spy in a thriller movie."

"Interesting. Okay, thanks for the call."

"You're welcome. But if you're thinking about making another wellness check on her, I wouldn't wait too long. She said she was just home to pick up a few things."

I glanced at Marco as I put my phone away. "Sounds like Lavinia is going to be on the move again."

"We still have half an hour," he said. "Let's go."

CHAPTER THIRTEEN

Lavinia opened the door of her apartment just a crack and one eyeball moved over me. She couldn't see Marco; he was standing to one side of the doorway. "May I help you?"

"Hi, Lavinia. I'm Abby. Remember me?"

She continued to study me. Seedy was wiggling in Marco's arms, wanting down, and I hoped Lavinia didn't hear her. "Sure," she said slowly, not sounding sure at all. "You live on the floor above."

I didn't correct her; she had no idea Betty had let us into the building. Instead, I said with a light laugh, "We nearly collided last Monday in front of the deli, remember?"

"And you had your funny little dog with you." Opening the door a few inches wider, she asked, "Is there something you need, honey?"

"I bring greetings from your employer. She's a friend of mine."

"Rosie?"

"Yep. She was concerned because you'd called in sick all week."

Lavinia forced a cough, patted her lungs, and cleared her throat several times. "I'm finally getting over it, thank the Lord. You can tell Rosie I appreciate her concern."

She backed up, intending to close the door, so I said, "Wait, Lavinia. My husband has some questions for you."

"Your husband?"

"Marco Salvare," I said. "He's a private investigator."

Marco stepped into view holding Seedy, and Lavinia's friendly expression froze. Her gaze darted between Marco, Seedy, and me, and then, with her smile fixed in place, she asked tightly, "What's this about?"

"The murder of Dallas Stone," Marco said.

At that, her pretense of friendliness vanished. It took her a moment to decide what to do, and then she said, "One moment, please," and shut the door.

I glanced at Marco, fearing we'd lost our opportunity to interview her. Would she climb out a window and make a run for it? Before I could ask Marco what we should do, I heard what sounded like papers shuffling and a drawer opening and closing.

"Hear that?" I whispered, and leaned closer. Marco nodded.

The door opened partway and Lavinia stuck her head out again, saying in a low voice, "I don't know anything about the murder."

"You work on the town square and didn't hear about the murder victim found at the courthouse?" Marco asked.

"Okay, I heard about it. Ain't my problem, though. As you can see, I'm right in the middle of something, so this might have to wait."

"Considering that you're about to become a murder suspect," Marco said, at which point her jaw went slack, "I think it is your problem."

After a momentary internal debate, Lavinia stuck her head through the doorway, glanced up and down the hallway, and said in a whisper, "You'd better come in, then. This floor has nothing but busybodies on it." She held the door while we entered. "And I'm pretty sure they can hear me through the walls, too, so keep your voices down."

She had on a white blouse and jeans. She also had a bad case of hat hair, yet her bouffant do was still three inches above the top of her head. She wore little makeup and her eyes looked tired. As she led us through an immaculate living room, I glanced around to see what she could have been shuffling and noticed a maple desk against one wall, but the only thing on top was a calendar.

I opened my notebook. "Let's start with your trip out of town Tuesday when you were supposedly home sick."

"I didn't kill Dallas. Why am I a suspect?"

Marco put Seedy down but held on to her leash. "We didn't say you killed anyone. We just have a few questions."

"I'll give you ten minutes and then you gotta get out of here. I have a flight in a couple hours and I still have to pack."

She sat us at a square maple table in her kitchen, Seedy in Marco's lap. Lavinia didn't offer anything to drink. She merely sat facing us, her arms folded across her blouse.

"We're not here to torment you," Marco started. "We've been hired to find Dallas's killer and your name came up."

"Because I called off work? Is that all it takes to be a suspect in this town?"

"It takes a little more than that." Referencing my notes, I said, "According to our investigation, Dallas drained your bank account and left Springfield without signing the divorce papers. You followed him to New Chapel and took a job at Rosie's Diner. You were off work the day Dallas was murdered, went home sick after his body was discovered, and have been absent ever since. You lied about being sick, too, and—"

"I was not lying," she protested. "I was sick—*am* sick." She coughed again, making Seedy jump and look up at her. She had been dozing on Marco's knees.

"—*and* you were stalking Dallas Stone."

"That's crazy," she said, showing a spark of anger. "I'm no stalker."

"We have eyewitnesses, Lavinia," I said.

Jumping to her feet, she said in an angry whisper, "I just wanted an opportunity to talk to Dal in private. The only conversations we had were either at the diner while I was on duty or on the phone—when I could get him to answer my calls."

"This is why we wanted to speak with you," I said. "We need to get to the truth so we can take you off the suspect list."

She thought it over, then turned to leave the kitchen. "Keep talking."

"When did you hear the news about the murder?" Marco asked.

Lavinia came back with a suitcase and propped it open against a wall. "Monday around noon." She left the kitchen again and returned with an armful of clothing. "Everyone who came into the diner was buzzing about it."

Was she actually packing a suitcase while being interviewed as a suspect?

"Were you upset?"

She gave Marco a wary glance. "I went home, didn't I?"

"Wasn't that because of the cold you were coming down with?"

Her cheeks reddened but she didn't answer, only continued to fold clothes and lay them in the suitcase.

"Do you know who Jingles the window washer is?"

She lifted one shoulder and let it drop. "Doesn't everyone?"

"Are you aware that the police have arrested Jingles?"

"Yeah. I saw the write-up in the newspaper."

"What day was that?"

"Tuesday morning."

"Let's go back to when you first came to town," Marco said. "What were your conversations with Dallas about?"

"The divorce papers and my money," she said. "We didn't have anything else to discuss."

"In these conversations, did you ask him to sign the papers?" Marco asked.

"I *begged* him to sign them," Lavinia said. "I also told him I was struggling to pay my bills and wanted my money back."

"What was his response to signing the papers?"

"He kept telling me to mail them to him," she said. "Fat chance, I told him. I know your tricks. I told him he either signed them in front of me or I'd—"

She broke off, clenching the blouse in her hands, clearly realizing she was about to say something incriminating.

"Why didn't you hire a lawyer?" I asked.

"You try telling an attorney you need to go after a runaway spouse and see what happens. They want money up front, and I don't have it."

"Did you threaten to harm Dallas?" Marco asked.

Lavinia glared daggers at Marco. "Look here, mister. I'm not the kind of person who goes around hurting others. I told him I'd have a little chat with his new girlfriend and tell her what kind of jackass she was seeing."

I knew she'd said more than that, but I didn't want to get Betty Summers in trouble.

"What was his response?" Marco asked.

She shrugged her shoulders, flattening the blouse on the table. "He told me if I went near her, he'd make my life a living hell. Now I'm a suspect, so I guess he kept his promise."

"Did you talk to his girlfriend?" I asked.

Lavinia tried unsuccessfully to hide her smile. "I did. And then she dumped him. He claimed that was why he moved into the men's residence."

"Do you know her name?" I asked.

"Kandi Cane. That's Kandi with a *K* and an *i*. Sounds made up, doesn't it?"

"What did you hope to gain by stalking Dallas?" Marco asked.

"I wanted him to sign the damn papers," she said sharply. "He was supposed to meet me and my attorney at the courthouse in Springfield to sign them, but he never showed up. I found out later he'd beat it out of town."

She dropped her blouse into the suitcase, got her quilted floral-print purse from the kitchen counter, and flopped it down on the table in front of us. Digging into it, she pulled out a thick white envelope in a plastic sleeve and shook it at us. "I've been carrying this with me since the day Dal took off."

Seedy jumped down and went beneath my chair.

"When did you find out that Dallas had drained your bank account?" Marco asked.

"Not until after the weasel left town. I went to the bank

to take out money to pay my attorney fees and was told my account had been closed. Every penny was gone."

"Was it a joint account?" Marco asked.

"It was mine, but he talked me into putting him on it in case something happened to me." She gave an angry snort. "Something happened to me all right. Dallas happened to me."

"How much was in there?"

"One hundred forty-three thousand dollars—my entire life savings, which he probably used to pay off his debts. He had been gambling away his salary while I was using mine to pay bills. Now I have to start all over, and I'm fifty-four years old!"

"Didn't you think it was wrong that you had to pay all the bills?" I asked.

"He said he was investing his money so we could both retire in a few years and live high on the hog. What an idiot I was for believing him. But if you looked at him, you saw a smart, wealthy, attractive man who drove a fancy car and owned expensive clothes. Why wouldn't I believe him? He bought me nice things, too—fur coats, jewelry—until we were married. Then the leopard began to show his spots."

At the mention of jewelry, I asked, "Do you still have the jewelry he bought you?"

She gave me a wary glance. "Why?"

"Do you own a blue gemstone necklace set in gold?"

"Define blue."

"Any color blue," I said.

"I have a blue sapphire birthstone necklace that my mama bought for me."

"Do you have it in your possession?"

"Of course I do."

"Could we see it?"

Lavinia lifted her chin. "You got a search warrant?"

"Is there a reason you don't want us to see it?" I retorted.

"I just don't, that's all."

"Let's go back to the time of your marriage," Marco said. "Did you ever ask to see Dallas's investment portfolio?"

"I don't even know what a portfolio is," Lavinia said. "Dallas was the expert on money matters, or so he convinced me—until he got fired. At least I know I'm not the only gullible gal. He did the same to his first wife, too. Only difference is, he did sign those divorce papers."

"Why was he fired?" Marco asked.

"Got caught with his finger in the till. Dal was danged lucky his boss didn't press charges."

"Did you know Samuel Atkins?" I asked.

"Who?"

"Samuel Atkins, your husband's former boss back in Springfield."

A cautious look stole across Lavinia's face. "Oh. Yeah, I met him a few times. Work-related events, that kind of thing."

"Do you know where Samuel Atkins is now?" Marco asked.

She pulled at a thread from her sleeve, averting her gaze. "No."

"Did you know Dallas's first wife?"

"Nope. I'd never even talked to her until that jackass left me high and dry. Then I found her number and gave her a call to see if she had a clue where he might've gone."

"Do you still have her phone number?" I asked.

Throwing me a glare, Lavinia got her cell phone, scrolled through her contacts, and showed me the information, which I jotted down.

"Is that how you located Dallas?" Marco asked.

"Did that through LinkedIn. He'd put up his résumé to find a job, then posted about it when he got hired at the bank here. The idiot didn't know he did me a favor."

"How did you know to check LinkedIn?" Marco asked.

"When we were married, he was always on it," she replied. "Looking back, I realized he was probably searching for a new job so he'd have somewhere to go when he left me."

I was impressed with Lavinia's detective skills.

"What were you doing last Friday afternoon?" Marco asked.

She pursed her lips. "Friday, Friday . . . I think I just came straight home from work. Oh, wait—I stopped for groceries."

"We'll need a witness who can verify that."

"I didn't see anyone I knew," Lavinia answered quickly.

"Then we'll need the name of the store," Marco said. "I'll have to show your photo to the clerks to see if someone can back up your alibi."

Lavinia studied Marco a moment, her brows knitted. "What if you can't find anyone?"

"That would be bad. Why did you leave town Tuesday?"

"I went back home to visit my ma 'cause she's taken ill."

"Where is home?" he asked.

"Springfield, Illinois. I'm going back there now, in fact. I just came home to water my plants and get more clothes. I wasn't expecting to have to stay with her."

"What airline?" Marco asked.

"United."

"Why didn't you just tell Rosie about your mother?" I asked.

"I was afraid she'd fire me," Lavinia said. "I didn't know how long I'd be away."

"Rosie is an understanding boss," I said. "You need to talk to her."

"You're right," she said with a change of tone. "I haven't always had bosses as kind as Rosie. I'll give her a call before I head out."

"Think back to Monday morning," Marco said. "When Abby saw you heading toward the deli, where were you coming from?"

"Home."

"Abby saw you coming across the courthouse lawn from the direction of Franklin. Is that correct?"

"Yes." She made a slicing motion. "Straight across."

"But you live north of the square. Coming across from Franklin would be out of your way. Are you sure you didn't stop somewhere first?"

"Oh, wait—I remember now. I drove that morning."

"You live three blocks away. Isn't it faster to walk to the diner?"

"I was running late so . . ." She shrugged.

"Still, in the time it took to locate a parking spot, you could've been at work." Marco paused to watch her deal with that, and when she merely shifted her gaze away, he said, "When you came across the courthouse lawn, did you see anything unusual?"

"No, but I wasn't looking around. I was in a hurry to pick up my breakfast. I didn't want to be late for work."

"You bought food to eat before going to work at a restaurant?"

"Rosie doesn't allow us to eat on the premises. I picked up a bagel and ate it on the way."

I put an asterisk beside my note so I could check with Rosie later.

Make that *Marco* could check with Rosie.

"When you came out of the deli," he said, "did you notice the police swarming around the courthouse?"

"Like I said, I was in a hurry that morning. But yeah, I saw them out of the corner of my eye."

"Did you go over to see what was happening?"

She picked at the back of her hair, her aversion increasingly indicative of dishonesty. "No, I didn't want to be late, as I said before."

"Where did you park?"

She plucked at her lower lip. "On Franklin."

"When you went back to move your car, were the police still there?"

"I didn't move my car."

"Have you paid the parking tickets?"

"What parking tickets?" she answered slowly.

"Two-hour parking on Franklin. If you didn't move your car, you should have at least two tickets."

After a slight hesitation, she said, "Of course. Silly me. I *did* get ticketed. My memory of that day is off, see, because I wasn't feeling well. This cold thing was coming on . . . and that morning I was thinking about getting my food and hurrying to work and all and not wanting to disappoint Rosie by being late. She can give you a look that just makes you cringe." Turning to me, Lavinia said, "Well, you should know. She's your friend. I mean, she's nice and all, but she has that look."

When I didn't say anything, Lavinia continued to prattle on. "So I was coughing and digging for a tissue, not minding where I was going or what was happening around me, and then you shouted, 'Hey!' And that was the first time I really looked up ... Then I saw you and your dog and then I went and bought my bagel and got myself to the diner, and that's the God's honest truth."

She made a grand gesture of checking her watch. "Listen, I really gotta go. You know, my ma being sick and all."

"Sure," Marco said. "Abby, anything before we wrap it up?"

"I have one question," I said. "You mentioned that when we almost collided, you were digging for a tissue. But when I saw you, you were stuffing something *into* your purse. Do you remember that?"

No need for an answer. Her expression told me everything.

CHAPTER FOURTEEN

"It was my scarf," Lavinia finally said. "It kept slipping, so I took it off and stuffed it into my purse. But I did need a tissue."

"What color is the scarf?" I asked.

"Black. To match my coat." She rose, rubbing her upper arms as though chilled. "I'm going to need you to leave now."

I tucked my notebook in my purse; then Marco and I stood. Seedy put her paw on my leg, so I picked her up.

"One more thing," Marco said, pausing in the doorway. "Do you keep any rodent poison on your premises?"

"Rodent poison? For what? If there are any rodents around here, I've never seen one."

"So when the cops search your apartment, they won't find any?" Marco asked.

Her eyes widened. "They're going to search my place?"

"I meant *if*," Marco said.

She fanned her face. "Whew. You had me scared there for a minute."

"Why?" Marco asked.

"Well, you know, the idea of cops tearing my place

apart isn't something anyone wants to think about. So they're not planning to, right?"

"That's up to them," Marco said.

"But poison isn't how Dallas died, so why would the cops care if I had rodent poison in the house? Not that I do."

"The toxicology results aren't back yet, so until they know if anything else played a role in his death, they'll look at all possibilities." Marco smiled. "Have a nice day."

"Yeah, okay, then."

The door shut quickly behind us. I noticed two other residents' doors open a crack and eyeballs tracking us. At least Lavinia hadn't lied about the busybodies.

"What was all that about the cops searching her apartment?" I asked as we headed to the car.

"I just wanted to see how nervous she is about police scrutiny."

"Clearly she is. I don't trust Lavinia at all, Marco. First, she hid something she didn't want us to see, then she got defiant when I asked to see her necklace, and then she was definitely rattled when I mentioned that I'd seen her stuffing that scarf into her purse. Or she claims it was a scarf, anyway. It could've been Dallas's tie."

If only I could remember.

Marco waited until after we were buckled into the 'Vette, then said, "What else?"

"Besides our suspect plainly packing a suitcase to leave town?" I opened the notebook. "Lavinia seemed nervous when you told her you had to find an alibi witness for her and when you questioned her about Monday morning. She wouldn't look at you when you asked if she knew where Samuel Atkins is now, and her story about parking the car on Franklin didn't ring true. The only thing that I do believe is that she was stalking Dallas to get him to sign the divorce papers."

"Agreed. I'm still working on how she could have pulled off the murder."

"I was thinking about that, too, Marco. Here's the scenario I came up with. Friday afternoon Dallas leaves the bank and goes to find Jingles, unaware that Lavinia is stalking him. She trails him to the shed, where they argue. He turns his back on her—maybe to walk away—and she loses it. She grabs him by his tie or throws her scarf around his neck, dragging him back inside the shed, losing her necklace in the process. When she realizes he's dead, she panics, shuts the shed, and runs home.

"Soon the full extent of what she did starts to sink in, and she's a complete wreck, wondering whether she left any evidence behind. When nothing shows up in the newspaper about the murder by Sunday, Lavinia asks around, finds out that Jingles hasn't been seen, goes to the shed before dawn Monday morning, and moves the body."

"Why not leave the body? Why take that risk?"

"I haven't worked that out. Maybe she was having second thoughts about letting Jingles take the blame. Then, later that morning, she realizes she dropped the tie and/or scarf and returns to the courthouse to find it. And that's what she was stuffing into her purse when I saw her."

Marco shook his head. "How lucky could the murderer get to have a whole weekend to kill, hide the body, ponder what to do with it, and move it away from the crime scene?"

"What are you implying?"

"Doesn't it strike you as quite a coincidence, Sunshine, that Jingles was out of town while this murder was going down? Not only out of town, but incommunicado? With camping supplies readily available?"

"Maybe he camped out regularly. Have you asked him that? Is it beyond the realm of possibility that a person who camps out keeps supplies on hand?"

"Don't get defensive, Abby. We have to consider the possibility that Jingles killed Dallas. You know that."

"So you believe there's no way Lavinia could have pulled it off?"

"I'm not saying that. What if Lavinia and Jingles were working together? Doesn't it seem more likely that Lavinia would have been able to lure Dallas away while someone else did the dirty work? And then they both split before they knew what to do with the body. She didn't seem at all concerned about Dallas's death, so maybe she wasn't the one who committed the murder. When we look at Jingles, all we see is a kind old man. We know nothing about his past—but I'll handle that. Then I'll have Reilly check to see whether Lavinia got ticketed and whether a necklace was recovered. I'll follow up with the airlines as well."

"Thank you." As we pulled into the parking lot, I glanced at my watch. "I have ten minutes left. Do you want me to take a quick walk over to Rosie's Diner to verify that part of Lavinia's story?"

He handed me Seedy's leash and gave me a kiss. "Hoof it, babe."

Rosie was busy at the cash register when we arrived, so I had to wait several minutes before she was able to speak with me privately.

"So Lavinia *was* at the airport," Rosie said. "But she should've been straight with me. I understand what it's like to have a ma to care for."

"Do you have a policy about your staff eating here?"

"Sure do," she said. "They can't eat unless they're on a break. I don't want them chewing while they're taking someone's order."

"What about eating before they start their shifts?"

"Honey," Rosie said, "I don't care what they do before they're on duty as long as they aren't breaking the law. If they want to come early and grab a bite, they're welcome to do it. We've always got a cook on the griddle who'll make someone a plate of eggs."

Lie number two. "Was she late getting here Monday?"

"I sure don't remember that, and I'm a stickler about my employees being on time. Besides, Lavinia worked the ten-to-six shift and she's usually here early."

Lie number three. No matter what Marco thought, with a strong motive and all those falsehoods, Lavinia Stone just moved to the top of my suspect list.

Back on the town square, workers from the street department were loading the barricades onto a truck, and traffic was moving again. I saw Bloomers' OPEN sign showing in the glass pane of the yellow frame door, but there weren't any shoppers to be seen. Except for half a dozen workmen, the whole downtown seemed deserted.

As Seedy and I cut across the courthouse lawn, I spotted Marco standing in front of Down the Hatch talking to Bonnie from the printshop and Greg from the jewelry shop. By the time I reached Franklin Street, they'd gone their separate ways.

"Marco," I called as we crossed the street.

He strode toward us carrying a plastic grocery bag.

Seedy gave an excited yip and wiggled as though he'd been gone a year.

"Hey, little girl," he said, crouching to scratch her behind her butterfly wing ears. He rose and held up the bag. "Guess what went into the garbage bin behind Lavinia's apartment building."

"I'm assuming it's the rat poison." I sniffed his shoulder. "You might want to go home and shower before the bar opens."

"Yep. Ten minutes after we left, she came out with this bag. I've got photos of her shoving it down into the bin."

"Should you have removed it?"

"Rat poison wasn't the cause of Dallas's death. It doesn't prove she was involved in the murder, only that she lied to us."

"Lavinia lied to us three more times, Marco—once about not being able to eat at work, once about needing to bring food to the diner, and once about being late. Rose told me Lavinia wasn't due there until ten. I saw her at eight. She had plenty of time to get to the diner and have breakfast. No reason for her to race across the lawn unless she realized she left something at the murder scene that might point to her. The way I see it, she had the motive and opportunity, and if I could remember what I saw in her purse, maybe the means, too."

"Before you make your mind up that she did it, we still have another suspect to interview—Dallas's girlfriend."

Seedy was tugging on the leash, wanting to get back to Bloomers. "Just a minute, Seedy. Before I go, Marco, what's up with Bonnie and Greg?"

"They wanted to know how the case was progressing and to tell me how anxious all the shop owners are about Jingles. I promised them we're moving forward, but it looks like that's not going to happen tonight on my end. The bar will be jammed because of the basketball play-offs. Do you want to do some snooping from home?"

My ears perked up. Snooping was my favorite extra-curricular activity—when I wasn't under pressure, and unfortunately I was. Still, I couldn't resist asking, "What were you going to do?"

"An Internet search for Kandi Cane, contact United Airlines to see what they'd tell me about Lavinia flying to Springfield Tuesday, call Robert's mother to verify his story, and touch base with Dallas's first wife to see what she knows."

I sighed. "I wish I could. I even have questions for the first Mrs. Stone already in my head. But I know we'll be working all evening to catch up with the orders that have been accumulating."

"Then don't worry about it. Just take care of your business. I'll work on it tomorrow."

"I feel bad that we're having to squeeze in time for Jingles. Everyone here is counting on us, Marco, and I'm just as anxious as they are."

"We'll work it out, sweetheart. Go. Get busy." He gave me a kiss, rubbed Seedy's head, then strode up Franklin toward the bar. As always, I watched him go, wondering how I'd gotten so lucky.

My phone began to play "Flower" by Jewel, my theme song, which meant I was being called by someone inside the shop. Instead of answering, I stepped inside and saw Grace coming toward me.

"I was just ringing to tell you not to bother coming in. We've lost our Internet connection. The workers hit a buried cable under the pavement, so until it's repaired, we can't collect the orders from our Web site."

Which meant there would be even more to do tomorrow. My shoulder muscles began to tighten. "At least we can work on what's on the spindle."

"Lottie finished those last evening while you were at the meeting. Don't you remember me telling you this morning?"

"I guess I missed it." Seriously, what was wrong with my memory?

"How is Jingles's case coming along?" Lottie asked, stepping through the purple curtain.

My shoulder muscles tightened further. "We have two suspects so far, with more people to interview."

"There's an hour and a half left, no orders, and no customers," Grace said. "Why don't you take the rest of the day off and continue to work on the case?"

"Are you sure?" I asked.

"Look at her smiling," Lottie said, nudging Grace.

"First smile I've seen all week," Grace said.

"Get out of here," Lottie said. "If any customers show up, we know what to do."

"And if our Internet connection comes back," Grace said, "we'll ring you."

I almost hoped it didn't, but I also knew I needed revenue coming in to pay their salaries, especially now that I was adding another full-time employee. "Let's think positive on that."

"That's the spirit," Grace said.

"Thanks, ladies," I said. "See you bright and early."

I walked across the street to the courthouse lawn and sat on a cement bench while Seedy played in the grass. "Guess what?" I said to Marco on the phone. "No Internet connection."

"Same here. We'll have to write out all the credit card info until we're back online."

"This is a blessing in disguise for me, Marco. I'm going to use the time to take care of that list you mentioned, starting with a call to the first Mrs. Dallas Stone."

"Go for it, Buttercup."

I found the contact information Lavinia had given me and dialed the number. As I waited for an answer, my phone beeped to signal an incoming text. I checked the screen and saw my mom's name, but before I could read it, a woman answered.

"Is this Verna Stone?" I asked.

"Yes," she said warily.

"Mrs. Stone, I'm Abby Knight Salvare of the Salvare Detective Agency in New Chapel, Indiana. Has anyone from the police department here contacted you?"

"No," she said with a note of alarm in her voice. "Why?"

"I'm very sorry to report that Dallas Stone is no longer with us." It was always so awkward explaining that someone had been killed.

After a pause, she said, "And you're telling *me* because . . . ?"

That was cold. "Because you may be able to help. There's no easy way to say this, Mrs. Stone, but your ex-husband was murdered."

"I guess he finally fleeced the wrong woman."

No sympathy there. "My husband and I were hired to find the killer and we wondered if you would mind answering a few questions that might aid our investigation."

"Go ahead. I don't know how much help I'll be, but I've got nothing to hide. And by nothing, I mean *nothing*. Dallas left me bankrupt. But before you start asking me questions, would you mind answering a few that I have?"

"If I can."

"How did he die?"

"Dallas was strangled."

"Huh. How many girlfriends have you uncovered?"

"Just one."

"Just one *so far*, you should be saying. And how did you learn about me?"

"Lavinia, his second wife, is here in New Chapel. She gave me your number."

"Lavinia followed him there? I told her to let it go. I told her she'd never get a dime from him. But obviously she didn't listen. Is she a suspect, then?"

"I really can't comment on that." I heard a beep and held my phone away to see that I had an incoming call from Nikki. I ignored it and went on. "Did Lavinia tell you what her plans were?"

"She said she would hound Dal until she broke him or died trying. Her exact words. She called me to find out if I knew where he was. I told her I didn't know and didn't care. Him walking out of my life was a blessing. How did she find Dallas?"

"He posted his résumé on a social network."

Verna laughed. "For a smart man, he sure could be dumb."

"How well do you know Lavinia?"

"I don't know her at all. I spoke with her on the phone just that once. Poor woman. At least Dallas had the decency to divorce me."

"Did Lavinia make any other remarks about what she was going to do after she found Dallas? Anything hinting at murder?"

"Not that I remember, and I believe I'd remember a murder threat. She sounded determined to get her money back, though. And who could blame her? He left her high and dry, too. I wanted to scratch his lying eyeballs out."

"Have you made any trips to New Chapel recently?"

She laughed. "There was a time when I believe I could've murdered Dal, but I've been right here in Springfield, and you can check with the hospital where I work to verify it. I'd be happy to give you the information."

"Thanks." Hospital. *Nikki.* I had to make a note to return Nikki's call when I had some free time. I wrote down the information and thanked Verna for her help.

"You're welcome. Good luck finding the killer. I hope the judge goes lenient on the woman, whoever she is, because it's probably justifiable homicide."

I wasn't sure any homicide was justifiable, but I thanked her again and ended the call.

I pulled up Mom's message and read it: *How do you like this title? The Sunflower Also Rises.*

Children would never get the reference. *Keep hunting,* I texted back.

"Aunt Abby!" I heard, and turned to see Tara and a girlfriend come trudging across the lawn toward me, large backpacks hanging from their skinny shoulders.

Seedy looked up from sniffing the grass, momentarily alarmed. Then she recognized Tara and went as far as her leash would allow to wait for her, tail wagging, ears at attention.

"Hey, mama dawg," Tara said, crouching to snuggle her. "When are you going to come see your puppy?" She said this while giving me a quizzical glance.

"Maybe this weekend," I said hopefully. I gave her friend a smile. "Hi . . ." Could not remember her name.

"Jamie," the girl said.

"I was just going to say that." Seriously. Memory?

Tara stood up and linked arms with Jamie. "Just so you know, Rosa's advice was dead-on, wasn't it, Jamie?"

"We're BFFs again," Jamie said, leaning her head on Tara's shoulder.

"We'll never let a boy come between us again," Tara said. "Not even when we get married."

"Because we're best friends forever!" they chorused, then laughed.

I felt a pang in my heart. Nikki and I had been like that once.

"We just wanted to say hi," Tara said. "We're on our way to Brown's Ice Cream Parlor. Tell Rosa thanks for me."

"Will do," I called after them. *Not.* All I needed was Rosa giving me one of her *See what you're missing?* looks. I pulled out my phone and scrolled through my contacts. I needed to phone Nikki right now—not *when I had time.* The way my life was going, that might never happen.

But then I *noticed* the time. Nikki was already on duty at the county hospital. She worked afternoon shifts as an X-ray technician. She'd probably tried to reach me during her break. I texted Nikki instead: *Call me when you have a chance.*

The phone rang before I could get it back into my purse. "I'm off today, Abs. It's Thursday. Remember? I'm off on Thursdays."

"Great! When did that happen?"

"Before you moved out of the apartment."

"Oh, right. I remember now." Dear God, my memory really was failing. "So what's up?"

"I'm off tonight. I thought maybe, *maybe* you'd want to do something, like go see a movie or just hang out somewhere and catch up—if I can tear you away from your husband."

Nikki was not a snide person normally. When she sounded that way, she was actually covering hurt feelings. So although I really needed to work on the case, I also had to do this for Nikki. I'd just have to be creative about making the best use of my free time. "Sure. I'd like that."

"Which? See a movie or go hang out somewhere?"

A movie would require at least two hours, possibly three. Hanging out could be over in one and a half, leaving time to contact United Airlines, do an Internet search for Kandi Cane, call Robert's mom, and make up a list of questions for Marco. "Well—"

"How about both? There's a new chick flick playing at the cinema. It starts at seven thirty, and then we can grab dessert somewhere afterward and talk."

Not a good idea. That would use up at least three hours, maybe longer. Meanwhile, Jingles was sitting in the county jail waiting for us to find the real murderer. I massaged my tight shoulder muscles. The pain was now moving up my neck. "Well—"

Her voice grew sad. "I miss you, girlfriend."

Zing. Straight to the heart. Oh, the slings and arrows of a guilty conscience. "I miss you, too, Nik."

"So are we on?"

I hesitated. It wasn't what I wanted, but I didn't see a way out. "The evening sounds great."

"Are you sure? You don't sound sure."

"I'm positive." Positively ashamed that I was still trying to figure out how to squeeze in time for the case.

With a smile in her voice, she said, "I'll pick you up at seven."

I checked my watch. It was four o'clock now, leaving one hour until dinner with Marco—unless I moved dinner to six o'clock. That would give me two more hours to work on Jingles's case. But I couldn't get online at Bloomers or Down the Hatch and I didn't want to go to my parents' house, where they'd besiege me with questions and attempt to ply me with food. Where else could I use a computer?

CHAPTER FIFTEEN

"I love what you've done with the living room, Nikki.
You must have gotten tired of the violet-and-green
color scheme, huh?"

"That palette was more you, Abs. My taste runs to the
blue family."

We were standing on her new area rug, a modern design in blue squares with black-and-white accents. Nikki,
who towered over me, was wearing a navy down vest
over a long white tunic with navy leggings and navy ankle boots with silver studs. She sported red pendant earrings that nicely accented her blond spiked hair, and a
bright red chain around her neck added a bold touch.

Simon, her white cat, was rubbing against my legs,
wanting attention, so I picked him up and snuggled him
against my shoulder. He sniffed my nose, then rubbed
his head against my chin. He and I had been buddies
back in the day when life was simple.

I'd arranged to use Nikki's laptop in exchange for
grabbing dinner afterward and then going straight to the
theater. I'd dropped Seedy off at the bar and was now
itching to get down to business. However, it seemed
Nikki had other ideas.

She twirled around happily, her long arms out like

helicopter blades. "Don't you just love it? And look at my old sofa. I found these great quilted covers designed especially for pet owners. Now Simon's fur doesn't stick!"

"Nice." I glanced around for her computer desk.

Nikki started up the hallway. "Come see your old room."

I rubbed my tight neck muscles and traipsed after her, reminding myself that I owed this to my best friend.

Nikki's new office, my former bedroom, was furnished with a marine blue hide-a-bed sofa and bookshelves made with white bricks and glossy black shelving. She'd painted the walls pastel blue and had mounted photos in white frames on them. I spotted her computer on a new white desk and rubbed my hands in anticipation. Perfect.

Then I took a closer look at the photos and found that many of them were of the two of us at various stages of our lives. In the center of the bunch was a larger photo of Nikki standing at my side on my wedding day, holding my bouquet. Nikki had been my maid of honor.

Tears stung my eyes as I stepped back. "The room looks great, Nik."

She put her arm around my shoulders. "I'm so happy we're finally able to do this. Now get your computer work done so we can begin our girls' night out." She started out of the room, then paused. "How much time do you think you'll need?"

More than my impatient friend would probably want to give me.

After Nikki left the room, I put Simon down and sat at the computer, pulling up the United Airlines Web site first. I checked for flights to Springfield from the nearest airport, Chicago Midway, and then wrote down contact information for Marco.

I called Robert's mother next, and after introducing myself, explained that I wanted to verify some information for a case I was working on.

"Is my son in trouble?" she asked. She sounded curious rather than worried.

"No. He witnessed an event that may be crucial to our investigation. I need to make sure he got the dates correct."

The line suddenly filled with static, so I couldn't hear her answer. "I'm sorry. You're breaking up. Would you repeat that?"

"I said 'very well,' although I would question your assumption that he might be incorrect. My son is rarely wrong. He has a memory like a computer."

She talked just the way Robert did. "What day did your son arrive at your house last week?"

"Friday, six o'clock p.m. as usual. We're an hour ahead, so—would be five o'c—your time. I always—spaghetti with meatb—and red sauce on Fridays. It's his favor— Hello?"

"I'm here. The line keeps breaking up. And he was there Saturday as well?"

"Of cou— Rob—wouldn't miss my pot roast din— I marinate—beer."

It was a terrible connection, but I got the gist of it. "Did he head back to New Chapel after dinner on Saturday?"

"No, he left Sun—after breakfa— I make French toast and bac—Sunday mornings. That's also one—fav— meals. He likes to get to the uni—library by noon so he can help shel—books, otherwise he would stay for Sunday din— I make roast chick—for Sun—dinner."

Clearly mealtime was a big event in her house. "Has

Robert ever mentioned a man named Dallas Stone to you?"

"No, we've nev—discussed—Stone."

"Has Robert ever talked about a man named Jingles?"

The line finally grew clear. "Yes."

"In what context?"

"He was quite upset about the police's treatment of Jingles."

"Has Robert ever explained why that's such an issue for him?"

"There's no reason for him to explain. I'm already aware of why."

"Would you share that with me?"

"There was an incident during college. The police suspected some boys Robert was hanging out with of having drugs and got quite rough with them. It frightened Robert so much he had nightmares for months. A psychologist sorted all that out, but Robert remains wary of police."

"What college did Robert attend?"

"Is this important to your investigation."

She'd caught me off guard "No. I was just curious about—"

"Then I don't see why it's on your list of questions. But to be polite, I will answer. He attended the University of Illinois for one semester. It didn't agree with him. Is there anything else? I have an appointment in half an hour."

"No, I just wanted to confirm that Robert was at your house Friday evening and returned home Sunday."

"I believe I've already confirmed that. Have a good day."

And she hung up.

I crossed one thing off my list—Robert's alibi. Next I did a search for a Kandi Cane in New Chapel, Indiana, and a Facebook page popped up. I followed the link and found a photo of a blond woman around my age dressed in a revealing outfit, posing in front of a red Mustang. Her information said she worked on the Calumet Casino River Boat, about a forty-minute drive from New Chapel.

I glanced at my watch and began sketching a plan. Forty minutes would put us there in time for dinner at Tumbling Dice, the casino's chic restaurant. Marco and I had dined there when we were investigating a case for his army buddy Vlad Serban, who'd been accused of killing a woman by draining the blood from her neck. Everyone in town had believed Vlad was a vampire, including Jillian, who was certain she'd been bitten by him and was turning into a vampire herself. Fortunately, we were able to find the true killer, but to this day, I wouldn't swear Vlad *wasn't* a vampire.

The food at Tumbling Dice was excellent, so I knew Nikki would be happy with that choice. And with luck, Kandi would be working tonight and I could interview her. Two birds with one stone. I'd just have to make sure Nikki didn't think the evening was about the case.

I scrolled down through Kandi's recent posts, most of which were just trading comments with friends, until I found one dated the day the news about Dallas Stone's murder hit the papers. The post was from a girl named Marti and included a link to the newspaper's online article. Kandi had been tagged in it.

Marti's comment was: Totally shocking! Talk about karma.

That was followed by more comments.

Jackie: Yeah, Karma really can bite you in the butt.

Gayle: Wow. You never think a thing like that will happen to someone you know. Hugs, Kandi.

Nancy: OMG! Just heard, Kan. Are you doing ok?

Kandi: What do you think? ☺

A smiley face? Obviously Kandi hadn't been sad to see Dallas go.

There was no further mention of the tragedy. I kept scrolling back in time until I was stopped by what appeared to be a rant, all in capital letters, posted three weeks before the murder.

Kandi: LYING THIEVING PIGS DESERVE WHATEVER THEY GET. This was followed by an angry face emoticon.

Beneath that post were more comments from the same friends offering sympathy.

Marti: You'll be okay. You're free of Dallas now, Kan.

Gayle: Go out and celebrate, girl.

Jackie: Free at last, free at last.

Nancy: Consider it a lesson, Kandi. You'll never let another guy hurt you like that again. Xoxo.

Then a new name popped up.

Casino Web: Just say the word and he'll live to regret what he did to U.

Kandi: Thx. Appreciate it. You rock, Web.

He'll live to regret it? Had I found a new suspect—or had I found coconspirators?

I clicked on Web's image, which was a photo of a security guard's badge, and found myself on his Facebook page. He, too, was employed by Calumet Casino, working as—surprise!—security. He listed himself as looking for a relationship with a woman.

There was no other information about Web—not a last

name or family member or even a photograph of him—
but there were plenty of images of Kandi in his album:
some of her working at a blackjack table, some with other
casino workers, but she was in every single shot. Obviously
he had a crush on her. Was he offering to kill for her, too?

Returning to Kandi's page, I kept scrolling down through
older posts until I found another rant, this one not in capital
letters, but angry nevertheless.

> If D is stealing my coins, I swear I will strangle
> him with one of his stupid hand-painted neck-
> ties!

Below were comments from her friends:

Jackie: Maybe you misplaced them. Why would D take
them? He's rich and he adores you.

Nancy: Hey, rich people break the law too, Jackie. Be
careful, Kandi. Don't trust Dallas. You don't know his
history.

Marti: Get one of those hidden cameras and see if
more go missing.

Casino Web: U are too trusting. Get him out now.
Didn't like him when I met him. If U want me to get rid
of him, let me know.

There was Web again, offering to get physical with
Dallas. I took my notebook out of my purse and wrote
Web's name under our list of suspects. Then I began to
write down questions for Kandi.

1. How did you meet Dallas?

*2. Were you aware that Dallas was still married to
his second wife?*

3. How did Lavinia find you?
4. Did Dallas ever try to borrow money from you?
5. How did you get Dallas to leave your residence?

Nikki stuck her head in the doorway. "Hey, Ab, what do you think about this outfit?"

I swiveled for a look and saw her modeling a cute blue tie-dyed tunic dress over black leggings. "Looks terrific, Nik. You're lucky you have the height to pull it off."

"You could wear this," she said as I returned to my questions.

"Only if I want to look like a hippie Popsicle on a short stick."

"I'll change and you can try it on."

Wait. What? I swiveled around again to say, *I'm kind of in the middle of something*, but she was already out the door and on her way to her bedroom.

6. From his Facebook comments, I know Web was aware of the missing coins. Did you ever discuss the theft with him in person?
7. Did you report the loss to the police?
8. Where were you on Friday from about two o'clock on?

"Here you go." Nikki draped the tunic and black leggings across my shoulder.

"Tunics aren't really my style, Nik. I'm too short. And I definitely can't fit into your leggings. You've got six inches on me and I've got six pounds on my thighs."

"They'll stretch. Come on. Don't be a party pooper. You might like this tunic."

Nikki pulled the door shut as she left. I stifled an exasperated sigh and stood, tugging my T-shirt over my head. I donned the tunic, then checked my image on the mirror attached to the back of the door.

Yep, a Popsicle. Short and busty was not an easy combination to work with. I didn't even bother with the leggings.

Nikki knocked and called, "So?"

I opened the door and handed her the tunic. "Nope."

"It's the pattern, that's all. You need a solid color."

"Why is it so important that I wear a tunic?"

"It's in style and you wear too many T-shirts and jeans. Wait—I have a tunic in a green that would go great with your hair."

And once again she was off. I sat down with a sigh and read over my notes, trying to get back my concentration, only to have Nikki fly in with a dark green tunic. I obliged her once again and stood in front of the mirror while she tried to convince me I didn't look like a giant cucumber in it.

"Let's get Marco's opinion," she said. "We can stop there after the movie."

"You want me to wear this tonight?"

"Yes, with the leggings. Don't look horrified. I wouldn't let you walk out of here if it made you look bad." She plopped down on the hide-a-bed sofa and smiled. "So when do you want to leave?"

Clearly, I wasn't going to get any more work done. I shut the notebook and put it in my purse. "Give me five minutes and then let's go."

On the minus side, I'd never felt less stylish. On the plus side, leaving early would allow me more time to talk to Kandi and Web. I just hoped both would be there.

*   *   *

The Calumet Casino River Boat wasn't as large as the Blue Chip or Horseshoe, but that didn't keep people from flocking to it. We waited in line inside the reception area to register and show our IDs, then entered a gigantic room filled with slot machines, roulette wheels, craps, cards, and blackjack tables, and more slot machines. Bells were clanging, people were laughing and talking, and one-armed bandits were clinking as we made our way to the Tumbling Dice restaurant at the prow of the boat.

A twentysomething brunette in a revealing black dress, gargantuan silver hoop earrings, and silver heels stood at a podium just outside the entrance. I saw her do a quick visual sweep of our ensembles, which made me want to apologize for wearing what now felt like a Halloween costume. I was considering asking whether she knew Kandi, but people lining up behind us put an end to that idea. Not only that, but I didn't want to start off on the wrong foot with Nikki.

"Dining with us this evening?" the hostess asked.

"Yes, please," I said. "Table for two near a window if possible."

"Just a minute." She stepped into the restaurant and came back a few moments later to lead us to a white-linen-covered table against a window that overlooked the harbor. We sat on elegant burgundy crushed velvet chairs and unrolled flatware inside burgundy linen napkins, laying the cloths across our laps.

"I'm sorry, but that's an ugly flower," Nikki said about the white alstroemeria in a crystal vase in the center of our table.

Our waiter, who, unbeknownst to Nikki, was hovering behind her, his pad in hand, said snidely, "Would you like me to remove it?"

Nikki reddened and gave him a sheepish smile. "It's fine. No need for that. Would you bring me a margarita, please?"

He sniffed as he wrote it down, as though margaritas were too common for his restaurant. He was around Marco's age but had none of my husband's aplomb.

Without even glancing my way, he said, "And for you?"

"A glass of Malbec."

He handed me a leather-bound wine list. "We have several Malbecs. Which one would you like?"

I looked over the list and pointed. "This Argentinian sounds promising."

"Very good."

"How did you know which one to order?" Nikki asked as the waiter sailed off.

"I didn't. I just chose the cheapest."

Nikki giggled. "You sounded so knowledgeable."

"It's all in the presentation, Nik."

Nikki gazed at the opulent décor and sighed happily. "This is fun. We should do it more often."

And even though my legs were going numb from the overly tight leggings, I said, "We should! And just so you know, if I were the florist that supplied their flowers, I'd take out all the alstroemeria and replace them with single stems of peach calla lilies."

"Absolutely. And if I were their decorator, I'd take out all the burgundy chairs and linens and replace them with a bright, cheerful color like robin's egg blue."

"It would definitely brighten up the place. And if I were the manager, I'd take out the snooty waiters—"

Our waiter appeared at my right and began to fill our water glasses. I sank down in my chair, mortified, while Nikki clapped one hand over her mouth to keep from laughing. He'd barely left the table when she burst out with a guffaw, which prompted me to laugh, and soon we had tears running down our faces.

I glanced around to see whether we were disturbing anyone and noticed that the hostess was alone. Perfect time to question her.

Wiping away my tears, I said, "I'll be right back, Nik."

I hurried to the front of the restaurant and said quietly, "Excuse me. Do you know Kandi Cane?"

"Yes. Are you a friend of hers?"

I didn't want to tell her my true purpose, so I just said, "A Facebook friend. I was hoping to say hi in person."

"She's at a table. When you're finished eating, I'll walk you over there."

"Thanks. And your name?"

"Marti."

I recognized the name from Kandi's Facebook friends. "Nice to meet you. I'm Abby and I'll be back." And then I scooted over to my table before Nikki felt abandoned.

"Don't tell me you complained about our server," Nikki said when I returned.

"Yes, I told her we wanted a calla lily and a new waiter, both of them peachy."

Nikki chortled. "Seriously, what did you tell her?"

"I asked about a woman who works here. Turns out she's on duty tonight, so I can stop by and say hi."

Nikki regarded me suspiciously. "What woman is that?"

"Her name is Kandi."

"A new friend of yours?"

"Every woman is a new friend, Nikki—a friend just waiting to be met."

Nikki gave me a quizzical look, but before she could

question me further, the waiter delivered our drinks. "Any appetizers tonight?" he asked.

"No, thanks." I wanted to hurry the dinner along, not stretch it out.

Nikki looked surprised, so I amended my answer. "None for me, that is. I'm not very hungry."

"I'll have the crab cake appetizer," Nikki said.

"Can we order our main course now?" I asked the waiter, ignoring Nikki's increasingly disgruntled looks.

"Whenever you're ready," the waiter said.

I scanned the menu. What was fast? "I'll have lasagna."

"Excellent choice," he said. "It's one of the house specialties. Just so you know, we don't prebake it, so it will take twenty minutes."

"Then let's make that spaghetti with Bolognese sauce."

Nikki lowered her menu to stare at me. "Are you in a hurry?"

"No!" I said with a tad too much conviction. "I'm in the mood for spaghetti."

"Any soup or salad?" the waiter asked.

"Nope." I handed him the menu.

"So just spaghetti, then." He was judging me. I could tell by the way his eyes narrowed.

"Yes," I said slowly, giving him a steely look. "Just spaghetti."

"I'll have a Caesar salad," Nikki said, "and the chicken marsala."

I stifled a groan. Appetizer, salad, entrée—what next? Dessert?

As soon as our server left, Nikki asked, "Did you see they have chocolate lava cake on the menu?"

And there it was.

CHAPTER SIXTEEN

Nikki raised her glass. "We need to make a toast."

My cell phone dinged. "Hold on. That might be Marco." I checked the message only to find it was my mom with a new title idea: *How about this: Leaf Well Enough Alone?*

I wished she'd leave *me* alone! I texted back: *Having dinner with Nikki. Will get back to you later.*

"Important?" Nikki asked. She knew I didn't interrupt meals for calls or texts unless I had to.

"My mom. She keeps sending me titles for a children's book she's writing. I'm sorry she interrupted. Go ahead."

Nikki waited until I raised my glass, then said, "To our long friendship. May it endure through thick and thin and husbands and boyfriends."

"Hear, hear." We clinked rims and then before Nikki could return to the subject of my new friend Kandi, I asked her to catch me up on her love life.

Over the next ten minutes I heard all about how she and Deputy Prosecutor Greg Morgan had decided to call it quits, but, after a week apart, had realized their mistake and were now seeing each other again. When her crab cakes came, Nikki offered to split them with me, but I glanced around and saw that our hostess was working the keys on her cell phone, obviously bored, so I decided to take advantage of it.

"No, thanks, Nikki. I'm saving room for the spaghetti." I pushed my chair away from the table and rose. "Be right back. I need to use the restroom."

At the hostess's station I said, "Would you direct me to the ladies' room?"

Marti pointed toward the wide entranceway. "Outside and around the corner to your left."

"Is Kandi's table anywhere near there?"

Marti stepped away from her podium and followed me through the entrance to point in the opposite direction. "Behind that section of slot machines is the blackjack area. Kandi will be at one of the tables. I'm sure you'll recognize her from her Facebook photo."

Why hadn't I thought of that?

As soon as Marti walked away, I hurried to the row of slot machines and peered around the first one in the line. Across a wide aisle I saw a group of blackjack tables positioned so that the second, fourth, sixth, and eighth ones were staggered back. I had to wait until people moved out of the way before I could catch a glimpse of Kandi, and then I thought I recognized her behind table two. I snapped a photo of her with my cell phone so I could compare it with her Facebook photo before I got back to the table.

"Something I can help you with?"

I turned toward the voice and found myself facing a large, muscular, brown-haired, ruddy-complexioned man in a gray blazer, white shirt, red tie, and black pants. He had a badge pinned to his jacket pocket that read *Security*. I'd seen the identical badge in Casino Web's Facebook photo. Was it too much to hope that this would *be* Casino Web?

"I was just checking to see how full the blackjack tables are. My name is Abby. And you are?"

He folded his arms across his chest and regarded me with a wary eye. "Skeptical."

That wasn't good. I didn't want to be asked to leave because I was acting suspicious. Sliding my phone into my purse, I forced a light laugh, trying to act nonchalant. "I meant your name, but that's okay."

Backing away, I pointed toward the restaurant. "I'm having dinner with my friend and thought maybe we'd play blackjack later—that is, if the tables aren't too crowded. You know how crowds wax and wane. Full one minute, empty the next."

I was babbling like I had something to hide.

"What's the photo for?" he asked.

"What's the *photo* for?" Restating the question gave me time to think of the right way to answer it.

"Yeah, what's it for?"

"Posterity."

That confused him. With a quick smile, I walked away, pausing outside the restaurant to check the photo against Kandi's Facebook image.

Bingo! The only difference in the photos was that now her hair was up and she had a black bellboy's cap on her head. I returned to the restaurant, where Nikki was about to start on her second crab cake. She frowned as I sat down, obviously annoyed.

"Took you long enough."

"There was a line. You'd think they'd have more stalls in a place this size."

She pushed the small plate toward me. "Have some crab cake."

My stomach growled at the thought, but I didn't want

her to know I'd lied about not being hungry. "Maybe one tiny nibble."

The waiter served her salad at that moment, so she said, "Just finish it."

The crispy cake was gone in thirty seconds.

While we waited for our main course Nikki talked about her job and how the new hospital had changed since the move, but not for the better. Newer and bigger hadn't translated into better care. Now it was all about profit and Nikki was ready to quit.

Our entrées came and she was still complaining. I kept sneaking glances at my watch as we ate, wondering how I was going to convince her that I needed to spend some time interviewing suspects when she said, "Enough about that. What's happening with Jingles's case?"

Perfect timing. I told her about our investigation and that at least one suspect, possibly two, were right there in the casino.

She put her fork down. "So that's why you wanted to come here—and why you're ostensibly not hungry yet you're scarfing down your food like you haven't eaten all day."

I put my fork down, too. "Are you angry?"

"Yes, I'm angry—that you didn't trust our friendship enough to tell me what you needed to do. I honestly don't care what we do as long as we get to hang out together. If you want to interview this Kandi person, let's do it. I'll take notes for you."

"You're awesome, Nikki. Thank you for understanding."

"Just one favor, though. Chocolate lava cake first."

"Done." I raised my hand. "Waiter?"

We chatted and laughed fondly at old memories, savored every forkful of our decadent desserts, paid our bill, and proceeded to the blackjack tables. I spotted Kandi dealing cards at table six in the center of the area. She wore her long blond locks in an unkempt updo under the hat and had pearl studs on her earlobes. She was wearing the standard dealer's uniform of a tailored white shirt, black armband on her right forearm, black slacks, and shiny black flats. Her crystal-edged name tag sparkled in the overhead lights, making her name easy to read: *Kandi*.

Nikki pulled me aside to whisper, "Do you know how to play blackjack?"

"No. I hadn't really thought this far ahead. Do you know how?"

"Nope."

We stood behind some players and watched for about twenty minutes before another dealer came to relieve Kandi. We caught up with her as she walked toward a door marked EMPLOYEES ONLY.

"Kandi?" I called.

She turned with a smile, displaying a mouthful of stained smoker's teeth. "Yes?"

"Hi. I'm Abby Knight Salvare. Do you have five minutes to talk?"

"Why do you need to talk to me?"

"I'm a partner in the Salvare Detective Agency working on the Dallas Stone murder investigation."

At the mention of Dallas, she bristled. Her thin stenciled lips clamped together. "Dal and I broke up a long time ago."

"How long ago?" I asked.

She put her hands on her hips, her eyes blazing. "How the hell is it any of your business?"

"Your Facebook posts put your breakup at about three weeks ago."

She was about to retort, then thought better of it and turned to exit. Apparently she needed more convincing. "I understand Dallas may have stolen some valuables from you."

She stopped cold. Her head turned toward me and as it did she was clearly sweeping the crowd. As though talking to someone over my shoulder she said in a loud voice, "So because of that you're investigating *me*?"

"As I just told you," I said in a hushed voice, "we're investigating a murder. All I want from you is to know more about Dallas's actions in the weeks before he was killed."

"What's going on here?" a man called.

I turned to find my security guard friend striding up to our little conclave.

"They want to talk to me about Dallas, Web," Kandi said with a little girl's pout, making me suspect that she knew how to manipulate people.

"Casino Web?" I asked. "Kandi's Facebook friend?"

He didn't dispute it, just said in a belligerent tone, "Kandi doesn't have anything to say to you."

"Then Kandi needs to tell me that." Turning back to her, I said, "Just five minutes to clear up some questions."

Web stepped between us, blocking her from my view. Folding his arms across his wide chest, he said, "Kandi wants you to go and so do I."

"I'm not hearing Kandi say that, Web," I said.

He put a beefy hand on my shoulder, an obvious attempt to intimidate me, causing Nikki to step back, her eyes wide. With a sneer he said, "I'm saying it for both of us."

Too bad Web didn't know I had a revulsion for any

kind of bullying behavior. It always brought out the tigress in me, sometimes to my own detriment. I glared at the hulking security guard and then at his giant paw. "Take your hand away."

Nikki stepped into my view, signaling that we should go. She looked frightened. I, on the other hand, undoubtedly looked like a short, freckle-faced, redheaded cucumber with a lit fuse.

Web squeezed my shoulder just enough to make me feel it. "I think maybe it's time for you to leave."

"I think you should think twice about threatening me." I gave his hand a pointed look.

He squeezed harder. "You want a threat?"

His grasp sent a tinge of pain down my side. Reflexively, my knee flew up at full force and before I knew it Web doubled over in pain, then fell to the floor, holding his groin with both hands.

Kandi knelt down with a look on her face that switched between horror and hilarity. She tried to help Web, but he winced every time she touched him. I bent down slowly and looked Web straight in the eyes.

"Considering that there's a murder investigation surrounding Dallas's death and that both of you have come up in the suspect list, it would be smart to answer a few questions to help clear your names."

Kandi looked at Web for guidance, but all he could do was shake his head no.

Channeling one of Marco's tactics, I said nonchalantly, "Or you can just wait until the New Chapel Police come calling, although I've heard it can be rather embarrassing when that happens in front of customers—or pit bosses."

They locked gazes; then Kandi gave him a slight nod

and helped him to his feet. Thank God the tactic had worked. I didn't have a backup plan.

As Web hobbled next to her through the employee door, I turned to give Nikki a look she knew well: *Bullies are only bullies when they aren't being bullied themselves.* Marco would be so proud . . . Maybe not so thrilled by my knee-jerk reaction, though. That might have to remain a secret between Web and me.

We followed them up the stairs, one deck above the gaming room of the Calumet Casino River Boat, and down a long stretch of windowed hallway. On our right, a group of men and women sat before a bank of television monitors in a brightly lit security room, their gazes fixed on the activities going on below. Their boss, Paul Van Cleef, the chief of security, was standing behind them, computer tablet in hand, taking notes.

I knocked on the window and he waved. Seeing Nikki, Kandi, and a red-faced Web in the hallway, he stepped outside. "Well, hello there, little missy. Long time no see. Now, what exactly do we have going on here?"

Paul was a large, friendly man in his sixties with a full white mustache and goatee, and long heavy sideburns down his deeply lined face. He wore a blue twill shirt with blue jeans and cowboy boots, allowing him to move through the casino without being pegged as security. Paul had helped us immensely when we were working to clear Marco's buddy's name, and we'd remained friends ever since.

"A friend of ours is about to be charged with a murder that we are certain he didn't commit. Two of your employees here have come up in our investigation and I'd like to talk to them."

Kandi and Web remained silent, Kandi still acting as a crutch for her personal bodyguard.

Paul stepped across the hall and unlocked the door to another room. Like the security room, it had windows to the hallway, with a long table and chairs inside. He motioned for Kandi and Web to enter, then said quietly, "I read about the case in the newspaper. Do you think those two were involved in the murder?"

"All we know at this point is that they've had contact with the victim recently. My hope is that they will have information that will help with the investigation."

He pondered my words for a moment, then gave a nod. "I'll be right across the hall if you need any assistance."

CHAPTER SEVENTEEN

Minutes later, Kandi, Nikki, and I were seated in burgundy leather swivel chairs at one end of the long walnut table in the plush conference room. Paul had asked Web to step into the hallway so both Paul and I could see him while I conducted Kandi's interview. Web had been either too weak to argue or too embarrassed to try.

I sat at the head of the table with Kandi on my right so I could get a good look at her face. Nikki sat on my left, my notebook and pen ready.

"Okay, I'll keep this as brief as I can," I said to Kandi. "My friend Nikki is going to take notes."

The manipulative pouty-girl routine Kandi had displayed in front of Web had vanished. Now she sat back, one leg crossed over the other, arms folded in a guarded position, eyes wary. "I need a cigarette."

"Answer the questions and you can go smoke. How long have you worked here?"

"About a year."

"Where did you work before that?"

"Olive Tree Day Spa. Hairstylist."

"Downtown," I prompted. "On Lincoln?"

At her nod, I asked, "So you're familiar with the layout of the town square?"

She swung her foot. "I guess so. It's a square."

"Ever use the alley behind Franklin Street?"

Kandi's foot stopped but her twitching didn't. She folded her arms tighter and drummed her fingers on her sleeves. "No."

Interesting. Her body language wasn't agreeing. "Do you know who Jingles is?"

"I guess so."

"Ever been near the shed where Jingles keeps his window washing equipment?"

"Didn't know he had a shed." Kandi's tone was brusque, challenging.

"How did you meet Dallas?"

"He came to my table every night and flirted with me."

"When did you decide to live together?"

"He kept pestering me to have dinner with him and I kept saying no, but finally I thought, what the hell? He's nice, he has money, and he makes me laugh. So we had dinner, he bought me stuff, and a month later he moved in."

"Whose idea?"

"Dal's, of course." She made a scoffing sound. "He was full of ideas. And he was full of BS."

My phone dinged. "Excuse me, this might be important." I dug it out of my purse only to see that it was another text from my mom: *Running late? What time will you be home?*

Honestly, did she think I was ten years old?

A second text popped up: *Do you like this title better? Foiled by Foliage.*

More like fuming at the folly. I ignored her message, set the phone on the chair beside me, and tried to remember where I was in my list of questions. "Were you aware that Dallas was still married to his second wife?"

Kandi's foot began to swing again. "The SOB told me he was divorced. And he never mentioned anything about a first wife. I learned that from Lavinia."

"Let's talk about Lavinia. How did she find you?"

"She followed Dal to my place, then waited until he was gone to fill me in on Mr. Wonderful." Kandi made another scoffing sound. "All his promises to marry me just as soon as he came into money—lies. Nothing but lies."

"That must have stung."

"Stung?" she cried. "*Ha!* You think I was gonna marry that guy after three months? No way. I was waiting around to see what kinda money he was coming into. Then maybe see what'd happen. I'll tell you what stung—that A-hole pawned the gold coins my grandmother left me. He's promising me a fortune and ends up robbing me of my life savings. And I wouldn't have even known they were missing except that Lavinia said if I had any valuables not to let him know. So right away I got out the jewelry box that I keep hidden in the back of my closet and every single coin was gone. Dallas denied taking them, of course. He said I must have been robbed and to call the cops."

Kandi leaned forward, resting on her forearms, intent on telling her story. "So guess what? I did call the cops, but there weren't no fingerprints or nothing that pointed to Dallas. The cops said I should go look for the coins at the pawnshops, and guess what? I did. And I found them. And get this. If I want them back, I have to buy them."

She scoffed again and changed positions. "Ten thousand dollars' worth. As if I could come up with that kind of money. Can you believe that crap? Those coins came from my *grandma.* They were my *inheritance.*" She blinked back tears. "And now I have *nothing.*"

Pushing away from the table with an angry huff, she folded her arms again. Her foot was swinging so fast, it was a miracle she didn't bounce off the chair. "Dallas knew that was all I had and he took them anyway."

I kept finding more and more reasons to be disgusted with Dallas. My phone dinged a second time, so I checked the screen discreetly and saw that my mom had texted me once again: *Abigail, are you all right? You didn't answer my last text.*

Growing more annoyed by the second, I put the phone on mute and set it down without replying, then had to remember where I was in the interview. I glanced at Kandi, who was still radiating anger. Oh, right. Her lost coins. "You must have been devastated."

"I still am. I let the jerk mooch for almost three months rent-free. I bought the groceries, paid the bills . . . I hope he's rotting in hell." She wiped tears off her cheeks.

I looked at Nikki, who was writing as fast as she could, so I paused a moment to let her catch up. "Did the people at the pawnshop tell you who sold them the coins?"

"No, but I know it was Dal. The cops questioned him, but he swore up and down he didn't steal nothing."

"Did he steal anything else?"

"I don't have anything else worth taking."

"Did Dallas ever try to borrow money from you?"

"That's what started it all. He said he was in a bind and needed money until his next paycheck came in. And I said, 'What money? I'm a working girl. I make enough to pay my expenses and that's it. The only thing I have to my name are my grandma's coins.'

"Stupid me. I can't believe how stupid I was for telling him about the coins and falling for his lies and letting him move in and—*everything.*" She slapped the table with her palms, then laid her head on her arms and wept.

Nikki paused to look at me and mouthed, *How awful.* I gave her a little nod. How could we not feel sorry for the girl?

"No," Kandi said suddenly, straightening. "I'm not going to cry. I've suffered enough because of him."

I handed her a tissue from my purse. She was playing the martyr role to the hilt. I wanted to believe her, but there was something about Kandi that didn't ring true, and I had nothing to base that on except my internal radar.

"Was Dallas living with you during the coin investigation?" I asked.

"Yes," she said, kicking her foot again. "Ballsy, wasn't he?"

"How did you get him to leave?"

Suddenly the martyr was gone and a subtle slyness stole over Kandi's face. She examined her purple fingernails. "I just, you know, told him I wanted him out."

"You said to him, 'I want you out,' and Dallas left with no problem?"

"Well, he said he wanted some time."

"Did you give him time?"

"Hell no. I didn't want him in my apartment when I wasn't there. Who knows what kinda trouble he'd get me into?"

"Did he leave, then?"

"No. The next day he told me the only place he could go was the men's shelter because he didn't have enough money for a security deposit on an apartment, but the shelter wouldn't have a vacancy for at least a week. And you know what? I didn't care."

"So back to my original question, Kandi. How did you get him to leave?"

She shrugged and wouldn't meet my gaze, her lips pressed into a furious line. My guess was that she'd done something to feel guilty about.

"Nikki, may I see the notebook please?" I said.

Nikki handed it to me and I flipped back a few pages to the notes I'd made from the Facebook posts. Kandi was watching me sideways as I scanned them, so I made a point of tapping the one I wanted before meeting her gaze. "So did you strangle Dallas with one of his stupid, hand-painted neckties?"

Kandi's eyes opened wide. "No! Oh, my God—I wrote that when I was angry. I would never—" She covered her mouth and shook her head, either too stunned to finish the sentence or pretending to be.

"That *is* the way he died," I said, handing Nikki the notebook.

"Look, I wrote that when I was angry. I am *not* a killer. Dallas was crazy about his ties to the point of making me nuts. He made me clean out a dresser drawer so he could line up those stupid ties to have a better view of them. Even when he claimed to need money, he was still buying ties. Talk to Web. He's the one who got Dallas out of my apartment. He's who you should be focusing on, not me."

She sure was quick to throw her friend under the bus.

"How did Web handle the task? Ask politely? Toss Dallas out the door? Strangle him?"

Kandi held up her hands. "All I know is that when I got home from work one night, Dal was gone. The next day Web told me they'd had a little talk. I swear that's all I know."

"Weren't you curious about what had transpired between them?"

"I figured I was better off not knowing in case—well, just in case." She rubbed her arms as though suddenly chilled by a thought.

"In case Web hurt Dallas?"

"I don't want to say anything against Web. He's been good to me."

And yet she sure was trying to give the impression that Web was dangerous. "Did Dallas ever contact you after their talk?"

"He came back to the casino one time trying to sweet-talk me into giving him a second chance, claiming he was about to come into a lot of money. Like I'd ever believe that line again. I called Web over and asked him to escort Dal off the boat. That made Dallas so angry, he and Web nearly got into a fight. But Web finally got him to leave."

"How long ago was this?"

She shrugged and fumbled in her pocket. "I don't remember."

"Was it right after the little talk the two men had, or was it recently?"

She took out a pack of cigarettes and shook one out. "Maybe a week ago."

"A week would put it the day before Dallas was murdered."

"I suppose so. I hadn't thought of that."

Kandi wasn't convincing. She wasn't even looking at me anymore. "Did Dallas say where this newfound money was coming from?"

"Something about an old friend who owed him."

"Was the old friend Jingles?"

She glanced at me warily. "*Old friend* is all he told me."

"You know who Jingles is, right?"

She nodded and rolled the cigarette between her fingers.

"You're sure Dallas didn't mention Jingles?"

She jabbed the cigarette between her lips, then slapped her hand on the table. "I already said he didn't."

Ignoring her childish outburst, I asked, "Did you discuss the incident with Web after Dallas left?"

"Web asked if I was okay. I said I was really pissed off that Dallas had the nerve to show his face here, and Web said not to worry, he'd make sure it didn't happen again."

"What did he mean by that?"

Biting down on the filter end, she said, "Didn't ask. Didn't care."

"So if Web chose to murder Dallas, that was okay with you?"

With a glare, Kandi pulled the cigarette from between her lips. "Of course not. I meant any other way Web wanted to handle it was fine with me."

"In light of that, when you heard the news about Dallas, did you wonder whether Web had had a hand in the murder?"

She paused as though she had to debate something. "You want me to be totally honest, right? So, yeah, it crossed my mind." She looked at her watch, pushed back her chair, and got up. "My break is over in two minutes and I gotta smoke."

"I'm sure Paul won't mind us taking another minute or two," I said with a smile.

Scowling, she sat down, crossed her legs, and started swinging one foot again.

"From his Facebook comments," I continued, "I know Web was aware of the missing coins. Did you ever discuss the theft with him in person?"

"Yeah."

"What was his reaction?"

"Kind of angry."

"I believe Web's comment to your post about the theft was that if you wanted him to get rid of Dallas, just let him know. How did you interpret that?"

"That he'd get Dal out of my apartment."

"Why didn't you accept Web's offer at that point?"

"Dallas gave me a ring that night. I thought maybe he actually had come into some money." She held out her hand to show me a gold ring with a blue topaz setting surrounded by tiny sparkling stones. "See this? Real diamonds."

Bam. Just like that, Robert's description of the necklace he'd found echoed in my head: *It was a blue gemstone surrounded by small clear stones that may or may not have been diamonds. It was set in gold dangling from a thin gold chain, though whether it was solid gold or merely gold plated I couldn't tell you.*

Could it be a coincidence? Trying not to tip my hand, I said, "It's a gorgeous ring. I hope he got you matching earrings or a necklace to go with it."

"Both." She huffed impatiently. "I lost the necklace."

Ding ding ding! No way was that a coincidence. Had I found the murderer? Or at least one of them? My brain was doing cartwheels of excitement, so I had to force myself to sound sympathetic. "That's a shame. Did the chain snap?"

"I don't know. I just looked down and it was gone."

I couldn't wait to tell Marco.

My phone vibrated against my leg. "Excuse me a second." Once again, on the off chance that this one *was* from Marco, I checked the screen and saw a text from my dad: *Mom's worried because you haven't answered. All OK?*

Gritting my teeth, I hammered out *BUSY!*, then dropped the phone into my purse. Why wouldn't they leave me alone?

Thrown off course, I couldn't remember what else I'd wanted to ask Kandi. I glanced at Nikki for help; she flipped back two pages, ran her finger down my list, and read, "Is Web currently your boyfriend?"

"I don't consider him my boyfriend, no," Kandi said.

"What does that mean?" I asked.

"He kind of thinks he is."

"And you *kind of* let him believe it since he did you a favor?"

"Kind of, yeah." She glanced at me from the corner of her eye to see how I was reacting.

Little gestures like that always made me suspicious. "Do you go out on dates with him?"

"I wouldn't say we're *dating*. Just, you know, he'll ask me to go see a movie or hit a club for some late-night dancing."

"Are you aware that you're in all of his Facebook photos?"

She snickered as though she found it funny. "Yeah."

"Why don't you consider him your boyfriend?"

"He's not my type."

"Then why go out with him?"

She shrugged.

I was betting it was because Web knew too much. What that knowledge was remained to be seen. What I wanted to know was how loyal Kandi would be if she thought Web could or would be blamed for the murder.

"What would you say if I told you Web is one of our prime suspects?"

She glanced at me, her gaze hard, angry. "Are you basing that on what I told you? Because I never said I believed he did anything to Dallas. Don't try to pin that on me."

"I'm basing it on what we already know about him. But you did say the thought that he might have murdered Dallas crossed your mind."

"You're not going to tell him I said that, are you?"

"Everything said in this room is confidential."

"It better be," she shot back, her voice jittery.

Her foot was shaking fast now and she was tapping the cigarette on the table. What did it mean? "Are you afraid of Web?"

She started biting the skin around her thumb. "No. I just don't want everyone thinking I'm a double-crosser."

"How would you be double-crossing him?"

She shrugged. "You know, like pointing a finger at him."

"So you're one hundred percent certain that Web *didn't* kill Dallas?"

She darted a glance at the clock on the wall. "I need to smoke."

"Answer and then you can go."

She glared at me, rising from her chair. "My answer is no, I'm not one hundred percent certain. Now *I've got to go.*"

"How certain, then? Ninety percent? Fifty?"

"Ninety," she blurted.

"One more question," I said as she reached the door. "Where were you on Friday from about two o'clock until midnight?"

She called over her shoulder, "Here."

"Are you sure? It'll be easy to check."

At that, Kandi paused, hand on the doorknob. "I *think* I was here, okay?"

"I'll have Paul find out," I said just as she stepped outside.

She came back inside, shut the door, and said quietly, "Okay, look. My days get mixed up. sometimes. You know how it goes. You wake up, think you have to go to work, jump out of bed, and then remember it's your day off. So I'd have to see my schedule for last week to know for sure—and I can't do that right now because I'm *already late.*"

She pulled the door open and was gone.

I'd bet anything she didn't work on Friday.

Because I hadn't had time to prepare for my interview with the security guard, I had to play it off the cuff, basing my questions on Kandi's responses. I tore a few blank pages out of the notebook for Nikki to write on, then placed the tablet in front of me.

This time Nikki and I took seats on the opposite side of the table. After what had happened earlier, I wanted a clear view of Paul in the other room in case we needed his help. Web took a seat across from us, his chair several feet from the table, his legs splayed and arms crossed, his expression dour. He didn't say a word, just kept his gaze on the wall behind me.

"How long have you been a security guard?" I asked.

He shrugged.

"Can you hazard a guess?"

Another shrug.

"How long have you known Kandi?"

He shrugged again.

"You don't know? How about a guess, then?"

No reply.

"Six months? A year? Since high school?"

He brushed something off his shirtsleeve.

A little pilot light flared in my gut; my Irish temper was on the rise. I needed a way to get him to talk before it came to a boil and I said something I'd regret. It had been known to happen.

Maybe if I stirred his jealousy. "Were you aware of the flirtation going on between Kandi and Dallas?"

Still focused on the wall, he shrugged again.

"It must have gotten hot and heavy for Kandi to ask Dallas to move in with her. Did you witness any of that at the casino?"

No response.

Fact one: Redheads had short fuses. Fact two: *Short* redheads had even *shorter* fuses. Trying to keep the irritation out of my voice, I said, "Seriously, Web? You're going to play this game with me?"

He looked at me, his expression inscrutable. "What game?" Then he looked away.

I glanced at Nikki. She rolled her eyes.

I inhaled and held my breath to the count of five. *Patience, Abby. Make Marco proud.*

Okay, time to poke the bear. I just wished I had a really sharp stick to help the process along. "Your comment on Kandi's Facebook page about the coin theft was that if she wanted you to get rid of Dallas, she needed to let you know. How should I interpret the phrase 'get rid of'? Because to me that looks like an offer to murder Dallas."

Web's eyes narrowed dangerously as he gazed at me, but he merely clamped his lips together and looked away.

A small rise was better than a shrug. Time to poke harder. "Is that what you did, Web? Did you take Kandi up on her idea and strangle Dallas with his own necktie?"

He drummed his fingers at a fierce staccato on the chair arms, still turned away.

I looked at Nikki and shook my head to let her know I was ready to blow. Now I had a choice to make. Either I had to call it quits and let Marco interview him, get Paul Van Cleef to sit in on this interview, or frighten Web into talking. The quickest route would be to call in Paul, but then I'd look weak. Ditto for Marco handling it.

Bottom line was that I wanted to score this interview so bad I could taste it. This bully was *not* going to get the best of me.

CHAPTER EIGHTEEN

I stared at Web, wondering what I should do. *Okay, Abby, think*. How would Marco handle this situation?

Easy. He'd call Web's bluff. I'd used that tactic successfully earlier. No reason it wouldn't work again.

I let out a sharp sigh. "Looks like it's time to bring in the cops."

Web snorted, obviously ridiculing me now. It was a common bully tactic. "We're done here," he said, rising. And what could I do about it? My bluff hadn't worked and I couldn't physically stop him, although the idea of putting out my foot and tripping him did sound incredibly appealing.

At that moment Paul Van Cleef opened the door, eyed Web, who had frozen in midair, then said, "Abby, the police are here. Would you and Nikki step outside, please?"

Nikki and I rose at once, gazing at each other wide-eyed, while Web sank back into his chair. We followed Paul into the hallway, where we found Reilly and two other cops waiting. Reilly moved us away while his men stood with their backs to the door.

"What's the situation?" he asked. "Did the security guard threaten you?"

Perplexed, I said, "Reilly, I'm in the dark here. What's going on?"

"Your dad said he received a distress text from you and asked us to move in."

"A distress text?" I pulled out my phone and held it up so he could read my message. "Does that look distressed to you?"

"What the hell does it mean?"

Completely confused now, I looked at the screen and felt my cheeks heat up. In my hurry to reply, I'd typed *BUST!* instead of *BUSY!*

That explained my dad's response. To a former cop who'd instructed his children on how to alert someone when they were in a dangerous situation, that had sent up flares.

"It was a mistake, Reilly. My dad overreacted to a typo in my text message. We're not in danger. I was interviewing this security guard for an investigation Marco and I are working on."

Silence ensued. Nikki put her hand over her mouth to hide a grin while Paul slipped silently back to his command center.

"So everything's copacetic?" Reilly said.

I motioned for him to step away from the other cops. "Actually," I whispered, "I'm working on Jingles's case and have an uncooperative suspect inside. So as long as you're here, will you do one small favor for me?"

Reilly turned to his men and said, "I'll meet you outside." He watched them leave before saying, "What's the problem?"

"This jerk is playing the *I don't know anything about anything* game, and I know he's lying. I told him if he didn't answer I'd let the cops take over, but that hasn't fazed him. So if you'd just stand inside long enough for him to get the message, I'd appreciate it."

"Why isn't Marco here?"

"He's busy at the bar."

Reilly thought it over and gave a nod. "For Jingles. Let's do it."

He opened the door, stepped in behind us, folded his arms, and stood like a sentry, his frowning gaze on Web.

"What's going on?" Web asked me in a hushed voice, his gaze darting from Reilly to me.

"Apparently the police are taking your Facebook comments seriously. I talked to the sergeant over there and he might be willing to let me finish the interview if you start giving me honest answers and stop playing games. Otherwise, he's going to cuff you and lead you out of the casino in front of your boss and everyone. So what'll it be?"

He glanced at Reilly again and said quietly, "I'll answer if I can."

I gave him a look of disbelief. "If you *can*? This isn't an aptitude test, Web."

"I'll answer, okay? No games."

I studied him for a long moment, letting him squirm, then stood up. "Let me see what the sergeant has to say."

Reilly and I stepped outside, where I gave him a thumbs-up and whispered, "It worked. I think he'll cooperate now."

Just up the hallway an elevator opened and Marco strode out, saw us, and came straight over to hug me. "Thank God you're okay." He held me by the shoulders and studied my face. "Tell me what happened."

With a wink, Reilly said to me, "I'll let you do the explaining. I'll phone your dad to tell him you're okay."

"Thanks for your help," I said.

"No problem," Reilly called as he walked away.

"It was a mistake on Dad's part," I told my anxious husband. "Mom has been sending me texts all day about title ideas for her book, including during the interview. I didn't want to interrupt the flow of conversation to answer her, so I ignored the last two. I mean seriously, Marco, she treats me like a little—"

"Make a long story short, Sunshine."

"Okay. Then Dad texted me next wanting to know why I was ignoring Mom, so I replied with one word: *BUSY*. But my fingers hit a *T* instead of a *Y* and he thought I was sending him a distress code—*BUST!*"

"I'd be alarmed if I got that text, too, babe."

"Anyway, it worked out to my advantage, because I've got an uncooperative suspect in there who now believes I have influence with the cops."

"But you're okay. That's all I care about."

"I'm fine."

"Do you want me to sit in on the interview?"

"I don't need you to, but if you want to, that's fine."

"Just yes or no, Abby."

"Are you angry?"

"Sunshine, after your dad phoned to alert me that you might be in a dangerous situation, he had me wishing that I'd never involved you in this business. All the way over here I kept imagining all kinds of scenarios—" He stopped, uncharacteristically emotional.

I put my arms around his waist and laid my head on his shoulder, touched by his concern. "Thank you, Marco. It's nice to know how much you care."

He wrapped his arms around me and held me tightly for a long moment. "I'm not going to lose you, Mrs. S."

"You won't, Mr. S." I stepped back and took his hand with a smile. "Come sit in on the interview. You're not going to rest easy unless you see that I'm not in danger."

"Lead the way and the interview. I'll only intervene if you give me a signal."

A few feet up the hallway I paused. "Guess what Kandi lost? A necklace that matches the description Robert gave us! She showed me the matching ring, and the whole set was bought by Dallas Stone."

"Did she seem hesitant to talk about it?"

"Nope. She couldn't remember where she lost it. So that necklace wasn't in Dallas's pocket, Marco. It was around her neck. That means Kandi was at the shed sometime before Robert got there Monday morning. Now we need to find out whether she acted alone or had Web help her."

"Not so fast, Sunshine. There's another possibility. Dallas might have stolen it from her to pawn later. It still could have been in his pocket."

How did he always manage to shoot down my theory? "She made it sound as though she looked down and it was gone, Marco. I think she'd know if it was missing from her jewelry box."

"I'm not saying you're wrong. Just that we need to consider all possibilities."

Marco could consider whatever he wanted. I was certain we'd found one person who had a hand in Dallas's death.

When we entered the room, Nikki looked up, then smiled in obvious relief. Marco gave her a nod and took a seat where he could watch Web.

"Web, this is my husband and partner, Marco Salvare," I said.

"Mr. Salvare," Web said, extending his hand in an obvious show of cooperation.

Marco merely gave him a nod, then sat back and crossed his arms, focusing his penetrating gaze on Web.

"Okay, let's start at the beginning," I said. "What's your full name?"

"Webster Alan Meridian." He crossed one leg over the other knee, his shiny black shoe resting casually on top. I wasn't certain whether he was trying to give the image of being relaxed or was actually more comfortable with Marco in the room.

I waited as Nikki questioned him on the spelling, then asked, "How long have you been a security guard?"

"A year."

"And what did you do before that?"

"Bouncer at a bar in Maraville. Before that I worked security at New Chapel Savings Bank."

"Which branch?"

"Downtown. Indiana Street."

"So you're familiar with the square?"

At his nod, I asked, "And you know who Jingles is?"

"The window washer the cops are holding for Dallas's murder."

"Have you ever been inside the shed in the alley behind Franklin Street where Jingles stores his equipment?"

He fidgeted with his shoelaces. "No. I didn't even know he had a shed."

"How long have you known Kandi?"

"About seven months."

"Did you date her prior to Dallas moving in with her?"

Web shook his head.

"Your comment on Kandi's Facebook page about the

coin theft was that if she wanted you to get rid of Dallas, to let you know. What did you mean by 'get rid of'?"

Trying to look earnest, he said, "Just that I'd get him out of her apartment."

"Get him out by what means?"

He shrugged.

"Were you going to rough him up?"

"Only if, you know, he wouldn't listen to reason."

"Kind of like when I wouldn't listen to reason?" I watched Web swallow hard and look back and forth between me and Marco. I guessed I'd have to explain that comment later. "And if roughing him up hadn't worked?"

"I've never encountered a situation like that." He looked at Marco as though to gauge his reaction to that statement, but my hubby had his poker face on.

"So what did it take to get Dallas out of Kandi's apartment?" I asked.

"We had a talk."

"And in that talk you said . . . ?"

"I just, you know, made some minor suggestions of what might happen if he didn't leave." Web was using a completely different tone of voice now, making himself sound like an old softy instead of a bully.

"So things like rearranging his face? Breaking a knee-cap?"

"No, nothing like that. More like helping Kandi file harassment charges against him." Looking at Marco, he said, "I was just trying to help out a friend. I didn't want to hurt the guy or anything."

Marco nodded toward me. "You need to speak to her."

Web reddened. I slid the notebook back to Nikki. I was on a roll now.

"Did Kandi file those charges?" I asked.

"She didn't need to. Dallas left."

"In one of your Facebook comments you indicate you didn't like Dallas the first time you met him. Why?"

"He was way too slick, too much of a show-off, flashing his money around, wearing an expensive gold watch and bracelet, bragging about his expensive suits. I don't trust guys like that. They're usually blowhards."

"Did you warn Kandi?"

"I told her to be careful, but she had dollar signs in her eyes when it came to Dallas."

"How did that make you feel?"

He shrugged. "It was her life."

"You didn't get jealous?"

With a forced smile, he said, "Kandi's my friend. I didn't want her to get hurt."

"You have a lot of photos of Kandi on your Facebook page."

"Again, she's a friend."

"But Kandi is in every single photo, Web. That feels like a serious crush to me."

"Feel however you want."

"When Dallas showed up at the boat trying to get back into Kandi's life, you escorted him off and, according to Kandi, told her you'd make sure that didn't happen again. Do you remember that?"

"Sounds like something I might have said."

"How could you guarantee it wouldn't happen again?"

"To tell you the truth, I couldn't guarantee it." He glanced at Marco. "I just told Kandi that so she'd feel safe. You know how it is. You want to protect them."

Marco nodded toward me again. "She's conducting the interview."

"Why were you so concerned about protecting her?" I asked. "Did you think Dallas was dangerous?"

"Not exactly dangerous. Just the kind to take advantage of a woman. I didn't want anything bad to happen to Kandi."

"Because she's your friend."

"Right."

"But she wasn't safe, was she, Web? Not as long as Dallas was alive."

Web blinked at me for a second. "I don't know what you want me to say. I didn't kill the guy."

"The post Kandi wrote about strangling Dallas with his tie didn't give you any ideas?"

"Why would I need to kill him? I got him out of her apartment and that was all she wanted."

"But maybe *you* wanted something more, like to have Dallas out of her life so that you'd have a chance with her."

He took a breath as though to calm himself. "Like I said, I was just doing Kandi a favor. Besides, it wasn't me who had a beef with him."

I wondered how long it would be before Web threw *her* under the bus. "Are you insinuating that Kandi might have killed him?"

"Take it however you want."

"Do you think Kandi's capable of strangling a man?"

"Under the right circumstances, sure. That doesn't mean she did."

"Is there any chance she did?"

"I wouldn't say *no* chance."

I felt as if we were talking in circles. "Would you say you're one hundred percent certain Kandi didn't kill Dallas?"

He tilted his head as though considering it. "Ninety-nine point nine percent."

"Interesting. She said you probably didn't do it, either, only her figure was ninety percent." I let that sink in a second. "Do you consider yourself Kandi's boyfriend?"

"Wait a minute. She was only *ninety* percent sure I didn't kill Dallas?"

"That's what she told me. Did I get that right, Nikki?"

Nikki flipped back a few pages, then pointed to one entry. "Yes. Ninety percent."

Web slapped his hands on the armrests. "I don't believe her."

"So again, do you consider Kandi your—"

"No, hold it." Looking at Nikki, he said, "I want to change my percent to eighty."

Nikki glanced at me to verify that she should make the change, so I said, "Then you're only eighty percent sure Kandi didn't kill Dallas?"

He folded his arms and grinned as though he'd done some fancy maneuvering. "Yeah, eighty percent."

"In other words, there's a twenty percent chance she did kill Dallas?"

"Hell, if she can have doubts about me, I can have doubts about her. And no, I'm not her boyfriend. I just did her a couple of favors. And for that I get her saying she thinks I might have killed her ex-lover. Seventy percent!"

"Actually," I said, "at ninety percent, she's pretty sure you *didn't* kill her ex."

"Yeah, but she told you she's ten percent *not* sure." He shook his head. "After what I did for her, too."

"Do you want to change your statement about what you did for her?"

"I already told you. I had a talk with the guy and he moved out. Then I escorted him off the boat and had another talk. And that's the full extent of it. Swear to God." He held up his hand at his last statement.

"And that brings me to the last question, Web. Where were you last Friday from about two o'clock until midnight?"

He pulled up the calendar on his phone. "It was my day off, so I was probably home." He paused for a moment, then looked at me as though shocked. "Hold on. That was the day I sat at home waiting for a call from Kandi. She asked me if I'd be available to help her—and then she never called. I wasted the whole day because of her."

"You were waiting to help her do what?"

"Move some furniture, an old chest or something. She said she might need help because it would be too heavy for her to manage."

"When did she ask you?"

"Thursday after the new work schedule came out. She saw that we were both off on Friday. That's how she knew I'd be available to help her."

"Did she tell you why she never called?"

"Just that she'd managed on her own." He gave me an innocent glance. "You don't think she wanted me to help her move Dallas's body, do you?"

Boy, was Web transparent. "Do *you* think that's what she wanted?"

He rubbed his chin. "Now that I look back, maybe she was trying to set me up. She was so friendly before Dallas died and now if I ask her to go see a movie or something, she acts like she's doing me a favor."

Kandi hadn't seemed cool when she'd called on him

to protect her twenty minutes before—but then, she *had* needed him again. "Back to my original question. Is she capable of murder, Web?"

"I wouldn't have thought so, but now I'm going to say there's a sixty percent chance."

"Are you worried that that might get back to her?"

Web's jaw twitched angrily. "I don't care if it does or not. What's the worst that could happen? She'd kill *me*? I don't think so."

"Okay, that should do it. Thank you."

"So I don't have to talk to the cops now, right?"

"Not at this time," I said.

Web left the room, muttering, "I can't believe Kandi turned on me."

Marco smiled. "Good job, Sunshine. Well played."

"You were amazing, Abby," Nikki said. "You sounded just like a TV detective."

"I had a great teacher," I said, linking my arm through Marco's. "And thanks, Nikki. I couldn't have done it without you."

"Can I just say I'm really glad it's over?" Nikki asked.

"Didn't you enjoy it?" I asked.

"Are you kidding? My hands were shaking so hard I'll be surprised if you can read my notes. Did you see the size of his hands? He could've snapped my neck in two. I was really happy to see you, Marco."

"Web is a bully," I told Marco. "He tried to intimidate me."

"But Abby stood up to him," Nikki said. "She kneed him in the groin and then made him think the cops were ready to take over the investigation. And then they showed up!" She chortled. "Talk about perfect timing."

"You what?" Marco asked me.

In a case of perfect timing, my phone vibrated, saving me from explaining my actions. But when I pulled it out and saw my mom's name on the screen, I put it back again. "Let's get out of here. I'm exhausted."

"Aren't you going to check your message?" Nikki asked.

"Why? It's Mom." The phone vibrated as another message came in. "There she goes again. She's probably sending more title ideas."

Marco held out his hand. With a sigh, I pulled out my phone and placed it on his palm. He unlocked it, read the messages, then handed it back. "You're right. It's your mom—*and* your dad."

As we followed Marco into the hallway, I said, "What did they say?"

Marco smiled as though he had a secret. "You'll have to read it yourself."

"Just tell me if I need to reply."

"You don't *need* to," Marco said.

"Good enough," I said.

"You might *want* to, though," he added.

"Want me to check it?" Nikki asked.

I handed her my phone. She read the message and smiled. "Marco's right. You should read it, Ab."

I took the phone off mute and dropped it into my purse. "Maybe later." Or maybe never.

"It's only eight o'clock," Nikki said. "We still have time to stop at Marco's bar for a nightcap. Girls' night can't be over already."

I was mentally exhausted after all that questioning, but I couldn't disappoint Nikki, especially when she'd been such a sport about helping. Outside the boat, I gave Marco a kiss and said, "We'll meet you at Down the Hatch."

"Not so fast, babe. You've got the car. I had to get a ride here."

"Marco, the 'Vette's a two-seater."

He put his arm around me. "Then we'll let Nikki drive and you can sit in my lap."

That was the best idea I'd heard all day.

Going to Down the Hatch turned out to be the worst.

Chapter Nineteen

While sitting on Marco's lap, I told him everything I remembered about Kandi's interview, with occasional assistance from Nikki.

"Kandi is a hard woman," I said. "The only time I saw a softer side was when she was crying over her grandmother's coins. And it was obvious that she used Web to get Dallas out of her life. The question is, to what extent — just out of the apartment or into the afterlife?"

"I think it was just out of her apartment," Nikki said. "Otherwise Kandi wouldn't dare stop seeing Web, and he could potentially blackmail her forever. Personally, I think Web killed Dallas out of love for Kandi. No more competition."

"But Dallas was already out of the picture," I said. "And I believed Web's story about waiting for Kandi to call him all day. Kandi is manipulative and has the stronger motive. She knows her way around the square and was off Friday. And there's her necklace, which I still believe she dropped. Means, motive, and opportunity."

"But Web is in love with Kandi," Nikki argued back. "That's a strong motive, too. And he's familiar with the square and was off on Friday as well. I think they did it together."

"Give me a scenario," Marco said to me.

"Okay. Kandi has the murder all planned, so she arranges for Dallas to come over to her place on Friday. After she kills Dallas, she worries that Web might not keep his mouth shut, so she stuffs the body into a chest and gets someone other than Web to help her move it to Jingles's shed after dark."

"Why would Kandi take the body to the shed?" Marco asked. "She'd have to have someone help her dump it and then haul the furniture away. That's a lot of work, and risky as well to involve someone else, when she could just as easily have taken the piece of furniture to the dump."

I shrugged. "I haven't worked that out."

"That's why I think Web was involved," Nikki said.

"Let's forget about the furniture for now," Marco said. "For all we know, Web made up the story about moving it to cast suspicion on her. It seems more likely that Kandi simply followed Dallas to the shed," Marco said. "Then the same scenario you had for Lavinia could apply. Except that I'm still having a problem with why either one would pose the body on the courthouse steps and how one woman could manage that."

"Lavinia is strong, but you're right—Kandi isn't very big."

"That's why I keep saying Kandi and Web are in it together," Nikki said.

"Are you moving Kandi and Web to number one and two on our list?" Marco asked.

I shook my head. "There's still more convincing evidence pointing to Lavinia."

"Until the lab results come in, it's all circumstantial," Marco said, "and that's a problem for us. It could be weeks before the detectives have proof. We need a confession if we're going to clear Jingles."

"What can we do?" I asked.

"Keep up the pressure on our suspects until little cracks appear in their stories," Marco said. "First thing tomorrow I'll call Paul Van Cleef to get Kandi's address so I can talk to her neighbors. They might be able to shed light on this piece of furniture Web claimed she moved and who helped her. Then we'll need to do a second interview with her to follow up on the new information. I'll also call Reilly to see what he can find out about the blue necklace."

"Evening seems like a good time to catch Kandi," I said. "Let's go tomorrow after supper."

"Thank goodness I'll be busy," Nikki said. "I'm not cut out for this stress."

"You work in a hospital, Nikki," I said.

"That's what I'm saying, Abby. There's less stress at the hospital."

When we reached the town square, we parked on a side street and walked to the bar, where Marco resumed his bartending duties and Nikki and I were lucky enough to get a booth that had just been vacated. I retrieved Seedy from Marco's office and held her on my lap until our drinks came. After that, she sat under the table by my feet as Nikki and I chatted for an hour, until I couldn't keep my eyes open any longer.

"Are you getting old?" Nikki teased. "You can't even stay out past nine thirty."

"I'm sorry, Nik. I was up early and I haven't been sleeping well."

"After hearing about your situation at home, I understand why. So let's call it a day. Just promise we won't go so long between our girls' nights out."

Holding up my right hand, I said, "I do solemnly swear that I will not—"

Seedy began to growl and suddenly darted out from the table and headed to the front of the building, weaving in between customers' legs. I scooted out of the booth and went after her, but before I could catch her, the door opened and a group of people came in. Seedy hobbled around them and out onto the sidewalk, where I could hear her barking excitedly. I wove through the crowd and dashed after her, only to see her disappear around the corner onto Lincoln Avenue.

"Seedy!" I called, running after her. "Seedy, come here."

"Abby?" I heard Marco call.

I turned and saw him and Nikki standing outside the bar. Walking backward and rubbing my arms for warmth, I called, "Seedy got out."

"You need your jacket," Marco called. "I'll grab it and follow you."

I ran to the end of the street, turned the corner onto Lincoln, and saw Seedy running after a shadowy person. Under the streetlights I couldn't tell whether it was a man or woman, but when the figure cut across Lincoln, Seedy followed, seemingly unaware of a big pickup truck headed toward her.

"Seedy!" I screamed as the driver hit his brakes.

Narrowly avoiding the truck's tires, Seedy ran on until she turned another corner and disappeared from sight.

"Here," Marco said, catching up to me. I slipped my arms into the jacket sleeves; then we dashed across Lincoln Avenue in pursuit of our dog.

"She almost got hit by a truck, Marco. This is all so unlike her."

"Did you see what she was chasing? Was it another dog?"

"No, a person. I couldn't see that well with these old-fashioned streetlamps, but it seemed the person had on dark clothing with a hat or a hood or something standing up from his or her head."

"She couldn't have been going after a man. She'd have run in the opposite direction. Could what you saw over the head be just a tall hairdo?"

"You mean like Lavinia's? She's supposed to be in Springfield."

"If she told us the truth."

"How about a bellboy's hat?" I asked. "That's what Kandi wears when she's working."

We came to a halt at the intersection of Franklin and Chicago Streets, another east-west route that ran through downtown. There was no sign of our dog or the mysterious figure, so we were unsure of which way to go.

"If Seedy keeps going, she'll get lost, Marco."

He pulled out his cell phone and dialed my number. "Let's split up. I'll head left; you go right. Just keep your phone in your hand and stay on the line with me."

I started west on Chicago Street, calling Seedy's name.

"See anything?" came Marco's voice through my phone five minutes later.

"Nothing. And I'm almost to the old Y building. You?"

"Not a sign of her. I'll go one more street south and then double back."

"Seedy!" I called, making a circuit around the huge YMCA building. I went inside through the main doors and found Chester and Sol watching the small television on the counter. I explained my mission but neither man had seen Seedy pass by through the big front wall of windows.

"Sorry we can't be of more assistance," Chester said, "but if we do see your little rescue, I'll phone."

"How about someone running past that might have had a hat or a hood on, or had a tall hairdo?"

"Like Mr. Stone's stalker?" Chester asked. "Sorry. No one has been by."

I thanked him, but he and Sol had already returned to their TV show, so I doubted they would have noticed anyone running by. I was about to leave the building when I heard a ding. I glanced back to see the elevator open and Robert Hall step out. He had on a brightly colored T-shirt with a Spider-Man logo, black jeans, and black sneakers. He spotted me as he slipped on a gray hooded sweatshirt. "I hope you're not here to report a problem with Jingles's case," he said, striding toward me.

"I'm looking for my dog. She came this way and I was hoping someone saw her."

"Don't you keep her on her leash?" Robert asked, gazing down his nose at me in that superior way of his.

I gave him a polite smile. "Actually, we were inside, and I leave her off the leash when we're indoors. She escaped when the door opened."

"If your dog is that prone to escape, I suggest you keep her *on* her leash."

"We were at Down the Hatch," I said carefully. "People come and go there all the time, and she's never run after anyone before."

"Ah, yes, Down the Hatch," Robert said, tapping his chin. "A 1900s-era bar in desperate need of a total renovation. I've eaten there only once, when I ordered a barbecue beef sandwich that oozed sauce that was both excessive *and* excessively sweet all over my clean T-shirt. It's a mistake I'll never make again."

His attitude made me wish I could ooze more sauce onto him. "I'm sorry."

"What you should be sorry for is housing a dog in an establishment that sells food." Robert did a neat pivot and marched across the tiled floor toward the hallway.

I huffed as I headed for the exit. To think that our picky little Seedy had actually rolled on her back and thumped her tail for him. *Wait wait wait.* Seedy *liked* Robert. Maybe it hadn't been Lavinia outside the bar after all.

"Robert, hold on," I called.

He paused with his hand on the handle of a gray metal door. "What is it?"

"Were you outside just now? Maybe walking past Down the Hatch?"

"No, I was upstairs just now."

Rats. That would have explained Seedy's escapade. "Okay, thanks."

He pulled open the door and was gone.

It was a very straightforward response. Yet for some reason my inner antennae were rising.

When I stepped outside, Marco was coming up the street toward me empty-handed. "No luck."

My heart began to pound in dread. "What do we do now? We can't leave Seedy out here in the dark."

"Let's get the car. We can cover more territory that way."

We walked to the corner and were about to head north toward Lincoln when I heard a little yip. I turned just as Seedy popped out of the shrubs alongside the Y. She hobbled toward us, shaggy tail wagging as though she didn't have a care in the world.

Tears filled my eyes as I scooped her up and hugged her. "Bad girl! Do you know how worried we've been?"

She licked my chin, then wanted down.

"No way, Seedy." I handed her to Marco. "You've had your fun for one night."

"Why did you take off like that?" Marco asked her. "Were you protecting Abby?"

His chin got a bath, too. Licking was her most effective defense.

"Who would she be protecting me from?" I asked. "Lavinia knows Seedy. It'd be hard not to recognize a three-legged dog. If it was her, why would she have run away?"

"Maybe the barking frightened her. Or she didn't realize it was Seedy."

"I was yelling Seedy's name, Marco. She would have heard me."

"Then maybe she didn't want us to know she was outside the bar."

"There's another possibility," I said. "Robert."

On our way back, I told Marco about my strange encounter with Robert. "He claims he was in his room, but it's not sitting right with me and I think it's because of the way he answered. *I was upstairs just now.*"

"Remember, Robert is a literal person, Abby. Did you use the words 'just now' when you asked him?"

I tried to recall my exact words, but the fear that I'd lost my dog made things a bit blurry. "Maybe. At any rate, I want to question him again. We know Seedy likes Robert. Chasing him makes more sense than chasing Lavinia. She lives on the opposite side of the square. She would have looped back toward her apartment, not run toward the Y."

"We don't know that she ran toward the Y. That's just where Seedy ended up. And I'm not sure Robert being outside the bar is pertinent, but we'll talk to him again. Right now let's find out whether Lavinia is back in New Chapel."

Closeted in Marco's office, we phoned Lavinia. She answered after four rings, sounding breathless. Putting her on speakerphone, I said, "Lavinia, it's Abby."

"Oh. Hi, Abby." Still breathing hard.

"Did I catch you at a bad time?"

"No." She coughed. "I was just sacked out on the sofa trying to get over this dang cold."

Then why was she breathless? "Are you home?"

"Uh, no, at my mom's. Something I can do for you?"

I glanced at Marco for assistance and he whispered, "Ask her if she's filed for death benefits yet."

"Lavinia, I just wanted to see how you were feeling and make sure you've filed for death benefits."

"That's mighty nice of you. Yes, I sure have."

"Okay, great. That's all I wanted to know."

"Wait," she said. "I forgot to ask how the murder investigation is going."

Marco mimed taking aim at a target, so I said, "I think we're drawing a bead on our suspect."

"Wow, that's fast. So—" She paused. "Anyone I know?"

"I can't comment on a case. Sorry."

"But you think you're close to naming the killer?"

"We're getting closer by the minute. Anyway, sorry for the interruption. Take care."

As soon as the call ended, Marco grabbed the car keys. "Let's take a ride over to her apartment to see if she's telling the truth."

CHAPTER TWENTY

We left Seedy at the bar under the care of Marco's brother, dropped Nikki at her place, then headed for the Hampton Arms Apartments. We called upon Betty Summers to let us in and she happily obliged in exchange for a few minutes of conversation. Unfortunately, she couldn't tell us whether Lavinia was home.

Thanking Betty, we proceeded down the hall, where I rapped on Lavinia's door. That was followed by a shuffling sound, but no one answered.

"Did you hear that?" I whispered to Marco.

He nodded.

"Lavinia?" I called. "It's Abby. Sorry it's so late, but I'd like to ask you something. It'll only take a minute."

I rapped again, then rang the doorbell, but still got no answer. "Lavinia, please call me tomorrow. You have my card."

And then we left.

"I'll bet she's home, Marco. I definitely heard something move."

"Maybe it was the rats."

"Or maybe she lied about going back to her mom's."

"Imagine that. A suspect who lies."

I was still mulling over the events of the evening as we

pulled up in front of the bar. Marco came around and opened my door for me, holding out his hand to help me out. "We'll work on it tomorrow, babe. You look exhausted."

I *felt* exhausted. It had been a long, busy day.

Marco gave me a kiss. "Go home, take a hot bath, and get to sleep. I'll keep Seedy here with me."

"So I'll just have my parents to deal with?"

"Be nice." He kissed me again and left.

I walked into my parents' house through the back door and found both of them sitting at the table having tea. They turned to gaze at me expectantly.

"What?" I asked.

They exchanged looks that I didn't even try to decipher. Then Mom said, "How are you?"

"Fine."

"And?" Mom prompted.

"Tired. Long day."

Translation: *Not in the mood for chitchat. Still angry.*

"Anything unexpected happen?" Dad asked.

Did I want to go into the whole dog-on-the-loose story with them? No.

"Nothing at all." I took two chocolate chip cookies from the cookie jar and paused at the doorway. "By the way, I was trying to conduct an important interview when you kept bombarding me with texts today. I'm not a child. Don't do that to me anymore." I said a curt good night and headed up the hallway to the staircase.

I soaked in the tub, started to read in bed, and fell asleep with the book in my hand. I never even heard Marco come in. Turned out that I hadn't lied to my parents. I was tired. But not tired enough to erase the hurt looks on their faces.

Well, too bad, I told myself. I was all grown-up now. Independent. Self-sufficient. Married, for Pete's sake. They had to stop crowding me.

Friday

Armed with self-righteousness, I marched down to the kitchen and made my toast with almond butter, ignoring the omelet Mom slid onto my plate and staying silent while Dad read articles from the newspaper. I also didn't look either one in the eye in case they were still giving me those expectant gazes.

"What was that about?" Marco asked as he drove us downtown.

I stroked Seedy's soft fur. "What was what about?"

"You wouldn't look up from your breakfast."

"I was thinking about Jingles's case."

"Abby."

It was only one word, but his tone said, *You're not fooling me.*

"Okay, fine. When I got home last night, Mom and Dad were in the kitchen having tea, and when they saw me, they gave me this look."

"What kind of look?"

"I don't know. Like they were waiting for me to say something. But I didn't feel like talking, so I went to bed."

"And this morning you were afraid they'd still be looking at you that way?"

Bingo. But I couldn't admit it, because then I'd be acknowledging that it bothered me. "I just want them to stop crowding me, Marco."

Marco drove on. "Are you going to avoid them every morning?"

"No. Of course not."

He didn't say anything else, but I could tell he was ruminating on the subject. It wasn't until we paused outside of Bloomers to kiss good-bye that I asked him what he thought about the situation.

"Doesn't matter what I think," he said matter-of-factly.

"It always matters, Marco."

"Okay." He pulled into the parking lot and killed the engine. "I think you should read their message."

"Because it's gooey with sentimentality so I'll feel bad about not answering Mom's texts? Well, sorry, but I'm not going to cave in. My parents have to stop treating me like a child." Then I kissed his cheek and led Seedy toward Bloomers.

"I told you it didn't matter what I thought," he said as he walked the other way.

"Yes, it does," I called after him. "Usually."

"Marco doesn't understand," I told Seedy. "He's never been in my situation."

Seedy wiggled to get down. She'd obviously never been in it, either.

It was business as usual that Friday morning. Shops and businesses reopened, people were back on the square, our coffee-and-tea parlor was crowded, and Rosa and I were working like madwomen on a thick stack of orders.

And yet I found myself humming contentedly as I finished an anniversary arrangement made of a mix of gerberas—pink standards, deep red miniatures, and another standard variety called fiction that was a mix of fluffy red-and-white petals. To accentuate the arrangement, I added tall, curling strands of veronica, with variegated pittosporum for greenery.

"You sound happy," Rosa said. "Did you have fun on your afternoon off?"

"Yep. Marco and I interviewed people for Jingles's case."

"All day?" she asked as Lottie stepped through the curtain and headed toward the walk-in coolers.

I pulled a sheet of wrapping paper off the roll. "All day and all evening."

"And that was fun?"

"Definitely. It's like working on a giant jigsaw puzzle, putting pieces together and seeing what kind of picture it makes. It's a lot like arranging flowers, to tell you the truth. You have an image in your head of what you want the finished arrangement to look like, and then you put the flowers together and see what happens."

Rosa turned her arrangement of roses, spider mums, and carnations to see it from all angles. "What do you think of this one, Abby?"

Before I could answer, Lottie looked over her shoulder. "Nice job, sweetie. Have any luck on the case yesterday, Abby?"

Why was I just plain Abby now? "We found two more suspects," I said, "at—of all places—the Calumet Casino River Boat."

"Is that the gambling boat?" Rosa asked me.

"Sure is," Lottie said, once again beating me to the draw. "Ever been there?"

Rosa shook her head, her luxurious curls bouncing over her shoulders. "Sergio's brother lost his savings gambling, so Sergio wouldn't step foot inside a casino." She smiled impishly. "But I've always wanted to see what it was like."

"Well," I said, "they're—"

"Noisy as all get-out," Lottie said, emerging from the walk-in cooler with a fresh supply of daisies and carnations. "And with all the bright overhead lights, you wouldn't know whether it was day or night. Still, many people love it. You just have to be careful not to get gambling fever."

"Sounds like fun to me," Rosa said.

"In the words of the late, great W. Somerset Maugham," Grace said, entering the room carrying a tea tray, " 'Often the best way to overcome desire is to satisfy it.' "

"Are you in favor of gambling, Grace?" Rosa asked.

"Not for myself," she said. "I wouldn't presume to decide for anyone else."

My cell phone rang, so I checked the screen and saw Marco's name, and my heart gave a little leap. I stepped away to answer in private. "I'm glad you called, Marco. I want to apologize for what I said this morning. I hope I didn't hurt your feelings."

"Abby, come on. They're your parents. You asked my thoughts, so I gave them to you. Okay?"

I was smiling when I said, "Okay."

"Good. Now down to business. I spoke with Sean Reilly just now and he had two things to report. First, Lavinia doesn't have any parking tickets, which means that either she didn't park on the square or she didn't drive down at all."

"So we add another lie to Lavinia's list. Now we need to know her real reason for coming from the direction of the courthouse."

"And it may be as simple as that she parked in a free lot off the square and forgot. Granted, that's a stretch."

"A big stretch, Marco. She'd be driving to a lot two blocks from home and still have a three-block walk to the diner."

"In any event, we'll have to talk to her again. Reilly also told me that they have yet to determine what was used to transport Dallas's body to the courthouse, but they do have a print of the tire treads. By the width of the tread and the span between the marks, it might be a mover's dolly."

"Something a woman could handle," I said.

"Yep. Also, forensics turned up synthetic black fibers on the body that they believe came from the garrote. That fits with my theory that Dallas was wearing a black tie."

"Dallas bragged about his ties being expensive, Marco. Wouldn't they be silk?"

"I've already got that on my list to check. I'll call David's Men's Store to see if there is any record of the purchases Dallas made. Last thing, and this is the biggie, as Robert reported, a blue topaz necklace was found in the gravel outside the shed. It's been entered into evidence and sent away for testing."

"I'll say it's a biggie. That just moved Kandi into the number one slot on my list, Marco. We're really going to have to put pressure on her tonight."

"Don't worry. I've got it all scripted in my head. I'll keep coming back to her missing necklace, and when she's good and annoyed, I'll let her know where it was found and when. With any luck, we may solve the case tonight." The excitement was evident in Marco's voice.

"On another front," he said, "I phoned Betty Summers, and she promised to let me know if she saw Lavinia. I also did some research on Jingles, or rather Samuel Atkins, and found several newspaper articles about him. Interesting guy, our gentle window washer. While he was the head of his investment firm, he lived in a two-million-dollar mansion in an exclusive suburb of Springfield, bought hand-tailored suits from England, and owned five luxury automobiles."

"Wow. Just—wow."

"According to the newspaper, Samuel and his family lived the high life for years—until an undercover investigation revealed that he had been taking money out of client accounts."

"Our Jingles did that?"

"Samuel Atkins spent five years in prison for his crime, sweetheart."

I was speechless. This new vision of Jingles just didn't match with the one of the kindly old man who helped everyone. Those five years in prison had clearly changed him. But why had he turned his back on his family?

"That could explain why Jingles didn't file charges against Dallas," Marco said. "He might not have wanted the scrutiny."

"Maybe Dallas knew what his boss was up to and that's why he felt free to steal from the company, too, never expecting that Jingles would fire him for it."

"I hate to point this out, Abby, but that strengthens the case against Jingles. Besides saying he was going to write to Jingles's sons, Dallas may have threatened to spread the news about his incarceration around town. That's quite a motive for murder."

"I still don't believe he did it, Marco."

"I'm with you on this one, Sunshine. And you'll be happy to know that Jingles is a free man, temporarily at least. Dave called earlier to tell me that the DA wasn't prepared to bring charges against him yet, so he's been released on bond. The DA still plans to move forward with his investigation, so Jingles isn't in the clear yet, but at least he's home."

If both hands had been free, I would've clapped. "We've really got to step up our investigation, Marco, so that doesn't happen."

"I'm heading to Kandi's apartment building now to interview her neighbors. I want to be prepared when we meet with her tonight."

"Okay. Keep me in the loop. I'll see you at the bar for dinner."

Rosa and I whittled down the pile of orders all morning, until there was just an inch left when she left at noon. She offered to walk Seedy for me, so I took her up on it and then ate my turkey sandwich while I worked. I kept my eye on the clock, looking forward to dinner with my husband and then a trip to the casino boat afterward to, I hoped, pin down our killer.

Those plans were scotched when Marco told me over dinner that, due to the basketball play-offs that evening, he and his entire staff were needed to work the bar.

"Seriously, Marco? After we just talked about how we had to step up our investigation, you can't get anyone to sub for you?"

"I tried, Abby. Believe me, I tried. Why don't you ask Nikki to go with you?"

Disgruntled, I gave him a look. "Did you miss her saying yesterday how stressful it was? Besides, she's working tonight. I'll just go alone."

"Don't even think about it. You need someone with you. How about your dad?"

I paused, a French fry halfway to my mouth. "I'm trying to *detach* from them, Marco, not reattach."

"Jillian?"

"Now you're just being annoying."

"Lottie?"

"She's bowling tonight—with Grace, so don't even bother asking."

"One of your brothers?"

"They're doctors, Marco. They work ungodly hours. The chances of either being free are slim to none. Besides, I know they'd tell everyone about it Sunday at dinner, and that would wound my dad. My parents would never speak to me again." I paused to eat a fry. "Huh. That's actually not a bad idea."

"Then I'm out of ideas."

"Let me think about it, okay? What did you find out from Kandi's neighbors?"

"Only one person saw her that day, a lady by the name of Lynn Keltner, who said she heard noises and peered through the peephole to see Kandi dragging a black trunk into the hallway and down the hall to the elevator. She estimated the trunk to be about two feet deep by three feet wide by two feet high."

"Big enough to hold a body?"

"Yep."

"Any sign of Web?"

"The neighbor didn't see anyone else with her, but that doesn't mean someone wasn't waiting on the main floor to help her. I'll contact Kandi's landlord tomorrow to see if they have a security camera on the premises."

I took the notebook and pen out of my purse and began a list. "So I'll need to ask Kandi why she didn't admit to being off work Friday, who helped her move the trunk, and what was inside. What else?"

"Where it is now." Marco sipped his beer. "You know who'd be a good assistant? Rosa."

I pretended I was going to blow my drink through my straw at him. "No."

"You're right. I forgot about her son."

"Did you also forget Rosa's habit of blurting out whatever thought comes into her head? Or that she has no volume control? Or that every male eye in the casino will be on her? Rosa is not a person to have with you when you're quietly trying to trap a suspect."

"You need to think of someone, babe. Otherwise the interview waits until we can go together. I'm not taking a chance with your safety."

"I'll be on a boat full of people, Marco."

"With a river beneath it and a big parking lot beside it with lots of places to hide. You finish your interview, debark, and are never seen again. Not gonna happen."

I crossed my arms and scowled at him. He crossed his arms and scowled back. It was a stalemate.

But I was hungry and needed to eat, so I uncrossed my arms and picked up my sandwich. I knew Marco was only being protective, and I loved him for that, so while I chewed I contemplated my choices. But after I ran through his list of prospective assistants again, Rosa was starting to look better. She wanted to experience a casino, she had street smarts, and she had a built-in babysitter living across the street.

I pulled out my cell phone. "Fine. I'll ask Rosa."

Marco smiled, so I smiled back. Better to get it in now, I decided. I had a strong hunch I wouldn't be smiling at the end of the evening.

CHAPTER TWENTY-ONE

Rosa and I were on our way to the casino an hour later. The air in the 'Vette was charged with energy, both of us excited for different reasons. I was so sure Kandi was guilty that I could already see myself squeezing a confession from her and successfully closing the case. Rosa just wanted to have fun.

Under my tan jacket I wore a cream-colored sweater and brown slacks with brown ankle boots, a look designed to help me blend into the crowd. I hadn't thought to give Rosa instructions, so it was my fault that she was wearing a knee-length V-neck leopard-print dress beneath her black trench coat and shiny red stilettos.

I prepped Rosa as I drove, making sure she knew what to do and what not to do to help me. Basically, I told her to stay silent.

"So all you want me to do is write down answers," she said.

"That's all. Kandi is a tough young woman, but she can also be a good actress and make you feel sorry for her. So just listen, write, and don't show any emotion."

"I can do that."

That remained to be seen. "And afterward, if you want to, you can try your luck at the slot machines."

Rosa patted her purse. "Good thing my mother gave me twenty dollars to spend."

I glanced at her to see whether she was being sarcastic. But no, she seemed perfectly happy about it. Was it just me, or didn't she feel silly being given money as though she were a child?

"I'm going to ask her about a particular piece of jewelry," I told Rosa. "It's a blue topaz necklace that matches a ring Kandi wears. As I'm talking to her, I want you to pay close attention to her facial expressions and write them down."

"Like, if she smiles, I write down that she smiled, and if she frowns, I write down that she frowned?"

"Perfect."

"What if she sneezes? Should I say she wrinkled her nose and shut her eyes?"

"Just leave out sneezes."

"What about coughs?"

My fingers tightened on the steering wheel. "Yes, leave those out, too."

I pulled into an empty parking space facing a border of tall maple trees at the back of the nearly full lot and killed the engine. "Ready?"

"One more question. Do you think this Kandi is the killer?"

"I think there's a strong possibility."

Rosa slapped her palm on her knee. "Then we will get her to confess tonight."

"Not *we*, Rosa. Me. *I* will try to get her to confess."

"*Dios mío*, Abby. Did you hear what you said? You will *try*. And what did I say? We *will* get her to confess. *This* is why you need me here."

I pulled the notebook and pen out of my purse and handed them to her. "No, *this* is why I need you here."

She gave me a coy smile. "We will see." Then she opened the car door and slid out.

I took a deep breath, closed my eyes, and counted to ten. Then I followed.

We went through the check-in process and entered the main room, which was hopping that Friday night. Amid the clanging slot machines, the cacophony of voices, the stench of tobacco smoke, and the bright lights overhead, Rosa stared around her with a smile of pure joy, reminding me of a child in a toy store.

She stopped and pointed. "Look at all those slot machines." Pressing her hands together, she was practically bouncing on her toes. "I can't wait to try them."

"There'll be time later. The blackjack section is right behind that row of machines. Let's go see if Kandi is working."

As we wove through the crowded room, I kept one eye out for Web, and although I saw several security guards circulating among the players, I didn't see him. But I did spot Kandi, so I pulled Rosa back to whisper, "That's her—the blond at table seven."

"She's pretty," Rosa said loudly. "I don't like her monkey cap, though. Why do the women have to wear those ugly black caps?"

"I think they're called bellboy caps," I said softly. "And you need to keep your voice down."

"Why? It's so noisy here I can hardly hear you."

A man at the nearest slot machine turned to see who was speaking so loudly and ended up ogling her. Rosa smiled at him and elbowed me, saying out of one side of her mouth, "Look, he is flirting with me. Should I flirt back?"

"Nope." I took her arm and led her away from the machines. Why did I think this was a good idea again? "I need to go upstairs and talk to the chief of security. Do you want to come with me or stay here and keep your eye on Kandi?"

"Stay," she said instantly. "I want to watch the people play so I can win."

"Trust me, Rosa, you'll need more than ten minutes to master blackjack."

I left her at the fringe of a group of curious bystanders watching the players around the horseshoe-shaped table and took the elevator to the second floor. I let Paul Van Cleef know that I needed to interview Kandi again and asked whether the conference room was available.

"I'll make it available," he said. "And I'll see that Kandi's relief is down there to take over for her. Give me about ten minutes to arrange everything."

When I returned to the blackjack section, I had to elbow my way through a ring of men watching the game at Kandi's table. It wasn't until I got inside the ring that I realized it wasn't the game that had their attention; it was Rosa, sitting front and center between two men at the table. She was clapping and cheering for another man who'd just won, seemingly oblivious of their admiring gazes.

She saw me and motioned for me to join her. "Abby! Abby, come watch!"

I put my finger to my lips to warn her to be quiet just as Kandi's head snapped up. She searched the bystanders until she saw me; then her expression hardened immediately.

"Look, Abby, I'm playing the blackjacks!" Rosa cried.

Kandi's mouth formed a hard line as she dealt the cards, her gaze jumping from the deck in her hands to Rosa, then to me without losing track of what she was doing.

"I bet the whole twenty dollars," Rosa said as I took a position behind her.

"You shouldn't have. You won't have any to play with later."

Kandi turned over the last card and a big cheer went up.

"Twenty-one!" Rosa cried, stretching her arms toward the ceiling. "I win! I win!" She turned and hugged me, laughing. "Five hundred dollars, Abby! I am rich!"

I was speechless.

And Kandi was gone.

It took me a second to process that there was now a man standing where Kandi had been. I pushed through the onlookers, frantically searching for her, but my height combined with the people milling about made it impossible. I spotted several empty chairs at table five and climbed onto one, ignoring the dealer's cry of "Hey, get down from there!"

"Wait, Abby," Rosa called. "I have to collect my winnings."

Seeing Rosa depart, the entire group of men groaned. Just then I spotted a blond wearing a black hat on the opposite side of the ship moving rapidly toward the check-in room. I jumped down and wove through the crowd, calling, "Make way!" But it seemed everyone I encountered was maddeningly slow. I finally broke free and dashed into the check-in room to find a line of people that snaked around twice.

I pushed into the center and turned in a circle, looking

at the faces around me, but Kandi's was not among them. I checked the coat room and the ladies' room, but she wasn't there, either.

"Did you find her?" Rosa cried, hurrying up to me.

"No. I think she got off the boat."

"Maybe we can catch her in the parking lot," she said, and headed for the exit.

I was about to follow Rosa when I heard a deep voice say, "Miss Abby?"

I turned to see Paul Van Cleef behind me. He motioned for me to step outside the room, then asked quietly, "What happened?"

"I think Kandi left the casino."

"She left? Did you tell her you wanted to talk to her?"

"I didn't get a chance. She took off when her relief came. She saw me and must have gotten spooked."

"Well, next time she sees me, she's going to get canned."

"Please don't do that, Paul. I don't want to be responsible for her losing her job."

"If Miss Cane didn't do anything wrong, there'd be no reason for her to run, would there? But she did leave, so now I don't trust her. That young lady is history."

When I left the boat, I spotted Rosa clattering on her high heels along a row of cars, ducking to check under and between them. She saw me and called, "I haven't found her yet."

"Come on, Rosa. Kandi's gone."

Dejectedly, I walked to the 'Vette and got in, sighing as I turned the key. I'd so wanted that interview, so wanted to prove Jingles's innocence and close the case.

Rosa patted my knee. "Don't feel bad, Abby. At least one of us had good luck."

Naturally, it was Rosa.

*   *   *

"We need to find Kandi's trunk, Marco."

I was sitting at his office desk, my chin propped on my hand, when he stepped inside and closed the door. I had phoned him on my way home to get Kandi's address and fill him in, but the bar had been too noisy for a long conversation. So I came to pick up Seedy and ended up staying to do research on Marco's computer.

Before dropping Rosa at home, I'd taken her with me to Kandi's apartment, but, as I'd expected, no one answered her door. Now my hope was to learn more about Kandi so I could figure out where she might go to hide.

"We need to talk to Web first," Marco said, sitting in one of the slingback chairs opposite the desk. "He may know where the trunk is. You're off tomorrow, so we can go see him in the morning."

"I'm *supposed* to be off tomorrow, but I already promised Lottie I'd work until two so we can get caught up. How about after that?"

"Let's do it. Give Paul Van Cleef a call this evening and find out if Web is scheduled to work tomorrow. We need to know where to find him."

I pointed to the computer screen. "Look here. Kandi graduated from Plymouth High School, and she's got her whole family listed on her Facebook page. Plymouth's not far from here, Marco. I'll find out where her parents live, and if Web isn't any help, maybe we can take a ride there after we talk to him."

"Don't forget we've got your family dinner tomorrow night. I arranged to be off so we could attend."

I collapsed onto my arms, burying my head. Not the family get-together!

"We can continue working Sunday, babe."

I lifted my head. "Or we can skip the dinner."

Marco gave me a frown. "Abby, you can't hurt your family that way."

"How is that hurting them? We have a job to do—an *important* job. All of the downtown merchants are counting on us. Time is of the essence, Marco. We can't waste a whole evening. We need to clear Jingles once and for all."

Marco folded his arms across his shirt. "Are you trying to convince me or yourself?"

I collapsed onto my arms again with a loud sigh. Was I turning into my diva cousin?

That thought brought me upright. "Be honest, Marco. Wouldn't you rather work on our investigation than sit at a table with drama queen Jillian and her amazing wunderkind Harper, nervous Claymore, texting Tara, snobby Portia, my know-it-all brothers, and parents who will probably want to cut my meat and wipe my chin?"

"You certainly make it sound enticing. Our alternative, of course, is to have dinner with my family."

"No, Marco, not with either family. Our first obligation is to solve this case."

"Is that what you honestly believe?"

"Why is that coming as a shock? You're all about work."

Marco rubbed his chin, thinking, and finally stood up. "Okay. Tomorrow we'll work all day. But I want to go see Jingles before we do anything else on the case. I'll invite him to have lunch with us, our treat. Can you get away from Bloomers for half an hour?"

"Yes, but why before anything else?"

"I have some questions for him."

Marco was being evasive. What did he have up his sleeve? "Do you know something?"

"I know a lot of things. For instance, I had a talk with Jingles's oldest son this evening."

"And you're just now telling me about it? What did he say?"

"You'll have to wait and see."

Whatever. I was just happy that I'd gotten out of those dinners.

Saturday

Despite my eagerness to get to work and bring the investigation to a close, Marco still had to shake me awake and hand me a cup of coffee. But once recharged, I was ready to go, as was Seedy, who'd been walked and fed and was wiggling with energy.

"Since it's Saturday," I said, applying mascara in the bathroom mirror while Marco shaved over my shoulder, "let's do something different and grab breakfast at Rosie's Diner."

"That's fine, but you still have to tell your parents we're not coming tonight."

How was he able to read my mind? Seriously, maybe he *was* psychic. "I'll text them from the diner. It'll be fine."

Marco's gaze met mine in the mirror and I saw it in his eyes. I was being a coward.

I jabbed the wand back into the tube and tossed it in my makeup basket. "Fine. I'll tell them before we leave. But the plan is, we walk straight through the kitchen and I pause to speak just before we step out the door."

Marco was shaving around his mouth, so his lips didn't move, but his eyes crinkled at the corners as though he found my plan humorous. Personally, I thought it made good sense.

The morning drama began the moment we stepped inside the kitchen.

"I see Jingles was released," Dad said, peering at me over the newspaper.

"Do you two want scrambled eggs with or without bacon?" Mom asked, stirring eggs in the cast-iron skillet.

Holding Seedy in one arm, I kept moving toward the back door, my hand on Marco's back to keep him moving, too, as my parents continued to talk at us.

Dad cleared his throat. "It says in this article—"

"Did you get a chance to think about that last title I texted you?"

"—that District Attorney Darnell—"

"And don't forget to be at the country club by six tonight."

As we stopped at the door, I glanced at Marco and he gave me a nod of encouragement.

"Mom. Dad. Stop a minute." I waited until they were both looking at me. "We won't be able to make it tonight."

"Why?" Mom asked.

"We have to work. We're very close to solving the case."

"On a Saturday night?" Dad asked.

"Jingles was released," Mom said, looking hurt, "so what's the hurry now?"

"The DA is still pursuing him," I said. "If we don't move fast, Darnell can still bring charges against him."

"But your brother is going to make a big announcement tonight," she said.

"You can tell me about Jonathan's big announcement tomorrow. Let's go, Marco."

When he opened the door, I ducked under his arm and slipped out. But Marco paused to say, "We're sorry we'll miss the dinner. Give everyone our regrets."

I glanced back to see their reaction and flinched at the disappointment on their faces.

As we buckled ourselves into the 'Vette, I said, "See how well that worked out?"

Marco looked at me but said nothing.

What did he know about my parents? They were fine with it.

I hummed all morning as I arranged flowers, feeling as free as a bird. No family dinner to get through, no country club to worry about, not even Rosa to deal with. Just doing what I loved. I could hardly wait for noon so I could do the other thing I loved with the man I loved.

Jingles was already in a booth when I arrived at Down the Hatch with Seedy. Marco took her to his office, then returned just as Gert came for our orders. Jingles seemed embarrassed to be our guest, but Marco soon had him laughing with some funny bar stories.

I'd never really looked closely at Jingles, but now that I had a chance to observe him, I could see deep lines of sorrow etched into the skin beneath his eyes and around his mouth. Was it from his years of incarceration?

We chatted about inconsequential matters as we ate our sandwiches, and then over light beers—only root beer for Jingles—Marco began to discuss the case.

"First of all, we wanted to update you on the investigation," he said. "We have two strong suspects and are especially focused on one of them. We'll be working on that part of the investigation all afternoon and for however long it takes to close the case. And just so you know, we always close our cases."

Jingles held his frosty mug with both hands and said earnestly, "I don't know what I've done to deserve such kindness from you and the people in this town."

"You're a good worker and you've helped a lot of people," I said. "You wouldn't believe how many stories we heard about your charitable works. You have very little and yet you're so generous."

"Thank you." He sighed and for a moment just stared into his mug. "Unfortunately, it wasn't always so. There was a time when my sole focus was on giving my family the best of everything, which to me meant making money."

"There's nothing wrong with wanting the best for your family," I said.

"You're right. There's nothing inherently wrong with having the finer things in life, unless getting them *becomes* your life. I wanted my family to live in the biggest house, ride in the best cars, wear the most expensive designer clothes, and have every new toy that came on the market. I saw how much my kids enjoyed taking trips to Europe and I wanted more of that for them. So I worked nonstop, eighty hours a week, and when that wasn't enough, weekends, too. But it got to where I couldn't make enough to support our extravagant lifestyle, so—" He sighed. "I stole from my clients. And then I got caught. And then my life came crashing down around me."

I was going to say something encouraging, but Jingles

kept talking, almost as though he needed to get it all out and clear his conscience.

"Being incarcerated was tough, but even tougher was hearing what my boys had to say to me on their first and only visit. 'All you did was work, work, work, and we hate you for it. We hope you stay in here forever.'"

"Oh, Jingles," I said, reaching out to touch his hand, imagining his grief.

"And then my wife took her turn. 'Who was there to help me when the boys were sick or their teachers wanted to talk? Not you, Sam. Where was I supposed to wear all those beautiful dresses and furs and expensive baubles when you were always at the office? What good were they to me without you? I needed a husband, a partner, and your sons—your *sons, Sam*—needed a dad. So have a great life, Samuel Atkins, Jr., because I hope I never see you again.' Then she divorced me and took the boys to another city.

"You know what my reaction was? Anger. Those ingrates. After all I did for them, how dare they turn against me? So good riddance.

"But then a pastor came to visit me in prison and opened my eyes to what was really causing my anger. It was shame—deep, dark, ugly shame for misplacing my devotion and in so doing abandoning the people I loved most. So I came here and started over. New name, new identity, and new outlook. I wanted to prove to myself that I could live without wealth and be happy, and I have. I wanted to make up for hurting my family by helping others, and I've done that, too. Then that fool Dallas came along and made contact with my sons. Now the past is all stirred up again."

"It's been decades since you went to prison," I said. "Why wouldn't you want to see your sons now?"

"Because I hurt those boys, Abby. They don't need me resurfacing in their lives to remind them of that terrible time. They've been doing quite well all these years without me. I want to keep it that way."

I suspected he would not be open to the suggestion that he had no way of knowing whether his sons missed him, or to the observation that they weren't boys any longer.

"I don't know what made me tell you that," Jingles said. "I don't like people to know my past. Everyone thinks highly of me now—well, they *did* think highly of me."

It did seem odd that he'd confessed all that to us. But maybe he just had no one else he could trust.

"That's just it, Jingles," I said. "It *is* in the past. It's not going to change anyone's mind about you. We know you're innocent."

Marco signaled for me to cool it. I gave him a questioning look, but all he said was, "Tell us about your dad, Jingles. You mentioned him before when we asked about the money clip you carried."

Jingles smiled wistfully, shaking his head. "Ah, my dad. What a pioneer ol' Sam Senior was. Smart, brave, daring. He was my role model for what a real man should be."

Marco's phone rang, so he excused himself to check the screen. Rising, he said, "Business call. I need to take this in the office."

"You were telling me about your father," I said to Jingles.

"Yes. What a great businessman he was. Sam taught me everything I know, and in return I took his firm to even greater heights. We spent hours poring over the financials, strategizing, planning for the future . . ." Jingles broke off and looked away, his eyes filling with tears. "Oh, how I loved working with that man. And then one day he wasn't there anymore. But I kept on working because that's what he'd taught me to do. Turns out I was a workaholic just like him."

Jingles continued to talk, telling me stories about his dad, and finally he looked at me, his expression pensive. "You know what I realized years after Sam Senior was gone? It had never been about learning the business from him. It had been about being *with* him. That's what my sons had been trying to tell me."

He paused to take a sip of root beer and I did the same with my beer, thinking about what he'd said, trying to imagine my life without my dad in it—or my mom for that matter. Then my phone beeped and Mom's name popped up on the screen. Clearly bad timing on her part.

"Excuse me a moment," I said, and read her message: *Your brother is very disappointed that you're not coming tonight.*

She was trying to guilt me into going! I shoved the phone into my purse, too annoyed to respond. I thought I'd put a stop to that behavior, but apparently not.

"Now look what I did. Got you all upset."

"Oh, no, it wasn't you. It was my mom—a long story. What were you saying?"

"I didn't mean to bend your ear for so long. Let me change the subject and ask a silly question. Do you know why everyone calls me Jingles?"

"Because you jingle the coins in your pocket when you talk to people."

He reached into his pants pocket and removed the coins, opening his palm to count them. "Eighty-seven cents. Never more, never less."

"Why?"

"Because when I first came to New Chapel, that's all the money I had in the world. I'd used up the rest getting here. Now it serves as a reminder of how far I've come."

"How did you get by?"

"Asking for handouts. Then a kind man took pity on me. He found a tiny studio apartment and paid my first month's rent; then he took me to the grocery store and bought food."

"Wow."

"And he didn't stop there. He talked the city into hiring me to wash windows for businesses on the square. All he asked was that I, in turn, help others. And that's what I've done ever since."

"That's awesome, Jingles. Do you still keep in touch with the man?"

"Yes, ma'am, and so do you. His name is Sergeant Jeffrey Knight, late of the New Chapel PD. He wasn't a sergeant at the time, of course. Just a hardworking, low-paid beat cop."

Tears welled in my eyes and I swiped them away. In a voice thick with emotion I said, "He never told me."

"No, he probably wouldn't. He's always been a humble man. It's why I liked him right from the start. I'll bet he's been a good dad to you."

I nodded. "He always made time for us."

"Tell him that, Abby. He won't always be around."

I reached across the table to take his hands. "Jingles, you won't always be around, either. I wish you would contact your sons."

At that, he pulled his hands back. "No. And don't you

dare blindside me by calling them for me. Promise me that, Abby."

Given the stubborn set of his face, I decided it probably wasn't a good idea to mention that Marco had already done just that. "I promise."

Seconds later, Marco slid into the booth beside me. He folded his hands on the table, waited a moment for our full attention, and said solemnly, "There's been a new development in the murder investigation, Jingles. And it's a game changer."

CHAPTER TWENTY-TWO

Jingles looked so stricken by Marco's words that my husband quickly added, "Don't be alarmed. This could work to our benefit. It seems the coroner miscalled the time of death. Dallas didn't die on Friday afternoon, as estimated. He died Saturday morning between nine and noon."

"How will that help me?" Jingles asked.

"If you'll think back to your first interview, you said you saw no one at the campground on Friday, but you talked to a park ranger on Saturday morning. If we can find him and get him to verify your alibi, you should be in the clear."

"That's wonderful!" I said.

Jingles just stared at Marco, shaking his head in disbelief. "All this trouble because of the coroner's error."

"It happens," Marco said. "A more exact TOD isn't given until the autopsy is performed. But now that we know, Abby and I have work to do, so you'll have to excuse us. One question, though. Do you remember what time you saw the ranger?"

"Midmorning, I believe. I was still in my sleeping bag because I'd gotten chilled in the night. I should have brought a coat, but my head was spinning so much when I left that I couldn't think straight."

"Yet you did think to pack a pair of leather gloves," Marco said.

Jingles blushed. "Yes, I packed them. They were in the drawer with my underwear and socks and I just grabbed everything."

That was answer enough for me, but Marco still seemed skeptical.

As soon as Jingles was gone, Marco said, "I'm going to put in a call to the Dunes Park Department to get them started on finding that ranger."

I raised the beer bottle to take a drink. "I hope they can locate him quickly."

"I hope they can locate him, period."

My hand stopped, the bottle an inch from my mouth. "You still don't believe Jingles is innocent?"

"Some of the things he said felt off to me. And what's the first rule?"

"Verify, verify, verify."

"You got it."

"But this new information means the alibis our suspects gave us no longer apply. We're going to have to reinterview all of them and that's going to eat up more time."

"Actually, we don't need to do anything but find that park ranger. If he can verify Jingles's alibi, the case against him will be dropped."

"But we still won't know who the murderer is."

"We were hired to clear Jingles, Sunshine. That's it. We'll turn our info over to the detectives and let them find the killer."

I put my chin in my palm and sighed. "We're so close, Marco. It's a shame to stop now. Wouldn't it be quite a coup for our agency to find the killer?"

"That was my first thought, so after Reilly called, I phoned Paul Van Cleef at the casino and learned that both Kandi and Web were at work by eight thirty the morning of the murder and didn't leave the boat until after four that afternoon. That effectively knocks them off the suspect list."

"Then why would Kandi run from me?"

"Because she has something to hide and you were getting too close to discovering what it was. She may not be the murderer, but it's within the realm of possibility that she knows who is."

"It can't be Web. He was working Saturday, too."

"Not Web. Remember that both Kandi and Lavinia admitted they'd talked to each other. For all we know, they plotted Dallas's death together. Maybe Lavinia realized we were getting close before Kandi did, and that's why we can't reach her. I also tried to call Robert's mother, but no one answered."

"Robert's mom verified his alibi for the whole weekend."

Marco finished his beer and set the bottle aside. "Would you mind looking in your notes to see what her exact statement was about Saturday?"

I flipped back several pages. "Here it is. I asked if Robert had been there on Saturday, and she said, 'Of course. Robert wouldn't miss my pot roast dinner.' Then I asked if he had driven back to New Chapel that evening and she said no, because he always stayed for her Sunday breakfast."

"So she said he was there for breakfast on Sunday but she *didn't* say that he was there for breakfast on Saturday. Think about how literal Robert is and how we had to be specific with him. If we were going to continue with the investigation—and that's a *big* if—I'd want to talk to her again."

Marco got up. "For now, all we're going to think about is Jingles. So I'm going to head up to Lake Michigan to find the ranger."

I drained the last of my beer and slid out of the booth. "We're both going to have a full day. Good thing we don't have to attend that dinner tonight."

Marco patted my shoulder. "Keep telling yourself that. I'll see you around two."

Lottie and Grace were doing a great job of handling the parlor and shop when I returned, so I stayed in the work-room and concentrated on filling orders. Or at least I tried to concentrate. My recalcitrant brain was still intent on putting the puzzle pieces of the investigation together. I kept replaying the events of Monday morning in my head, hoping they would trigger a clearer picture of what I'd seen Lavinia put into her purse, but it seemed the harder I tried, the fuzzier my memory got.

"Hola."

I glanced around to see Rosa tossing her bright blue jacket over the back of my desk chair. "I stopped to get a cup of coffee and Lottie told me you were working hard back here so you could leave by two, so I thought I'd help. I just took Petey to his karate class, so I have an hour to murder."

"Make that *kill*. And that would be great. Thank you."

Rosa took an order from the spindle and began to assemble her supplies, talking while she worked. "Are you and Marco going somewhere fun today?"

"We'll probably be working on Jingles's case."

Rosa paused just outside the walk-in cooler to wrinkle her nose. "You should take time off to do fun things, Abby. You work too much."

"Now you sound like my family. I enjoy working on cases with Marco."

"I'll bet you would enjoy going dancing with Marco, too, or bicycling—something besides work."

I kept my eye on the arrangement in front of me, tired of having to defend my decisions. Snapdragons, lilies, forsythia . . . What had I been thinking about before she arrived? Oh, right. Monday morning.

Rosa stepped out of the walk-in cooler with an armload of gerbera daisies, spider mums, and eucalyptus. "Why are you making the frownie face? You're working, aren't you? You should be happy."

"It's not that. I was just trying to remember a detail I saw last Monday while I was heading over to the deli. It might be important to the case."

"Do you have a foggy brain about it? If you want, I can help you get rid of the fog."

"No, that's okay."

She pushed up her sleeves. "It won't take long. I'm an expert at it."

Naturally. "No, really, that's okay."

She stood behind my stool and pressed her fingers into my tense shoulder muscles. "Just relax and take a deep breath."

"Rosa, I don't have time for this." But I couldn't stifle the sigh that slipped out as she kneaded the knots of tension away.

"Breathe in through your nose. Now hold—one, two, three seconds—and let it out through your mouth—one, two, three. Keep listening to my voice as you breathe. Now again, in, one, two, three . . ."

As I followed her instructions, she worked her way up the back of my neck, her fingers loosening stress I hadn't even known was there. "As you inhale, make the picture inside your head of what you want to remember. Keep breathing, in and out, in and out. What are you seeing?"

"I'm standing in front of the deli with Seedy."

"Keep going. What happens next?"

"I'm turning to see who's running up behind me. It's a woman and she's coming straight at us. She's not looking because she's stuffing something into her purse." I scrunched my eyes, willing the image to clear, but my mind wouldn't cooperate. "That's where I go blank. I can't see what she's putting into her purse."

"Something is blocking your memory." Rosa pressed on a particularly painful knot on my left shoulder. "Ah! It's your mother, something she said or did." She pressed on the right side and I flinched again. "Also something your father said or did."

"How could you tell that?"

"My fingers talk to me. We're going to have to go back to this thing they did if we want to unblock you."

She began to work on those knots. "Breathe again, Abby. Follow my voice and breathe with me, in and out. In and out. Now go back to the first thing that happened Monday morning."

"It's not just Monday morning, Rosa. It's every morning. Since we moved back home, my parents have treated me as though I'm still a child. My dad reads the newspaper to me, and my mom insists that I eat her breakfasts."

"Now your neck is tense again. This is a bad situation for you, Abby. But you want to see inside that purse, so close your eyes and breath again." She began to massage my shoulders. "Tell me just about Monday morning. Can you see your papa reading?"

"Yep, just like every morning. He's got his back to the refrigerator and his glasses perched low on his nose. 'You'll be interested in this article, Ab.' And then he starts reading it out loud."

"Aha! The knots are getting harder. This is where the memory block begins, but don't worry. I can untangle it for you. Now I want you to remember what he read."

"Can't. I tuned him out."

"That's not what your muscles are saying. You heard him on some level, Abby. Think back as you continue to breathe."

As Rosa kneaded my shoulders, my tension lessened. "It was an article about something happening downtown with VIPs . . . Oh, I did hear him! It was about the press conference, and how all the town bigwigs and bank VIPs would be there. My dad thought I'd want to attend, as if I had any free time—which he knew I didn't."

"Your shoulders are relaxing. I think we are fixing the problem. Now let's go back to when you were on your way to the deli."

Amazing. The images were coming in clearer. "I remember Grace telling me I'd forgotten the eggs, so I snapped on Seedy's leash and we headed for the deli. We crossed the street to the courthouse lawn and she immediately began to pull me toward the lilacs. Then I got a text from Tara and—" I was going blank again.

Rosa began to knead the bony knobs at the base of my skull. "Relax, Abby. Let your mind draw the picture for you. You read Tara's text and . . . ?"

I concentrated on my breathing for a few seconds and

then the image came in again. "I answered her text and then pulled Seedy away from a piece of a necktie lying in the grass." My eyes flew open and I turned. "I can see the tie! It's just like the police said—black with tiny yellow diamonds on it."

"See? I told you I could clear the fog. Now turn around and keep going."

This time I was an eager subject. As she kneaded my muscles, I slipped into the breathing routine and let my thoughts drift back. Then suddenly I was viewing everything through my own eyes as if it were happening right then.

"Okay," I said excitedly. "Seedy and I are standing in front of the deli. I hear footsteps and turn. A woman is coming at us so I shout at her. She looks up and narrowly avoids hitting us. I notice that her purse is still open as she rushes past . . . I can see it, Rosa! Her scarf is black and . . . black and . . ." My newly relaxed shoulders slumped. "It's a plain black scarf, just like Lavinia said it was." I opened my eyes and sighed. "I can't believe I was wrong. I would have bet any money that necktie was in her purse."

"Why do you believe that so strongly?"

"Because I saw that black-and-diamond pattern somewhere besides that first glimpse of the tie on the lawn that morning. But where could it have been?"

Rosa circled her index finger. "Turn. We will find out."

She began to massage my temples, giving her breathing instructions in a low, soothing voice. "Now go back to when you saw inside Lavinia's purse. What happened after that?"

As the images became clear again in my mind's eye, I began to describe the details I saw inside the deli, the nervousness Lavinia had displayed, and then my trip back across the lawn to the murder scene. But no tie appeared.

"Keep going," Rosa said softly.

"There's nothing left to tell. I came back to Bloomers with the food and that was it. No, wait. I had to stop outside because Seedy wanted to go see the window washer."

"Robert, right?"

"Yes. He was up on a ladder and I was afraid Seedy would upset either the bucket or the ladder or both, so I scooped her up and—" My eyes flew open. "The bucket. It was on the bucket handle!"

"The necktie was on the handle?"

"Yes! I remember having a fleeting thought about how smart it was of Jingles to pad the handle of that old tin bucket, never dreaming it was anything but a scrap of material." Then I stopped. "Oh. That's not good."

"Why?"

"The dead man's tie was on Jingles's bucket. *Jingles's* bucket, Rosa."

Her eyes widened. "So you think Jingles killed the man and then wound the dead man's tie around his bucket handle? Why would he do that?"

I jumped up and grabbed my coat. "I don't know, because the Jingles I know wouldn't."

"Where are you going?"

"To Jingles's shed. If I'm lucky, his bucket might still be there."

"Wait, Abby. Wouldn't Jingles have his bucket with him?"

Oops. She was right. Jingles worked on Saturdays. "Then I need to find him and take a look at his bucket.

Tell Lottie and Grace I'll be back in ten minutes. Watch Seedy for me."

I put my purse over my shoulder and used the alley exit to leave the shop. I hurried up the short alleyway between my shop and the building next to mine to reach Franklin, then began scanning the streets around the square. I finally spotted Jingles on Lincoln in front of Windows on the Square and began walking toward him.

He was wiping the glass panes with a cloth and then stepping back to make sure they were clean. His ladder was standing under the store's eave. And there beside him was a bucket—not the old tin one but a shiny blue vinyl one.

I stopped in surprise. Why did he have a new bucket?

I stood there trying to decide whether to approach him or not and finally did an about-face and headed for the alley behind Franklin. I glanced around as I approached Jingles's shed but saw no one, so I tugged on the handle and the old wooden door creaked open, revealing an unlit interior.

The shed was about four feet deep and seven feet wide, with a gravel floor and wooden shelves along each side wall, where stacks of folded white cloths, large bottles of vinegar, and several gallon containers of window cleaning solution were stored. Shining my phone's light on the shelving on the opposite side, I spotted pairs of blue rubber gloves and the yellowed Nike athletic shoe box that Robert had discovered.

I aimed the light toward a back corner, where I saw wooden poles with squeegees attached leaning against a green garbage bin, but there was no sign of the tin bucket or the necktie. Remembering what Marco had learned

about the tire treads being from a mover's dolly, I paused
to study the garbage bin. It had two good-sized wheels
on the bottom and a hinged lid on top. At about three
feet wide, two feet deep, and four feet high, it certainly
could've held a body inside.

I was pondering the implications of that when I heard
a crunch of gravel behind me. I turned to find Jingles in
the doorway, his new bucket in one hand, his ladder in
the other, and a scowl on his face. Marco was right. He
was stronger than he looked.

"Something you need?" he asked in a curt, decidedly
un-Jingles-like voice, setting the bucket down so he could
bring the ladder inside.

"I was looking for your old tin bucket."

He placed the ladder against the back wall. "I don't
have it anymore."

I edged toward the doorway. I couldn't understand
why Jingles was being sharp with me and it made me
uneasy. Was he annoyed because I'd invaded his space?
"What happened to it?"

"You'll have to ask Robert."

"Robert took your old bucket? Do you know why?"

"He said it was past its prime." Jingles knocked the
blue bucket with his shoe. "He bought this one to replace
it. A gift, he said."

"When was this?"

Jingles began to clean out the bucket. "He was using
it Tuesday when I got back to town."

That felt like way more than a coincidence. "What do
you think he did with—"

"Stop! No more questions until you tell me what's so
all-fired important about that old bucket!"

I weighed my options and finally decided to be honest. This was Jingles after all, the man my dad had taken a liking to all those years ago. "It may be the key to finding the murderer."

"Shouldn't you be verifying my alibi instead of chasing down that old tin pail? Where's Marco?"

I opened my mouth to tell him and found myself lying instead. "He's on his way. I'm just a few minutes ahead of him."

Jingles studied me through narrowed eyes as he wiped his hands on a towel, making me feel as though he could see right through my lie. Then he picked up the new pail and placed it on a shelf. "You know," he said slowly, "if Robert did take the bucket, I might know where it is."

"In his room?"

"No, no—you don't want to go up to his room. It's more likely to be in his storage locker in the basement." Jingles paused to shake a gallon of window cleaning solution to see how much was left, then said, almost grudgingly, "I can take you there now if you like. Robert is working at the hobby shop this afternoon."

I hesitated. A massive old building would have a massive old basement. Did I really want to explore it with a man Marco still suspected of murder?

But this was Jingles. Still, I found myself saying, "I need to wait for Marco."

The window washer came out and shut the door behind him. "Suit yourself. But I have to be at the hospice center by three p.m."

I checked my watch. That didn't leave much time.

"Marco can always meet us there," he said.

Except I had no idea where Marco was. I glanced at

my phone, but there were no messages from him. It could be that he had nothing to report or that he was in an area where the signal was weak.

I didn't want to lose out on a chance to find the missing tie, and perhaps the clue to naming the killer, but I couldn't be stupid about it, either. Thinking back, I realized there had been something off when Marco and I had met Jingles at the bar, almost a "those of us who are about to die" attitude about him.

I had to let someone know where I was going, just in case. "I need to get Seedy first."

Jingles turned and started trudging up the alley, calling over his shoulder, "I'll wait for you at the corner. Remember, we don't have much time."

CHAPTER TWENTY-THREE

Rosa was gone when I got back to the shop, so I told Lottie and Grace that Seedy and I were going to the Y building with Jingles to see whether we could find a piece of evidence in the basement. Neither of them seemed to find that alarming, and that reassured me. Plus, now they knew where I was going. I told them I shouldn't be gone more than half an hour and to tell Marco to meet me there if they saw him. I tried to call Marco, but the phone went to voice mail, so I left voice and text messages for him.

Seedy hobbled happily along at my side up Franklin Street until she saw Jingles waiting at the corner, and then she balked, which did not help my nerves.

I picked her up, talking to her in a soothing voice. "It's Jingles, Seedy. You've seen him many times. Everyone likes Jingles. No reason to feel apprehensive." The way I was feeling at that very moment. Maybe she was sensing my stress.

Seedy tucked her head beneath my arm as Jingles and I proceeded west on Lincoln. My phone beeped with an incoming text, so I stopped to dig it out of the bottom of my purse, praying it was Marco. But it was a message from Tara: *Sure will miss you tonight, Auntie A.*

Great. Now my niece was trying to guilt me into going. I slid the phone into my hip pocket to keep it close for when Marco finally called.

"Was that Marco?" Jingles asked gruffly.

"Yes! He's running just a few minutes behind."

We continued on silently for two more blocks, and then I couldn't stand it any longer. "Jingles, have I done something to anger you?"

The muscles in his jaw clenched. "What was the one thing I asked you not to do, Abby? The *one* thing?"

There was only one thing I could think of: contacting his sons. "I kept my word, Jingles, but Marco had already talked to them. And if you'll remember, he did tell you at our initial interview that he would probably have to do that."

The old window washer trudged on, his footsteps heavier, his hands knotted at his sides. "Now they're trying to reach me. One of 'em even talked to Chester, wanting to know when I'd be around. So now I've got Chester hounding me to see him."

"I'm sorry about that, but can't you just hear what your son has to say?"

"What for? All it would do is open old wounds. I cut my ties with them years ago for a reason, Abby."

The cutoff necktie Seedy had found instantly popped into my head, and I couldn't help wondering whether Jingles had cut his ties with Dallas, too—literally.

"You know what Sam Senior always used to tell me? Let sleeping dogs lie. Now drop the subject."

Seedy began to squirm as though she was finally willing to trust Jingles enough to walk, so I set her down and we continued on, with her hobbling on the grass beside the sidewalk. We turned the corner onto Chicago Street, where I could see the old Y a block ahead.

As we approached the building, I spotted a woman

coming up the sidewalk walking three golden retrievers. Rather than having to stop and wait while the dogs went through their normal sniffing routines, I held Seedy so they could continue past.

I set her down again near the building's main entrance, but before I could get a grip on her leash, Seedy spun around and ran after the dogs, which had just turned the corner and were headed down the cross street. Her three-legged gait was awkward, but she could move fast when she wanted to, and before I could catch up with her to grab the end of her leash, she had dived behind a cluster of large bushes at the corner.

I dashed around the corner in pursuit. On the sidewalk heading up the street I saw the woman and her dogs, but not my misbehaving mutt. I checked beneath several cars parked along the curb and then returned to the group of shrubs at the corner, poking through branches, calling her name.

Moments later Jingles called, "I think I know where she went."

He was on the front side of the Y crouched before a low window, holding back the branches so I could see. As I squeezed in next to him I saw that the window had been propped open.

"She can't be down there," I said. "It has to be a long drop to the floor. She wouldn't chance it."

Jingles stuck his head inside and looked around, then gave a whistle. "Seedy, come here, girl."

I heard an answering yip.

Jingles moved back as I got down on my knees and stuck my head inside. And there, a good ten feet below me, was my naughty dog sniffing around on the cement floor. She wasn't limping. How had she survived the fall?

Then I spotted a step ladder a few feet below the window that someone had apparently used to open it. "Come on, Seedy. Up the ladder. Let's go."

She finally stopped snooping to look up at me, then hobbled to the ladder and yipped, as if to say, *Come play!*

"No, you come up. Come on. You can do it. I have a treat for you."

But after putting one paw on the bottom rung, she thought better of attempting the climb and turned away to start sniffing again.

"She won't climb the ladder," I reported.

Jingles got to his feet with an impatient huff. "We'll have to go get her. You wanted to see Robert's storage area anyway."

He was so curt, so unlike the kindly old man I'd always known, that I wavered again, wanting to trust him yet not sure I should. I checked my phone, but still no call or message had come in. Should I wait for Marco and see the storage area later?

When I looked again, Seedy was at the foot of the ladder gazing up at me expectantly. "Are you okay?" I called. She wagged her tail and began to run in circles, returning each time to the ladder to gaze up at me and whine.

"If we're going to go, we'll have to do it now," Jingles snapped.

Again I hesitated, but Seedy's whines were becoming more distressed. I backed out of the shrubs and rose, dusting off my knees. Finding the bucket was no longer my concern. I just wanted to rescue my dog and get out of there. "Okay, let's go."

I started toward the main entrance only to have Jingles call sharply, "Side door. If we go through the front, Chester will talk our ears off."

When I turned the corner, he was holding a brown metal door open. I felt a fluttering of apprehension as I stepped inside. A large old basement with hairy spiders and a man with a grudge behind me. Marco would be so upset.

On the small landing, Jingles pulled on a door, only to find it locked.

"Sorry," he said grumpily. "I don't come in on this side." He started up a flight of cement stairs on the right, calling back, "There's another door at the other end of the building that I *know* is unlocked."

My nerves were jangling as I followed Jingles through the long building. To my relief, the door there did open, revealing age-darkened concrete steps leading to the basement. We headed down, our way dimly illuminated by a row of low-wattage security lights high on the wall, and emerged into a vast, eerie space lit by a few overhead fluorescent tubes that buzzed and flickered annoyingly. I suppressed a shiver as I glanced around. "Seedy! Here, girl."

"She can't hear you. She's all the way on the other side of the building, past the utility room." He pointed out a long row of storage areas, each enclosed by chain-link fencing. "There's the lockers. Fourth one down is Robert's."

I paused briefly for a look, peering through the metal fence to see an old-fashioned bicycle, a battered blue-and-white skateboard, and a basketball, something any ordinary young guy might own. I also saw clear plastic bins stacked along the back, each bin holding what appeared to be neat piles of comic books, again something any guy might have. What I didn't see was the tin bucket. I mulled that over as I turned to follow Jingles.

"Utility room is through here."

I peered around a wide doorway into a large, ancient room lit by several bare bulbs and filled with mammoth water heaters, noisy furnaces, metal ductwork, and thick copper pipes strung between blackened beams—and spiderwebs large enough to catch mice. The smell of fuel oil permeated the air and the heavy coating of gray dust on every surface made me cough.

There was no use calling for my dog until we were clear of the noise, so I followed Jingles through the room, slipping my phone out to see whether Marco had tried to contact me. It wasn't until I had emerged into another large, unfinished area of the basement that I heard barking. "That's Seedy!"

"Keep calling so she'll know you're close." Jingles pointed toward another hallway at the far end of the room. "She's through there."

I kept calling her as I hurried across the room and was relieved by her answering barks. At the mouth of the hallway I flicked a switch, but nothing happened, so I turned on my cell phone flashlight and used it to guide me to the door at the end.

"I'm here, Seedy," I said as she whined and scratched to get out. "Don't be scared." I turned the knob and then shook it, but the door wouldn't budge. I stood on tiptoe to check the top of the frame to see whether there was a key hidden somewhere and came away with a coating of dirt on my fingertips.

I turned to ask Jingles for help, but he hadn't followed me. It struck me then that I hadn't heard any sound from behind me for a while.

"Jingles?" I called. "Everything okay?"

There was no answer.

I felt a prickle of fear on my scalp. *Go back,* that little voice in my head whispered. *You can bring Marco later.*

But Seedy's barks were louder and more desperate now, and she was scratching the door frantically, as though she could dig her way out. I was torn, my stomach in knots at the thought of leaving her behind but afraid to ignore the warning voice in my head.

Seedy stopped scratching.

I put my ear to the door, listening. "Seedy?"

At first all was eerily silent, and then suddenly there was a scuffling sound followed by her surprised yelp— and then nothing more.

My heart began to slam against my ribs. Someone had silenced her.

I looked around in desperation. Dear God, where was Jingles? Frantic now, I began to shake the doorknob and throw my body weight against the door, and when it wouldn't give, I pounded it with my fists.

Hearing footsteps behind me, I turned to see Jingles coming up the hallway holding a massive wrench as though it were a baseball bat. I flattened myself against the wall as he raised it in the air, my heart pounding so hard I could barely breathe.

"Get back!" he shouted.

I jumped out of his way as he brought the wrench down, breaking off the doorknob. He thrust the heavy tool into my hands, then pushed against the door and finally began using the side of his body as a battering ram.

On his third attempt, the door burst open, the old frame splintering, sending shards everywhere and Jingles careening into the room straight toward a large workout bench in the center. I watched in horror as he hit the end of the bench and staggered back, tripping over a set of barbells on the floor and falling onto his back. His head followed, hitting the concrete with a hard *thud* and then lolling to the side.

For a second I was too stunned to move, not knowing whether he was unconscious or dead. Then I ran to his side and dropped down to check for a pulse.

"*What* have you done?"

I turned with a gasp as Robert stepped into view, my dog in his arms, his hand clamped around her muzzle. He wore a look of stupefaction that I'm sure matched mine. Dressed like a self-styled comic book hero, he had on a black T-shirt with big yellow letters SA emblazoned on it, a wide black belt, black tights, yellow rain boots, a yellow rain poncho over his shoulders, and yellow rubber gloves. Around his head he wore a black-and-yellow headband twisted like a rope and tied above one ear.

I would have laughed at the ridiculousness of it if Robert hadn't been so dead serious. I didn't dare move, my fear of his harming Seedy keeping me frozen in place.

His shocked gaze turned accusatory as it fell on the wrench in my hand, then shifted to the unconscious Jingles. "What *have* you *done*?"

Slowly, I placed the wrench on the floor and rose, rubbing my sweating hands against my khakis. "I didn't do anything, Robert. It was an accident. Jingles was—"

"I am *not* Robert. I'm the Secret Avenger. And *this*"— he pointed at Jingles with his oversized gloves—"is no *accident. This* is an act of evil."

I took a step back. "No, you don't understand."

"Oh, but I do understand." He circled around behind me, glaring with imperious disdain. "You were never investigating the murder of Dallas Stone. You were planning to destroy me and my good works. And now you've destroyed Jingles for trying to stop you from entering my secret lair."

When he paused to quiet Seedy, who was wiggling in an effort to get down, I backed farther away. "Shush, now," he crooned, petting her and talking in a soothing voice. "All will be well soon."

I took a quick glance around, seeking a way to grab my dog and escape. But from the dismal amount of light coming through the two windows high up on one cinder block wall, it appeared Robert was blocking the sole exit. The only other route would be up the ladder and through the window, and I wouldn't be able to make that dash with Seedy unless Robert was incapacitated.

Robert clicked his tongue at me. "Jingles didn't deserve this treatment. He was the perfect sidekick, a man to be trusted. And you took him from me."

"Robert—I mean Special Avenger—please listen. Jingles may still be alive. I didn't hit him. He fell and struck his head."

"A likely story. It's just what I would expect from the enemy." He stroked Seedy's head but kept his gaze on me. "But justice was served today when this special animal showed up to deliver me. You deserve better than her, Seedy. You have exceptional gifts. You need to be with someone who can utilize them for the good of mankind." He paused as though an idea had just occurred to him. "I think that henceforth you should be known as Speedy. Yes, *Speedy*, Secret Avenger's trusted sidekick."

And just like that he'd crossed Jingles off and moved on.

As Robert began to describe the outfit he was going to create for Speedy, I glanced around. Right behind me against a sidewall were old metal shelving units stocked with emergency supplies: a lantern, kerosene, packages of batteries, a tool kit, jugs of water, cans of beans, towels. And on the bottom shelf sat Jingles's old tin bucket. But nothing was wrapped around the handle.

At that moment my phone beeped to signal an incoming message. *Please, God, let it be Marco!* I thought.

"What was that?" Robert asked.

I was stunned. Could he possibly not know what a text message sounded like? But then, he didn't own a phone, so perhaps he really didn't have a clue. "What was what?"

Robert gave me a skeptical look, and when I didn't say anything further, he pointed to the large bench press in the middle of the room. "Lie down on that."

I stared at him in alarm. "Why?"

"You'll find out."

Not if I could help it. "Look, I won't tell anyone about your lair. I wouldn't want to stop the Secret Avenger's good work. Just let me walk out of here with my dog."

"It's too late for that," he said matter-of-factly. "Now go lie down."

I shook my head, trying to look confident. "No. I'm walking out of here now."

Before I could take two steps, he'd elbowed back his cape to show me a small black holster hanging from his belt. "Stop right there. Don't make me use the WOMP on you."

I stepped back, palms raised, until I hit the shelves, hoping that there was something on them I could use as a weapon. To keep his attention away from what I was doing, I said defiantly, "Is that how you forced Dallas into the shed? Threatened him with the WOMP? Or did you lure him there?"

"I didn't *lure* him. He came there looking for Jingles, trying to shake him down again. I told him Jingles was far away from his evil tentacles, and that if he should darken that gentle man's doorstep again, he would suffer dire consequences. He merely laughed at me and made some very unkind remarks. So I grabbed his tie." This was all said in a nonchalant tone.

"You just grabbed his tie and choked him? A man who's bigger than you?"

"Secret Avenger is a master of martial arts. I knew the right moves to bring him to his knees. Then it was just a matter of tightening the noose."

The more Robert talked, the more he revealed how delusional he was. I knew he'd use his knife to kill me—if he could get to it in time—and that was my one hope. I draped one arm casually along a shelf inches from a can. "So you stuffed Dallas into the garbage bin and left him there until Monday?"

"I was going to put him on display earlier, but then I read in the newspaper about the press conference and that seemed a more appropriate time."

"You told us you didn't see his body in the shed that morning."

"I didn't lie. Robert didn't see the body. Secret Avenger did." Robert motioned toward the bench. "Go."

"Weren't you worried about getting caught? You left the body in the shed for two days."

"Secret Avenger never gets caught."

Seedy twisted her head and whined, her little body trembling as she tried to shake his hand off. She was as frightened as I was. I had to do something fast.

I grabbed the can and hurled it at his head, but he ducked effortlessly. Before I could hurl another, he had tucked Seedy under his arm and used his free hand to pull out his knife. "Get over there."

I moved toward the weight bench as slowly as possible. The only thing I could do now was indulge his fantasy. "Fine. I'll do whatever you ask. I'm not trying to make trouble. But I can't help noticing your Avenger costume."

"Children wear costumes. This is a suit."

"I'm guessing the letters stand for Secret Avenger. Black and yellow, just like you described."

He began to preen just a bit. "Usually I wear a hood and mask so I can patrol the streets undetected. I'm not used to being caught off guard."

"So was it *you* Seedy was chasing the other night?"

"She wasn't *chasing* me. She was *following* me." He smiled down at her. "You wanted to be my sidekick even then, didn't you? And now together we can defend the weak and helpless against people like her."

"And Dallas?"

"Dallas was pure evil, blackmailing my friend and stealing his precious money clip. He had to be stopped."

"Why did you leave him at the courthouse?"

Robert lifted his chin and rolled his shoulders back. "To show the town that justice had been done and to let the public know that their hero was protecting them."

"Weren't you worried that someone would see you?"

"Absolutely. Avengers must work incognito. But it was a simple job, really. The body was already in the garbage bin. I merely waited until after the imbecile cops had patrolled and then wheeled the bin over. No one pays any attention to a lowly window washer. My plan worked perfectly until my sidekick spotted something I'd dropped." Robert held Seedy up, rubbing his nose against hers. "But you were just pointing it out so I could snatch it up before the enemy contingent arrived."

Tucking Seedy under his arm, Robert pulled a pair of handcuffs from his belt. "Now lie down and hold your hands out."

My heart hammered against my chest as I reached the bench and lay down on it, fearing not only my death but Seedy's future with this disturbed man. A barbell rack was on either side of my head with a barbell in its cradle. Each end of the barbell was loaded with heavy iron weights. I was afraid to imagine what Robert had in mind.

He set my dog on my chest. "Make sure she doesn't move, Speedy."

As he headed toward the shelves, I wrapped my arms around her and she burrowed against my neck with her wet nose, bringing tears to my eyes. "We'll be okay," I whispered. "Marco will come."

Robert took a yellow rope from the shelves and tied my ankles together. Then he lifted Seedy off me and put her on the floor. He had just clamped the cuffs around one of my wrists when I heard a telltale ding from my hip pocket. *Praise God!*

"What *is* that *sound*?" he demanded. "And don't tell me you didn't hear it."

An idea began to form. "It's a message from my husband. He's wanting to know why I haven't returned from visiting Jingles."

"How do you know it's from your husband?"

"Because we arranged for him to text me at this time. We're detectives, remember? If I don't answer him right now, he'll know something's wrong."

Seedy was on the other side of the bench whining. When I dropped my free hand down to stroke her, she pawed at it, making her high, loud yipping noises, wanting me to pick her up again. In the midst of her barking, my phone dinged again, and then once more. Two more messages. I prayed they were from Marco, sensing I was in trouble.

At the third ding, Robert pressed his palms against his ears, grimacing as though the noise was painful. "Do something to make that stop! Speedy, shut up!"

"Seedy," I said, trying to make my voice sound calm, "lie down. Be a good girl. That's my girl. Just lie down."

She lay just beneath my free hand so I was able to pet her head as I talked in a soothing voice. "If you want the noise to stop, I need to send Marco a text to tell him I'm okay. Otherwise he's going to be here with the cops in two minutes. The cops, your enemy."

"You're asking me to trust *you*?" he sneered. "I can't trust *you.*"

"So you'd rather have the cops come? You can watch me send the message. Please! All I need to do is type one word and he'll stop."

"Give me your phone. I'll type it."

No, no, no! That wasn't part of the plan.

He held out his palm. "The phone, please."

With my free hand I slid it out of my hip pocket and handed it over. Maybe there was a way out yet. "The message should be right there on the lock screen. Just open it and type the word *BUSY*."

He stared at the screen, then handed it back, just as I'd hoped. "I don't know how to work it. You open it and I'll type."

I swiped across the message and opened up the text

box. But it wasn't from Marco. It was from my dad. My dad, whom I had scolded for deluging me with texts.

Robert snatched the phone. "You're taking too long. You're trying to trick me."

"No, I promise. I was just about to open the typing screen for you."

He frowned as he studied me, then finally handed it back, crouching down to watch me. "Do it, then. Quickly."

With Robert's face near mine, I had a clear view of his headband—black with yellow diamonds on it—and I recoiled in horror. Robert was wearing Dallas's tie—a sick souvenir of his so-called heroism. I could see the cut end hanging over his ear.

"What are you waiting for?" he asked.

I pulled up the screen with the keypad and handed it back. I had no choice but to let him reply to my dad's message.

Robert scowled in concentration as he tried to type, only to realize that his rubber gloves were too clumsy to strike the small buttons. Rather than break costume, he handed me the phone again. "You'll have to do it. One word and that's all."

My heart was in my throat as I hit the *B. Please let my dad think this is the real thing,* I prayed as I hit the *U.* My fingers were shaking, but that was okay. I wanted Robert to see how nervous I was. I hit the *S,* then started to hit the *Y,* but struck the *T* instead. Before he knew what had happened, I'd hit the exclamation point and hit send. A blue bubble popped up that read, *BUST!*

Robert reared back and glared at me. "That's not *BUSY.*"

"My hand is shaking. Marco will know what it means."

"How would he know what *BUST* means?" Robert

grabbed the phone and flung it across the floor, then grabbed my free hand and snapped the open cuff around it. "I knew I couldn't trust you."

As he looped a cord through the cuffs and strung it around the barbell, pulling it until my arms were over my head, Seedy began to whine. I lifted my head and saw her nosing Jingles's hand as though trying to rouse him. She nosed him again and Jingles's fingers twitched. Then his eyelids fluttered open and he turned his head toward us.

Suddenly my vision was cut off as Robert dropped a towel over my eyes, twisting it behind my head. Then I could hear what sounded like chain links clanging as he fastened something above me, but with no view of what he was doing, all I could do was imagine the worst, which increased my terror.

"There. Now it's done. Justice will be served."

My voice was nothing more than a hoarse croak. "What did you do?"

"Wouldn't you like to know *that* secret? All I'm going to tell you is not to move. But you will eventually, and then you'll find out."

I heard Seedy whine and then abruptly stop and I knew Robert had picked her up again.

"Time to get on with our work, Speedy. Say farewell to your former owner."

"Wait!" I called, trying one last time to stall him. "Let me say good-bye to her."

"That won't be possible. I've wasted too much time already."

I heard Robert's rubber boots pad across the room. Then he gave a gasp as though something had frightened him, followed by a cry of alarm and a heavy thud as he fell to the floor. That was followed by the sounds of a scuffle and Seedy barking. And all I could do was yell for her to get away.

In the midst of the scuffle I heard Robert cry in rage, "You can't betray me like this."

The scuffling continued until suddenly there was the sound of flesh hitting flesh, then a grunt of pain. I heard Robert's boots hitting the floor as he ran, and then Seedy's barks fading as she chased after him. "Seedy, no!" I cried. "Seedy!"

"Abby," Jingles called in a wheezy, breathless voice. "Stay perfectly still."

"Jingles? Oh, thank God!"

I heard a slow, shuffling step and then the towel was removed from my eyes. Jingles stood beside me, bent to one side, his right hand holding his rib cage. He was staring at the weighted barbell that Robert had tied me to with a thick chain. If I moved my arms or, God help me, even sneezed, the barbell would be pulled forward and would crush my throat.

Wincing in pain, Jingles went to the tool chest on the shelf and brought back a pair of heavy-duty wire cutters. "Don't move a muscle. Hear me now?"

"Yes." I lay absolutely still, barely breathing, as he positioned the wire cutters between links and squeezed. He grunted with the effort, pausing to catch his breath, his eyes closing as he battled pain. Then he tried again, his teeth clenched, the cords standing out on his neck. Just when I thought he couldn't bear the pain any longer, the chain snapped and my arms dropped. I was free!

As Jingles braced his hands on the bench, drawing in ragged breaths, I rolled to a sitting position, so relieved I started to cry. It was then that I heard police sirens blaring and the sound of cars screeching to a halt nearby.

*   *   *

I waited for what seemed like forever for help to arrive, finally yelling to attract attention. When at last Reilly and his men stormed in, weapons drawn, they surrounded Jingles, who was seated on the floor, his back against the bench, doubled over in pain.

"No, Reilly, no! Jingles saved me. It's Robert Hall. He murdered Dallas and he almost murdered me. He can't be far—he ran out of here a few minutes ago. You can't miss him. He's wearing a black-and-yellow superhero costume." I started to cry again. "Please find him, Reilly. He's got my dog."

Reilly immediately started issuing orders. "Kerr, take your men and form a perimeter. We need to get this guy now. Jones, get that stretcher in here ASAP and see what you can do about those handcuffs."

With my wrists still locked together, I had to wipe my eyes on my shirtsleeve. "Reilly, where's Marco?"

He bent down to pick up my phone. "I haven't heard from him. Your dad called me. Is this yours?"

I nearly started crying again. *BUST!* had worked. I never thought I'd be saying it, but God bless Dad for ignoring my lecture. "How did my dad know where to send you?"

"He'll always be a cop, Abby. When he got your text, he phoned Lottie to find out where you were."

I thought about that as I watched the officer work on the handcuffs. A few hours earlier, I would have been furious with Dad, but now—I glanced up at the barbell—I had a different perspective. "Make sure you get Robert's headband, Reilly. It's Dallas Stone's tie—the murder weapon."

"Abby!"

As the handcuffs sprang open, I peered around the officer and saw my husband in the doorway. I jumped off the bench and ran straight into his arms. Marco kissed me, then gathered me close, stroking my hair. "I'm so sorry I wasn't here. Are you okay?"

"Robert has our Seedy, Marco."

"We'll get her back, Sunshine. I promise."

CHAPTER TWENTY-FOUR

We were on our way out of the building, walking arm in arm, when Marco's phone rang. "Salvare," he said. "Yeah, we're just leaving the Y. We're going to follow the ambulance to the hospital." He listened, then glanced at me and smiled. "That's great news, Sean. And Robert? No kidding. Our little hero. Okay, thanks, man."

He slipped his phone in his back pocket. "The police found Robert hiding in Jingles's shed, cowering in the garbage bin, still wearing the tie. When they pulled him out, he was rambling about Secret Avenger saving the town. And guess who led them right to the shed?"

I glanced up as a squad car pulled up in front of us and an officer got out carrying our furry little hero. "Seedy!" I cried and ran to get her.

After making sure Seedy was none the worse for her big adventure, we left her with Marco's brother, then headed to the hospital to see how Jingles was doing. On the way, I told Marco the whole story, starting from Rosa's massage and ending with Jingles's rescue.

"The most horrific part, Marco, was seeing Robert wearing Dallas's tie around his head. I wanted to throw up."

"The most horrific part wasn't following a man who

might have been a murderer into a basement all by yourself? Or being blindfolded and handcuffed to a barbell,
or threatened with a knife?"

"I've been threatened before, but this was different.
Seeing that delusional man in full costume with a dead
man's tie around his head, believing completely that by
murdering me he would be performing a heroic act, was
beyond frightening. It was horrific. He truly thought he
was a superhero."

"Can I tell you what horrified me? That you put yourself in danger again."

"You didn't hear Seedy crying when she was stuck in
that creepy old basement, Marco. You would have done
the same thing."

He reached over and took my hand. "You know I love
Seedy, sweetheart, and you're right—I would have done
the same thing. But I can't live without you, Abby. Please
don't do that again."

I squeezed his hand, then turned my head to watch
the scenery go by, wishing I could make that promise.

He glanced at me. "Did my message get through?"

"Yes, Marco, message received."

"I meant my text message."

Oops.

"I didn't have a signal. I was afraid it didn't go through."

I pulled out my phone and saw that his text had finally
come in. It said: *Just located the ranger. Will talk to him
and head back soon.*

"I'm relieved that you found the man, Marco, but I
guess he won't be needed now."

"Again, I'm sorry I wasn't here to help you, babe, but
I am so happy your dad was."

"That makes two of us. After what I said to him about

texting me, it was pure luck that he sent the cops anyway."

"I don't think it was luck, Sunshine. I think it was love."

I didn't answer. I was scrolling back through my dad's messages, none of which I'd stopped to read: He was concerned I was working too hard. He didn't like seeing me stressed. He wanted me to slow down. I scrolled forward again and stopped at the text that had come in while I was interviewing Kandi. It read: *Read your mom's message.*

Marco pulled into a parking space at the hospital then, so I put my phone away and followed him to the emergency room.

Nikki was waiting at the desk and stepped out to hug me.

"How did you know I was coming here?" I asked.

"Jingles was able to tell me a little of what happened on his way to the examination room. I'm so glad you're all right." She hugged me again.

"How is he?" I asked.

"He has a collapsed lung and broken ribs, and who knows what else they'll find." She began backing up a hallway. "They're taking him to surgery now. I'll try to keep you informed. I've got to get back to work."

Marco got cups of coffee for us and then we sat in the crowded waiting room, hoping to hear some word soon on how Jingles was doing. A text came in from Lottie, who wanted to know if I was okay. Dad had told her enough to make her worry. I texted back a brief paragraph and asked her to let Grace know, too. Then we sat back to wait some more.

As the hours passed, a few of the downtown merchants began to arrive—Bonnie from the printshop,

Greg from the jewelry shop, Donna from Windows on the Square—and soon the waiting room was at standing-room-only capacity. Finally a kind nurse, learning why we were there, gave us a quiet waiting room in the surgery wing.

Another hour went by before we heard anything. "Mr. Atkins will be taken to a private room in about half an hour," a new nurse reported.

"Then he's okay?" I asked.

"I'll let the doctor tell you more. Are you family members?"

"He doesn't have any family," I said. "We'll have to do."

Marco and I stood at Jingles's bedside holding hands and praying as machines beeped and pulsed around him. The emergency room physician had told us that his lungs were functioning normally again, his broken ribs were taped, his vitals were in the right range, and his blood pressure was steady, but he'd slipped into a coma and they hadn't been able to wake him up. When we asked what could be done, the doctor merely said that they would continue to monitor him and we'd just have to wait and see what developed.

But a sympathetic nurse had taken us aside afterward and said, "I've seen this in elderly patients before. Sometimes they lose their will to live. Try talking to him, give him something to hope for."

Which was what we were doing. "Jingles, it's Abby. We're here and so are a lot of your friends from downtown. The doctor said you were doing well. Now we're all waiting for you to wake up. And guess what? The entire downtown merchant association is going to throw a party in your honor. Marco's going to host at his bar.

You're our champion, Jingles. You saved my life and who knows how many others. Isn't that great?"

I waited for some sign that he'd heard and finally said, "Can you blink if you can hear me?"

There was still no response, so Marco took a turn talking to him, telling him about Robert's capture and Seedy's role in it. And then I tried again, but finally we went back to the waiting room to report to the others.

All of them stopped talking when we walked in. "Any news?" Bonnie asked.

Marco shook his head. "He's not responding."

There were sad sighs all around as we sat down again.

When Marco went to get more coffee for us, I took out my phone and checked to see whether any new text messages had come in. Then, remembering what I'd started to do earlier, I tapped on Mom's name and brought up her long list of texts, groaning inwardly at her book titles: *Shrubs and Shrapnel*, *Crime Doesn't Carrot All*, *The Sunflower Also Rises*, *Leaf Well Enough Alone*, *Foiled by Foliage* . . . She was writing children's books. Kids wouldn't get her corny puns. What could she be thinking?

Mom hadn't sent any messages after the one that came in while I was interviewing Kandi. It was the one I'd refused to read, the one Marco, Nikki, even Dad had urged me to read. Might as well get it over with.

But as soon as I saw the word *title*, I was so irked I could barely stand to read on. I skimmed through it instead until I got to the last line, which stopped me cold: *You will always be my precious little girl.*

Marco sat down beside me. "Are you okay?"

I had to count to ten before I could answer. Mom had effectively thrown the last piece of kindling on the fire of

aggravation that had been burning in the pit of my stomach since I'd moved back home. *I am not a little girl!*

"No, I'm not okay. I'm furious. No matter what I tell
my parents—or ask or beg them to do—they refuse to
listen, Marco. I suppose this is where I should throw a
tantrum because apparently I *am* still a child. It's a good
thing we're not going to that dinner tonight, or I might
say something I'd regret later."

He handed me a cardboard cup filled with hot coffee,
then put his arms around me. "I'm sorry, babe."

A nurse stepped in and motioned for Marco and me
to come to the hallway. We went outside, where two
husky, middle-aged men in black overcoats were waiting.
They looked solemn, and my first thought was that FBI
agents or federal marshals had come to tell us we'd over-
stepped our bounds by investigating Dallas's murder.

"This is Mr. and Mrs. Knight," she said to them.

One man stuck out his hand to Marco and shook it
vigorously with a quick hello, then turned to me and
clasped my hand warmly. "It's a pleasure to meet you,
Mrs. Salvare. The nurse told us what happened today and
all I can say is thank you."

"And you are?" I asked.

"I'm sorry," he said. "I'm Sam Atkins the Second, and
this is my brother Joshua."

I stared at them in surprise. Jingles's sons!

"I'm so glad you got here quickly," Marco said. "Come
with me."

For a moment the men stood just inside the door, staring
at Jingles as though trying to grasp that the wrinkled old
man lying in the bed with tubes running into his body

was their father. Then Sam tossed his coat over a chair and went to one side of the bed to pick up Jingles's hand.

"Dad, it's me, Sammy. Josh is here, too. Can you hear me, Dad?"

There was no response, but Sam kept trying. His brother stood back as though reluctant to take part, even keeping his overcoat on as Sam told Jingles about their families and promising to show him photos of his grandchildren as soon as he got better.

"You *are* going to get better, Dad," Sam said, his voice breaking. "The nurse said there's no reason you can't." He glanced at his brother. "Say something."

Joshua merely stood with his arms folded, gazing impassively at Jingles.

Sam tried again. "We have a lot of catching up to do, you know. Come on, Dad—give me a wink or something so I know you can hear me."

He stopped then, watching for any sign of life, any acknowledgment or recognition, but Jingles lay still, lost in a netherworld. Had the men missed their last chance to make amends with their father? My throat tightened as I folded my hands together and prayed. Marco put his arm around me and pulled me closer to his side.

Sam sighed heavily and looked at his brother. "Nothing."

"He never did respond well to affection," Joshua said. "I wouldn't know what to say to him if he *did* wake up—not that he would even want us here."

"After the way we treated him," Sam said, "could you blame him?"

"Let's just go," Joshua said.

I couldn't keep quiet any longer. "Your father's not the man you remember. He's a kind, gentle soul who lives in one room at a men's shelter and uses all his free time helping others. Ask anyone in town what they think of your dad. They'll go on for hours."

"Then maybe we should talk to them," Josh said. "Obviously he cares more for others than for his own flesh and blood."

"Josh," Sam said quietly, "let it go."

"No, Sam, I won't. Our father never showed us affection. After all these years, how am I supposed to feel anything for him now?"

"Because he's our family," Sam said. "And no matter what, you don't turn your back on family."

"Watch me," Josh said, and went to the window, where he stood gazing outside, his hands stuffed into his coat pockets.

"You know what, Josh?" Sam snapped. "You've spent way too long hating him for that. You're actually turning into him."

Josh turned and stared at his brother in shock.

Sam leaned over the bed and said in a stern voice, "Listen up, you stubborn old bastard. You left us once. You will *not* do it again. We're going to wait right here until you open your eyes." Then in a surprisingly gentle move, he leaned over and kissed his forehead. "We love you, Dad." Glancing up at Josh, he added, "And we forgive you."

After a few long moments of waiting, Sam straightened, his expression of disappointment mirroring mine. He looked around, spotted the chair in the corner, and pulled it up. "Okay, Dad. I'm here, and this is where I'm staying. Josh, you can leave if you want to."

Joshua gazed at him pensively, then turned toward the window again.

"Let's go, Abby," Marco said in my ear.

But as we started toward the door, Jingles made a rumbling sound in his throat, as though trying to clear it. And then his eyelids fluttered.

Sam got to his feet and grabbed his dad's hand as Jingles's eyelids squeezed tightly together and then opened to mere slits. He tried to say something, but it came out in a hoarse whisper.

Sam leaned down, clasping his dad's limp hand between his. "Dad, it's Sammy. I'm here for you. You're going to be okay."

Jingles's eyes opened wider and then he blinked as though he thought he was dreaming.

"There you go," Sam cried, brushing a tear off his cheek. "I knew you could do it."

Jingles squeezed his son's hand. Then, with great effort, he turned his head to see his other son and slowly lifted a trembling hand to him, a tear rolling down his face.

At that, Joshua strode to his father's side and leaned over to hug him, sobbing.

Marco guided me to the door, but I didn't want to leave. Something deep inside me was rising, painful feelings of guilt, and when I realized what it was, I felt weak in the knees.

"Let's go, Sunshine," Marco said quietly. "They need their privacy."

My last glimpse was of Jingles gazing at his boys, his hands clasping theirs as though he was afraid they might disappear if he let go. It was as though all of them had been given a brand-new start.

As Marco closed the door behind us, I had to sit down

on a bench in the hallway and take deep breaths. What was I doing to my family?

Right then I took out my phone and pulled up Mom's text. It read: *Not a title this time but I have decided on my dedication. What do you think of this? To my talented, courageous daughter who is the inspiration for my series. Thank you, Abigail. You will always be my precious little girl.*

I gulped back tears. I would always be Mom's little girl just as Jingles's grown sons would always be his boys. It wasn't that they saw us as children; they saw us as *their* children.

I stood up and shoved my phone into my purse. "Marco, we need to go to the country club."

"Are you sure? We're not dressed for it."

"I don't care about that. I just need to be there."

"I thought you couldn't stand those family dinners."

"I don't want to become another Sam Atkins, Marco, caring more about my job than the people who love me most in this world, or his sons, whose hearts were so closed down by resentment that it took a near-death situation to open them up again. I'm so sorry for the way I've been treating my family lately. Let's go join that dinner in progress so I can begin to make amends."

He put his arm around my shoulders. "Now you're talking."

CHAPTER TWENTY-FIVE

O n our way across town, Marco and I rehashed the events of our remarkable afternoon. What I hadn't known earlier was that he'd spoken with Reilly while he was out getting coffee and had some surprising news about one of our suspects.

"The police department got a call from the Lansing, Illinois, PD about a young woman with a New Chapel address by the name of Kandi Cane who was trying to sell a sackful of gold coins to a local pawnshop."

"The coins she claimed Dallas stole?"

"You got it. The dealer thought it was suspicious that a young woman in a beat-up old car would have that many valuable coins, so the police came to check her out. Guess what they found in the trunk. A chest of old clothing with several small bags of gold at the bottom, apparently her inheritance from her grandmother. Her story about Dallas selling some of the coins in the pawnshop in New Chapel was a fraud also."

"So Kandi ran because she was afraid of being found out."

"Yep. So the blue topaz necklace Robert saw outside the shed may have been the one item Dallas actually did steal from her."

"Huh. Then Lavinia probably is at her mom's house."

"It really doesn't matter. She didn't do anything wrong, and because Dallas never signed off on the divorce, she'll receive his life insurance money and pension."

"Good for her! I can't help but wonder, though, why she was running from the courthouse that morning."

"I think I can explain that. Remember the article your dad read to us Monday morning about the press conference?"

Another time I'd acted selfishly. "A little."

"I pulled it up online. The article listed the town and bank VIPs who were scheduled to attend, and Dallas, being a vice president, was on it. So my guess is that Lavinia read the article, too, and had decided to wait for him somewhere out of sight—perhaps behind the lilac bushes—so she could talk to him afterward. The police were able to trace the nine-one-one call back to her cell phone."

"Poor Lavinia! Can you imagine her shock when she stumbled upon her husband's body? That would definitely explain why she was running and why she kept peering out the deli window. She probably knew she would be a suspect because of the threats she'd made."

"As for the necktie," Marco said, "it's being sent to the forensics lab in Indy for DNA testing. When the detectives asked Robert why he was wearing it, he said it was a symbol of good triumphing over evil. He is insisting they call him Secret Avenger and is demanding an attorney who *gets* his mission."

"I feel sorry for the public defender who *gets* his case."

Marco pulled into the hilly, wooded parking lot in front of the low, sprawling, brick country club building and turned off the motor. "Ready?"

I hesitated, my fingers around the door handle. Was I

ready? Would my family be angry that I'd gotten myself
into another dangerous situation? Would they even want
me at their dinner? I got out of the car, took Marco's
hand—and a deep breath—and we walked in together.

Just outside the private dining room, I paused, taking in
a scene that almost felt like a Norman Rockwell paint-
ing. Everyone was seated at a long dining table covered
with a white tablecloth, with a lovely low-profile floral
arrangement in the middle. My dad was in his wheelchair
at the head of the table, leaning over to say something to
my mom on his right, who laughed in delight. My brother
Jonathan was next to her, his head close to his wife's to
hear what Portia was saying.

Then came Jillian cradling little Harper adorned in a
fluffy pink dress and her white seed pearl halo, with Jillian's husband, Claymore, at the end. On Claymore's other
side was my brother Jordan and his wife, Kathy, lecturing
my niece Tara, who was rolling her eyes and sighing.

Mom was the first to spot us. She rose with a surprised
smile. "Look who came after all!"

Tara bounced happily, clapping her hands together,
and Dad gave out a bark of laughter. "How about that?
Come in, you two. We've saved you seats. Sit down and
tell us what happened."

And then I saw the two empty chairs.

"Jeff, for heaven's sake," Mom said, giving his shoulder a playful poke, "they don't want to talk about that
now. They just got here. Let them get some food in their
stomachs first. You know how Abigail gets when she's
hungry."

"You saved seats for us?" I asked.

"Of course we did," Mom said.

"Well, I just want to say," said my sister-in-law Kathy, rising, "that we are so relieved that you're"—she got choked up for a moment, then cleared her throat—"that you are all right." She gave me a misty-eyed smile as she sat down.

After which Jillian quipped dryly, "How amazing that you took time out of your busy schedule for us."

"Jillian, darling," Claymore said in a placating voice, "you're just as relieved to see Abby as everyone else is."

"I *am*," she said in a tearful voice, making Harper start to cry, at which she promptly handed her off to Claymore. "I really *am*."

As I gave Dad and Mom hugs and then went to hold Jillian's little girl—she really was adorable—Jordan said, "Seriously, Ab, we're all really glad you and Marco made it."

"And you caught the killer in time for dinner," Jonathan teased.

"But really we need to talk about your work habits," Jordan stated firmly in a good-natured way.

"Stop it, you two," Mom chided. "This is not the place."

I couldn't help but smile. To my mom, Jon and Jordan were still her boys and not highly respected doctors who dealt with life-and-death situations routinely. And that was part of my lesson. No matter how old we were, Mom was always going to see us as her children.

Truthfully, whenever my family got together, we often acted like kids, ribbing one another, joking, shooting paper straw wrappers across the table, even arguing, because we felt safe in the knowledge that no matter what, we were loved and accepted.

A waiter began circling the table with a bottle of champagne, and when all the flutes were full, Jon used his knife to tap on his glass, getting everyone's attention. "Time for the surprise announcement."

I handed Harper to Claymore and took my seat beside Marco as Jon rose and held his flute aloft. "Portia and I would like to announce"—he turned toward my mom—"that we have a bona fide author in the family—"

Wait, what? That wasn't a surprise.

"—and in her honor, we will be hosting a celebratory book signing at the country club when her book is published."

Mom blushed with pride as Jonathan continued. "Because not only has Mom finished the first book in her children's mystery series, but—*ta-da*—she was just offered a contract by a New York publishing house."

As everyone applauded and cheered, my mouth could not have dropped further. A genuine publisher wanted her Seeky book? I looked at Marco in surprise. Words could not express my shock or my chagrin at not having read her book. I had simply dismissed it as another of her wacky projects, but apparently Mom had found her true calling at last.

"A toast to Maureen," my dad called, and everyone clinked glasses and took swallows of champagne, with the exception of Tara, who had sparkling water.

"Thank you," Mom said, rising. "Your support means everything to me. And, Jonathan and Portia, I could not feel more honored or excited. But now I think it's time to toast the real hero here today."

She held her flute toward me. "To my daughter, whose courageous acts have not only helped catch a killer but also inspired me to write this series. Abigail, this is to you, honey, for proving again what an amazing person you are."

Once again, words failed me. I was amazing? Me, the law school flunk-out? The pathetic loser whose first fiancé had dumped her two months before their wedding, humiliating her in front of the entire town? The snippy daughter who had said nothing nice during the entire time she'd been a guest in her own parents' home? *That* person was her inspiration?

No, the little voice of conscience whispered. *Not that person. That's not how Mom views you. You are the young woman who took over a floundering flower shop and made it a success, who met and married her dream man, and who helped capture sixteen killers.*

Wow. Just . . . wow.

Marco squeezed my hand, then leaned over and whispered, "They're waiting for you to say something."

I met my mom's twinkling gaze and tried to speak, but all that came out was a thready "Thank you."

She nodded and smiled at me again.

Hmm. Was I reading it wrong or was that little twinkle in her eye starting to look a little more devilish than delightful? Was she even now plotting to move in with *me* at some future date?

"Tell them the rest of your news, Mo," Dad said.

Mom looked around the table as she said, "You'll be relieved to hear that I've finally decided on a title for the first book. But instead of telling you what it is, I made a sketch of my imagined cover to show you. Hold it up, Jeff."

Oh, no. I gazed down at my lap so I wouldn't see the expressions on everyone's faces when they read her latest groaner. I was horrified when they laughed.

"A toast, everyone," Mom said, "to *Mum's the Word.*"

My head snapped up, my gaze taking in the drawing in Dad's hands. On the cover was a tall, skinny redhead who looked more like Jillian than me. But she was standing inside her very own flower shop looking out the window at her bright yellow Corvette.

Mom was gazing straight at me, waiting for my reaction. "What do you think, Abigail?"

"Where's Seeky?" I asked, still in shock.

"Seeky isn't the star of this book, honey. You are. So . . . ?"

I don't even remember pushing back my chair. I only remember throwing my arms around Mom and whispering tearfully as I embraced her, "It's perfect."

Abby and Marco move into their new home!
But their tidy suburban neighborhood
hides a not-so-tidy dead body in:

MOSS HYSTERIA

another Flower Shop Mystery by Kate Collins.
Available in paperback and ebook
starting on April 2016 wherever Penguin
books are sold or at penguin.com.
Read on for an excerpt. . . .

Sunday

"Marco, would you get the door, please?"
        I waited for a response but my request was
met by silence. The doorbell pealed again, so I stopped
unwrapping our mismatched wineglasses to call, "Marco?
Where'd you go?"

He didn't answer—he was probably taking our dog,
Seedy, to the backyard—so I stepped around the pile of
crumpled newspapers in the kitchen and hurried to the
front hallway. It was currently the only area in our brand-
new two-bedroom ranch that wasn't cluttered with boxes.
My nose itched from chemical overload—new carpet
fibers, wood-floor stain, paint, and draperies—so I
paused to give it a good rub.

I opened the door to find nine women on my porch.

They were stacked like bowling pins, the ones in front bearing casserole dishes, the ones in the rear leaning out for a better look. The kingpin of this merry band was forty-five-ish with long blond hair that swept over one eye and fell in bouncy curls past her shoulders. She wore an off-the-shoulder white pullover with a tight gold miniskirt and knee-high white boots, an outfit that would better suit my fourteen-year-old niece, Tara. Heavy gold hoops swung from the woman's ears as she tossed her hair away from her eyes.

"Hi. I'm Mitzi Kole," she said in a perky soprano. "We're the Brandywine Babes Book Club, more commonly known as the Bees. We all want to say"—she inhaled loudly and then the whole group chorused with her—"welcome to Brandywine."

"Wow. Thank you." I pushed back the sleeves of my paint-splattered yellow sweatshirt and stretched out my hands to accept Mitzi's dish, only then noticing the black newsprint on my fingers, which was undoubtedly all over my nose.

"We also want to invite you to our book—." Mitzi stopped, her fake black eyelashes fluttering madly as she focused on something behind me. Her fellow ninepins leaned out farther.

I glanced around to see Marco coming toward the door, wiping his perspiring face with a towel, ruffling his wavy dark hair in the process. We'd been unpacking since early morning and he hadn't shaved, a look I found sexy. Judging by the ogling going on, as nine pairs of eyes swept down his well-muscled torso, taking in his short-sleeved navy T-shirt and snug-fitting blue jeans, so did the Bees.

"As I was saying," Mitzi said, having suddenly developed a throaty alto, "we'd like to invite you *and* your husband to our book club Wednesday evening." She reached around me to offer a dainty hand to Marco. "Hi. I'm Mitzi

Kole, the president of the club. I live two doors down."
She tossed her hair. "Our backyards nearly *touch.*"

Marco wiped his hands on the towel, then gave her
hand a polite shake. "Marco Salvare. Nice to meet you."
He nodded at the rest of the group. "Ladies."

Sidestepping me, Mitzi moved in front of him and said
in a sultry voice, "I *do* hope you'll come Wednesday, Marco.
We'd *love* for you to try us on for size."

More like try *her* on for size.

"That's Abby's department," Marco said. "She's the
social director."

Mitzi swung around to size me up. "Well, then, I'll just
have to convince *her.*"

I gave her a polite smile.

"We'll let you get back to unpacking," Mitzi said to
Marco. "It's been a pleasure meeting you — both." She
did an about-face and raised her hand, and on cue the
Bees deposited their dishes on the table in my front hall
and swarmed back up the sidewalk behind her, buzzing
excitedly.

As I turned to go, I noticed my next-door neighbor
Theda Coros clipping back the winter-dead branches on
her rosebushes. She winked at me and shook her head as
though she found the Bees silly.

"Nice neighbors," Marco said as we toted casserole dishes
to the kitchen. He put his dish in the refrigerator, then
turned to take mine but instead used the towel he'd
thrown over his shoulder to wipe the smudges off my
upper lip. "Nice mustache, too, Groucho. Any interest in
going to their meeting?"

"I'm thinking about it." Actually I was thinking about
how Mitzi's lascivious glances in my husband's direction
would have made me furious when Marco and I had
been dating. But I knew without a doubt he wouldn't do

anything to jeopardize the love and trust we had for each other, so I blew them off. "Where's Seedy?"

"In the backyard. She loves watching the neighbor kids play."

We'd rescued our little dog the previous fall after I'd learned she was to be euthanized. No one had wanted Seedy, who aptly fit her name. She was a small, ugly mutt with brown, black and white fur, an underbite, large butterfly-wing ears with tufts on top, and only three legs, but she had the sweetest nature and most loving personality I'd ever encountered.

Before my second visit was over, I had fallen hopelessly in love with her. Seedy had proved to be a wonderful pet and had even kept me from certain death just weeks earlier when Marco and I had been tracking down a killer. I couldn't imagine life without her.

We'd barely stuffed the last casserole into the fridge when the doorbell rang again. "I'll get it," Marco said, and strode off.

I opened a box marked *Kitchen* and found it filled with shoes, so I trotted off to our bedroom with it. Both bedrooms and a guest bathroom were off a hallway that ran the width of the house, with the master at the far end. I put the box on the floor and glanced around, trying to visualize how the room would look when everything had been stowed.

On my way back to the kitchen, I stopped to consider the hallway and decided the long expanse of off-white drywall would be the perfect place for our family photos.

"Abby, would you come here, please?"

At the door was a new group of women, this time bearing pies, cakes, cookies, and a bottle of wine. We'd had the Bees. Were these the Birds?

"This is Reagan," Marco said, introducing the leader of the pack, a pleasant-looking thirtyish woman. Her conservative navy jacket, jeans, and gym shoes were a sharp contrast to Mitzi Kole's 1980s sex-kitten outfit. "Reagan, this is my wife, Abby."

"Everyone here knows Abby," Reagan said with a bright smile, "and you, too, Marco. You're the Brandy-wine celebrities."

I liked Reagan right off the bat.

"Reagan and her group have a book club, too," Marco told me, his eyes brimming with amusement. "Books and Bottles."

"Bottles as in wine," Reagan said, presenting me with a bottle of red. "I'm sure you and Marco are over-whelmed with all the unpacking, but because you've already been accosted by the Bees, we felt it important that we stop by to welcome you and invite you to *our* meeting. It's Thursday at my place. I live right around the curve in the road, the white house with the yellow shutters."

Yellow. My favorite color. Another plus in Reagan's column.

"So here." She took a foil-covered pie from the woman beside her and placed it in Marco's hands. "Think of us when you're having dessert tonight." As they trooped back up our sidewalk, Reagan called, "Thursday at seven. We serve appetizers and desserts."

"You should join one of the clubs," Marco said as I tried to make room on the crowded kitchen counter for all the sweets. "You're always looking for something to do in the evenings."

"We'll see."

"We got lucky deciding to build in this development, Abby."

I grunted. I was still digesting Mitzi's outrageous come-on toward my husband.

Marco was about to bite into an oatmeal cookie but paused to give me a skeptical look. "You don't agree?"

"I think one of the *Bees* is hoping to get lucky."

"What are you talking about?"

"Queen bee, Marco, Mitzi Kole. I was appalled by how blatantly she was hitting on you. I hope that's not a sign of things to come. I'd hate to start out life here having to avoid a neighbor."

"Come on, babe, she was just being friendly."

"Seriously, Marco? Did you just arrive on this planet?"

He pulled me into his arms. "I'm teasing, Sunshine. I've met many Mitzis, and trust me, I know how to deal with them. *Motto.* Be polite and keep my distance. What do you say we take a break? We've been unpacking since five a.m. Let's heat up one of the casseroles and open that bottle of wine."

I was too exhausted to argue, and it really was nice to have food already prepared. But I'd made up my mind. If I joined a club, it would not be the Bees.

The weather that April day was mild, so after dinner we took our wine and went outside to sit on the front porch swing. Seedy sat on the porch's top step, one eye on us, one eye on the cars going by. I'd always dreamed of having a cozy little house with a porch swing, and Marco had surprised me by installing one that morning. Now my new husband and I sat side by side, rocking gently, enjoying the stillness of the spring evening.

The chance to be together for an entire weekend was rare, as Marco usually had duties at Down the Hatch Bar and Grill in the evenings. He also owned the Salvare Detective Agency, something he'd dreamed of establishing since his Army Ranger days. But this weekend was special. We'd finally moved out of my parents' house and into our very own honeymoon cottage.

We'd met nearly two years ago, shortly after I'd bought Bloomers Flower Shop, when Marco helped me track down the hit-and-run driver who'd smashed my

newly refurbished 1960 yellow Corvette convertible. That
case turned out to be connected to a homicide, and after
we worked together to pinpoint the killer, my second
career was launched. Now I was not only Marco's partner in life but also in his PI business. He liked to call us
Team Salvare.

"Am I interrupting?" our next-door neighbor called
from her front porch.

"Come over, Theda," I said. "Have a glass of wine
with us."

Theda had been a great help as our house was going
up. Because she'd lived in the development for more
than a year and had been one of the first to move in, she
knew the ins and outs of the building process and had
kept us from making costly mistakes.

In her late sixties, Theda had the strong profile and strik-
ing good looks of her Greek heritage. She was a tall woman,
large boned and thick bodied but not obese, with thick,
curly dark hair sprinkled with gray and shrewd brown eyes
that didn't miss a detail. She had been widowed a decade
ago and had a man friend she saw occasionally.

"I was just about to take my evening stroll," Theda
said. "If you'd like to join me, I'll show you around the
neighborhood. We can have that glass of wine afterward
if the offer is still open."

I glanced at Marco. "Want to go?"

"I'll get our jackets."

We hadn't really had an opportunity to see much of
the Brandywine community. Because of our dual occu-
pations, plus the brutal winter snows that had hung on
through March, we'd only driven through it. The subdivision was a community of ranch homes developed by
Brandon Emmett Thorne. Its street looped around the
park and a large man-made pond before circling back to
the main entrance.

All three streets were named after Brandon—Brandonbury, Emmett Lane, and Thorneapple, which Theda said was just one example of Brandon's pomposity. We had met the developer only once, at our closing, but Theda assured me I would reach the same conclusion once I got to know him better.

With Seedy on her leash, we accompanied Theda around the curve of our street to the clubhouse situated near the main entrance to the subdivision. After pointing out various features, Theda said, "You've probably seen the park, so let's walk the length of the pond before the sun sets."

From the clubhouse we followed a path down to the south end of the pond, then walked in the grass along the water's edge as we headed north toward our house. The pond was about a city block long, a quarter of that in width and fifteen feet at its deepest point. The pond ended behind Theda's lot, giving her a view of both the water and the park.

"You've got the best location in the neighborhood," I said, holding tight as Seedy strained on her leash. She'd seen something interesting and seemed determined to explore it. "No, Seedy," I said, pulling back on the leash. "Too damp and mossy there."

"You're right about that," Theda said, stepping down to the shore to prod a mossy section with the toe of her shoe. "We have a problem with it on both ends of the pond, but this end is much worse. The moss was supposed to have been treated last fall, but no one has ever come out to deal with it. Now it's spreading into my lawn.

"And yet I love living here," she continued. "It's a great community. In fact, sometimes I feel like I live on a movie set. Neatly tended houses, well-kept lawns, our own park, a clubhouse with a fitness center . . ." She paused to stare at something a few feet out in the water and gave a shuddering gasp. "Oh, my — and a body floating in the pond."